The Innocent Dead

Maid, Mother, and Crone Mysteries #1

Jill Nojack

IndieHeart Press
Kent, Ohio

Cover designed by Lori Gundy.

Visit the series website for series related content:

www.jillnojack.com

Publisher's Note: This is a work of fiction. Names, characters, places, and incidents are a product of the author's imagination. Any resemblance to actual people, living or dead, or to businesses, companies, events, or institutions, is completely coincidental.

The digital edition of this book is a Kindle Scout winner and is published by Kindle Press, an Amazon Publishing imprint.

The Innocent Dead / Jill Nojack. — 1st ed.

ISBN: 978-1-947670-020

1

"Great galloping goblins! If we must have a cat, it should at least know how to behave." Natalie glared at the fluffy black kitten half-hidden beneath the lip of the overturned basket of herbal teas. The scent of mint, ginger, and roses wafted upward from broken packages, but she refused to yield to their soothing properties. The frown lines between her eyebrows—more like frown craters after decades of frequent use—were working overtime.

Gillian Winterforth slid quickly between them, her chubby body clad in a loose, embroidered white blouse and colorful tie-dye skirt, creating an effective wall between Natalie and the kitten. She bent over and scooped it up. It batted at her long white braid, and she flipped the plait behind her, removing it from harm's way.

When she was standing again, she rubbed a cheek against the kitten's glossy fur. "If you were in charge, I'm sure you'd have things running smoothly like in Eunice's day. Nothing like having an imprisoned citizen inside the cat to keep an eye on things," she said.

Her amused response betrayed a fading English accent.

"Yes, excellent idea," Natalie said. "Where *is* Tom?"

A young female voice answered from the hallway leading to the private parlor of the Victorian home that housed Cat's Magical Shoppe. "Hubby won't be sleeping around town in a fur suit any time soon just to make your life easier, Natalie Taylor. Tom has plenty on his hands with his adorable new wife, a café to run, and a mansion to renovate, thank you."

When Cassie Sanders emerged from the hall, she winked a blue eye at Gillian, who smiled in return. Natalie didn't respond. They both knew she hadn't really meant that Tom should continue to fulfill the role of store cat. Probably.

As she bent and picked up the scattered bags of tea and Gillian went for the broom to clean up the mess made by the broken ones, Natalie straightened to the tingle at her spine that signaled the near presence of newly created life, her heart beating fast; *the game is afoot!* She said, "You can hear my old bones creaking while I work to put things right, can't you? But at least everything—absolutely everything—will soon be back in place as it should be."

Cassie laughed. "Seriously, only a joyless old crone would complain about a playful kitten. Lighten up, Nat. Cat's Magical Shoppe has always had a cat, that cat has always been named Cat, and that's how it'll stay. It's a family tradition."

"Joyless old crone!" Nat snorted. "My dear, you have no idea. Look to that one"—she gestured with her chin at Gillian, who was capturing the last of the spilled tea in the dustpan—"if you're looking for a crone. In this trio of witches that's not an honor I can claim. And Gillian..." She rearranged the salvageable teas in the basket. "I'm surprised that you haven't noticed it, too...how our little trio has changed. A way that will allow us to cast the spell that will bring order to my little world again."

Gillian put the broom and dustpan back in the storeroom. "And that change is?"

Natalie's head shook as she hmphed, then said, "You're not paying attention, are you?" She nodded in Cassie's direction.

Gillian's eyes followed her nod and dropped to Cassie's middle. They lit up with recognition. "You mean she...is she?" Her eyes opened wide.

"There's definitely new life in the room." Natalie looked at Gillian meaningfully. "What do you want to bet it's not us senior citizens who are carrying?"

"What are you guys talking about?" Cassie asked. "And stop staring at me like that. You're creeping me out."

Gillian moved to her side. "Sweetie, you won't mind a little staring if Natalie's right. If I could just..." Gillian moved a plump hand to Cassie's stomach. Cassie didn't flinch, so Gillian left her hand there for a moment. Her smile turned into an all-out grin.

"Oh, it's true, all right! Nat, we're going to be grandwitches."

Cassie looked down to where Gillian's hand still rested on her abdomen. "You guys mean?"

Natalie nodded. "I mean that you weren't a mother yesterday, but you certainly are today."

Gillian still glowed, but she took her hand away. "Yes, sweetheart, we both know what you and Tom did last night."

"Yeah, like we don't do that every night." Cassie rolled her eyes and giggled. "I mean, guys, we're still newlyweds. But no matter what we've been doing, there's no way to tell if I'm pregnant that fast."

Gillian said, "The child hasn't quickened, sweetheart, but there's a tiny set of cells inside you that's destined to become someone who is part you and part Tom."

Cassie looked down at her flat stomach, then back up to her friends, her face a study in wonder. "Part Tom. Part me. Omigoddess..."

Natalie raised a hand dramatically to shade her eyes, playful now as she neared her goal. "I shouldn't have said anything. The radiant output coming from where you're standing is blinding." She half smiled as she lowered her hand. "Your full attention, please."

She walked behind the counter, squatted carefully and, keeping a hand on the countertop to steady herself, unboxed the red vintage purse she'd paid dearly for at auction and hidden in her under-counter cubby months ago. Red is so important for an effective ward against the spirits of the dead.

The rustling sound of unfolding tissue paper had drawn Cat's attention. He stalked closer, crouching close to the ground with the tip of his tail twitching, readying to pounce. She shot the kitten a warning glare and set the handbag carefully at her feet where she could snatch it up at a moment's notice.

She stood up. "I only mentioned it because I need your help. With the three of us: Mother..." she said, putting her hand out gently toward Cassie with a flourish, "and of course, Maid..." She put an identifying hand on her own chest.

Cassie and Gillian looked at each other quickly, eyebrows raised, before turning back to Natalie with disbelieving eyes.

Natalie knew what they were thinking and scowled. "I was busy. I didn't have time for romantic nonsense." Her focus moved to Gillian. "Given those circumstances, as I've already said, you can only be the Crone. I think that's obvious."

Gillian smiled. "The wisest witch in the room? I agree."

"Believe what you want about the qualities of the Crone." Natalie twitched her outstretched hand as if flicking away a fly, then let it sink to rest on one narrow hip. No point in wasting time arguing the subtleties. "Let's stop quibbling and talk about the spell, shall we? I'd like to perform it as soon as possible."

Cassie was staring at her own stomach again. "Go on, Nat," she said after a moment. "Everybody's listening."

"It will require extreme focus from all of us…"

Her audience leaned in, but their eyes were pulled away again when the shop bell tinkled as the door opened and birthed a gaggle of senior shoppers. They had their pocketbooks at the ready, their shopping bags unfurled, and gabbled at each other like turkeys as they spread out quickly toward the shop's gaudier offerings.

Cassie looked out into the suddenly crowded shop and grinned. "Oh. That's what I came to tell you before you guys distracted me—a bus load of tourists just pulled up in the municipal lot. The town's new publicist got Giles into the tour companies as a secondary stop to Salem."

"What good news!" Gillian turned back to Natalie and said, "You'll have to hang on to whatever you want for later. We've got punters!" She spun and bustled toward the clump of customers with Cassie following behind.

Natalie didn't follow. She folded her hands on the counter and glared. By the time the shoppers cleared out, Cassie would need to be off to her husband, Gillian would need to be off to her partner, and her own needs would be forgotten. But she was tired, bone tired, of seeing dead people, and even more tired of seeing William, who was the most persistent of them all.

She looked down when a brush of movement fluttered her pant leg.

At her feet, the kitten's head and front paws, so recently covered with the ingredients of subtly enchanted teas designed for healing, beauty, memory, and self control, had disappeared into the open mouth of the purse she'd spent days preparing with complex cleansing rituals. Even she hadn't dared to put a hand in there for fear of contaminating it before the casting.

Blast the cat! It would be hours and hours of meticulous work before the spell could go forward and she'd be free from the demands and desires of the dead again. The kitten was soon running scared across the shop to hide behind Gillian's skirt as Natalie picked up the purse, pleased by her show of restraint. After all, the kitten was still alive, wasn't it?

∗∗∗

After clearing up their dinner dishes, Giles's newest resident watched anxiously as his wife unwrapped the gift he'd bought her as a housewarming present. He held his breath, although Gerald Akers knew better than most that hope can be overrated.

"It's hideous! What were you thinking?" Caroline shoved the still half-wrapped picture away from her at the table, knocking over her gin so that it spilled into the tissue wrapping and threatened to encroach on the framed watercolor. She pushed away from the table as it fell, likely worried about ruining her expensive Carolina Herrera dress, but with no regard for the expensive artwork.

Gerald reached out for both the glass and the gift, righting the tumbler before all its contents escaped. With his other hand, he rescued the picture. It was an abstract portrait of an intriguing woman, hair piled on the top of her head, her face painted with vivid, brilliant colors in places, pastel in others. Gerald thought he could see straight through to her soul. Or, more accurately, that she could see into his.

He saw himself reflected in the frame's protective glass; acne scars, gray hair, and accountant's glasses ruined the view. Even though he kept himself fit and strong with a daily running and weightlifting regimen, he had never had a face anyone would look twice at.

He held the image to his chest, glad it was safe. "It reminded me of you when you were younger. It's beautiful. Delicate. A little bit dangerous. You can hang it in your room. Until you've forgiven me for moving us out here and come back to our room, I mean."

Caroline rolled her eyes. "Just get me another drink." He jumped to her command, as he always did, and shot to the counter where the bottle sat waiting. He leaned the picture against the ice bucket on the dark wood bar while he set about his assignment.

She continued talking, more to herself than to him. "I'll return it and buy myself something suitable tomorrow if I can find a decent jeweler anywhere near this backwater town. I still can't believe we sold our beautiful condo for this." She looked around at the newly refurbished family room, her sour expression telling him she found nothing there she liked. "It's horrid here, just horrid. These yahoos think my bringing a few buses loaded with senior citizens into their dreary town will save their puny economy. I should be in Boston, publicist to movers and shakers instead of new-age shopkeepers."

"You know how much fitting in here means to me. Can't you try? This is exactly what I wanted from my retirement, and I'm still young enough to enjoy it thanks to my smart investments. You could learn to like the peace and quiet. I know you could."

"And you could learn to be as quiet as this stupid town, you pathetic little man."

He felt his face redden. "I could have come on my own. I'm sure you would have found someone else to take care of you as well as I do while you play at being a publicist." He was going to pay for that crack, he was sure of that. She would never accept their new lifestyle; he should have left her. But he couldn't. He loved her. He always had. But sometimes he just....

He pulled back from the urge to throw the drink in her face and put it down carefully in front of her. He'd pledged to her for better or for worse, and he'd meant it. She was the only woman he had wanted on his arm when he arrived triumphant in Giles to buy one of the finest houses on the lakefront. He wasn't one of the summer people now. He belonged. He and his beautiful wife. He took the platinum card from his wallet and set it in front of her by the glass. He'd rather pay for his earlier angry comment with his plastic than endure days of the silent treatment. "Take the Mercedes into Boston tomorrow and find yourself something nice."

She barely acknowledged him. She snatched up the card and her drink and stalked out to the porch that overlooked the lake. The sliding glass door rattled as it slammed behind her.

✳✳✳

Natalie unlocked her front door and hung her keys on the hook. After the influx of tourists, things had turned out exactly like she'd predicted they would. There had been no time for her to finish her appeal to her fellow witches; it was another in a series of delays before she could complete the spell to repel the residents of Giles that only she could see.

She meant to sigh, but it came out like a groan. It would be good to get out of her not at all sensible but terribly amusing black high heels. Their turned-up, pointy toes added a touch of whimsy to her fitted black pantsuit, but they made it even more urgent that she slide her aching feet into a tub of warm water spiked with Epsom salts, herbs, and a touch of healing magic. She had retired from nursing at sixty-five, so why was she behind a retail counter at seventy-four wearing nonsensical shoes? Ridiculous.

She should have said no when Cassie had asked. But if she had, Gillian would have been left alone most days to keep up with the latest gossip and goings-on in the magical community. No, it would be wrong of her to saddle a friend with such a burden; Natalie had to be there to assure someone accurately took the pulse of the town.

After all, it had only been a little over five months since an ancient Egyptian demon-goddess had nearly sucked the town into the rift she'd created between the little town of Giles and the Summerlands. The town had survived, but who knew what the long-term consequences of tearing the veil between the land of the living and the land of the dead might be? They'd gotten through the winter without much trouble, but with spring now making itself known, there was no way to predict what might appear as the last of the snow melted.

Even though the goddess Anat was now bound and buried in a three-ton block of concrete, Natalie remained on guard. After all, Anat had possessed Eunice Grandby, Cassie's grandmother, for nearly half a century without anyone in town catching on. She wasn't convinced that all of Anat's magical machinations had been trapped with her. No, it was best to be right there in the middle of things in case the whispers started again.

The sweet-smelling zing of ozone that always accompanied the entry of a spirit into the living realm alerted Natalie to the presence behind her. She knew who it was without looking; William had been showing up more and more frequently since her ward had been destroyed. Sometimes she wished she'd run in the other direction and let the town disappear into the breach when Anat had torn the veil.

She steeled herself to turn, knowing the increased visits might be her own fault; sometimes, if she didn't look at him directly, his company was reassuring, as if he'd never left her. Truth is, she missed him. She remembered when he'd first appeared after the Witching Faire: smiling, disarming her, looking like he did the first day they'd danced, the first day they'd kissed, the first day he'd told her he loved her.

Looking just like he did now, she thought as she faced him. He was impeccably dressed, as he was at all times, in tan pants, a crisp, white button-down shirt, and his favorite argyle sweater vest. His hair, not long enough for a DA but not short enough for a crew cut, was slicked to the side with the slightest wave at the front. Her old heart squeezed in her chest.

She'd always hated that sweater vest, but she could never bring herself to tell him.

He moved toward her, reaching his hand out for her arm. It felt cold against her skin as he tried to settle it there. Then it glided through, breaking the illusion.

"Lolloping lizard lips! Get off me." She stomped to the kitchen where she kept a tub under the sink to soak her feet after a day of too much standing. "Go away, William. I don't want you. The dead should be dead. They shouldn't continue walking around to harass the living."

Despite her protest, he trailed after her. "Are you sure you don't believe I killed those people? That was why you made the ward, wasn't it? And now you're trying to make a new one."

"No, I never believed it, even though my mother and grand-mother did. We had bitter fights about you." She placed the foot bath under the hot water tap and turned it on, testing the water with her hand as she said, "Help me find your body, William. When I find it, it can lay all those old rumors to rest. I'll prove you weren't a killer who ran away, that you were dead before the final murder. Once that's done, I'll help you pass to the Summerlands. You'll have your peace, and I'll have mine. Now go! I don't have the patience for this today."

He reached a hand out to caress her face as he had done hundreds of times when he was alive. All she felt was a chill; there was no substance. Her neutral expression insisted it didn't mean a thing to her. Then, he was gone.

Natalie stood for a while with her eyes closed before raising a hand to her cheek, a sad smile on her face, while the stream of hot water she'd forgotten about dissolved the last of her mineral salts and overflowed with them down the drain.

＊＊＊

There was no way Taniqua "Twink" Johnson was going to go live in boring old Giles with her mean old aunt. No way. Did any normal people even live in Giles? She sure hadn't seen any during visits.

Even the names of the stores were weird. You'd have to be a freak to buy your food at a store called the Decent Food Mart, which was the only grocery store for miles. Too bad her opinion couldn't stop her cousin's car from driving steadily onward with Twink captive in the passenger seat.

She finished putting a final coat of gloss on her already shiny lips and shoved the visor mirror back up flat against the roof of the car. It's not like the sunset would blind her—the sun hadn't bothered to come out from behind the clouds all day, pretty much like every late March in Massachusetts. She'd rather have ear plugs than eye protection, though. Her cousin Daria, who used to be cool, had been lecturing her nonstop since her mother had shoved her into Daria's tiny toy car and hustled back into the house without even saying goodbye.

Things had been bad, but she didn't think they'd been that bad. And it wasn't her fault. She hadn't meant to start the fire. It was like the flame had jumped out of the lighter and lit whatever it wanted to light instead of the candlewick she'd been aiming for. And who cared if a bunch of stupid silk flowers got burned up anyway? She'd stopped it from getting to the couch.

Plus, she hadn't broken any of the things her mother said she had. It was like stuff decided to commit suicide when she walked in a room. Why else would a brand new 50-inch plasma TV screen crack all the way down its face when she wasn't anywhere near it? She'd been with Marcus when she'd heard the sound of fracturing glass from the living room. She'd had nothing to do with it.

But she couldn't tell her mother she'd been sitting on her bed, leaning in for her first kiss when the new TV—the thing her mother seemed to care the most about, more than she cared about Twink, that's for sure—bit the dust. It wasn't anybody's business what she and Marcus did. He was the one person who always knew when she was in the room, and she wasn't going to let anyone interfere.

"Are you listening, Twink?" Daria asked, taking her eyes off the road as they passed the green sign for Corey Woods Campgrounds. Whatever she was looking for from Twink, Twink didn't think she'd found it. Daria turned back to the road as she asked, "Well?"

"How could I avoid hearing you?" Twink answered. "It's a small car. It's not like I had time to grab earplugs while my mother was shoving me out of the apartment."

Daria kept going on and on the same way she had been for the last half an hour. It was getting old. "I'm telling you, my mama doesn't put up with anything. Anything! If you pull what you've been pulling with your mama, you'll find yourself out on the street. I'd put you up if I had a bigger place, but my efficiency isn't even efficient enough for me. So it's not an option. You...you gotta behave, Twink. Where you gonna go if mama throws you out? Keisha, maybe? No, that wouldn't work. She got a roommate for her extra room. Oh, I just..."

Twink tuned her out and looked out the window again, taking in the last of the woods and the tidy, older houses on the edge of town. Great. Out in the boonies. Livin' large. Land of split rail fences and lawn jockeys.

Wait a minute...was that a sheep in that yard? Or just a really big, fluffy dog? And did it even matter? It was all too rural for her. She'd never even had a cat because their place was so small, and who wanted to trap a cat the way she was trapped, anyway?

Twink pretended to be fascinated by the scenery passing by on her right. She didn't want to risk Daria catching her eye again, not when there was a big, fat tear in it. It was the same old, same old. Nobody wanted her. How could the stupid little town of Giles be any kind of place for a girl like her?

＊＊＊

Cassie was drowsy and needed a nap after one of Tom's amazing dinners that would probably someday make her as chubby as Gillian. Not that Tom cared. He loved Cassie's appetite—all of her appetites. Plus, even though his marriage to Gillian had ended when he'd been trapped inside the store's cat for over four decades because she'd thought he'd abandoned her, Cassie knew he still thought Gillian looked great the way she was. Nothing to get jealous about though. That was ancient history. Tom had only aged by a couple of years while enslaved. He was way too young for his ex now. They were good friends and cared about each other, but there wasn't any chance of romance between them.

She snuggled closer to him on the only modern piece of furniture they'd bought since Tom had won the Stanford mansion in the town raffle. It was comfortable too, but not comfortable enough for her to ignore the sound she heard in the hall. She startled and sat up abruptly. "What was that?"

Tom pulled her back, but she resisted him. "No. Didn't you hear it?" She stood up and walked across the large sitting room full of well-maintained furniture that was the height of fashion in the late 1800s. "Something fell over in the hall."

He smiled at her invitingly from the couch, patting the place beside him that she'd just vacated. "Stop jumping at every sound. This is an old house—they make their own music. Learn to groove with the beat and you'll be fine."

Cassie looked into the hall and then darted out, returning quickly with an old-fashioned letter opener in her hand. "See? I told you. This fell off the hall table." She shook it at him. "It's heavy. It didn't leap off that table on its own. We need to get Natalie in here to check it out. Do a clearing or something. This place is too spooky."

Tom moved to her, gently pushing her brown hair out of the way behind her ears so that it fell down her back in a long cascade, then placed his hands on her shoulders. "Sure," he murmured as he bent to sweep his lips along her neck. "We'll have the place checked."

Most days, she would melt and forget everything else when Tom's lips met her skin, but not today. She ignored the invitation and said, "Especially the kid's room at the end of the hall in the other wing. It's so...I don't know. Sad. And creepy. It's like everything is waiting for a lost little one to come home. I mean, leaving the house to the town in furnished condition is one thing, but leaving everything in place for the kid to return..." She shuddered, dislodging his lips.

"I can see there's no distracting you tonight," he said. "So, should I tell you the story about that room? Everybody knew about it when I was in high school. It was the town's campfire story. If you'd gone to school in Giles when you were young, I bet you would have heard it too."

"There's a story about it?"

He took her hand and led her back to the couch. Watching his tight backside, she almost wished she'd given in earlier. It didn't help the situation that his messy, wavy, longish brown hair made him look like he'd just gotten out of bed and would be totally willing to return. Maybe she should let him take her...*No!* She wanted to know about the creepy room. She might be bringing a baby into this house soon, and she had to learn everything about the place.

When she sat next to him on the couch again, she turned toward him with her bare feet in front of her and her arms snugged around her crossed her legs, subtly putting up a block to prevent any stealth moves he might try. He'd have no choice but to tell her about the house.

"There are lots of stories about the Stanford place. Why do you think the town was so happy to get rid of it? Who knows which ones are true. But old lady Stanford was one weird chickadee, the last of her line after her brother William disappeared. And William...now there's a story. Apparently, he was one bad guy. He'd make our old buddy Kevin look like a sweetheart."

Cassie winced. "Don't bring Kevin up. Just don't. He's not worth mentioning. If William Stanford was worse than a guy who poisoned people, he must have been really bad. Even Robert never mentions Kevin."

Tom shrugged. "He does, but not around you. He understands how you feel, and he respects it. But he was the guy's father, so he's not going to never talk about him. So I get that. There's something strong between fathers and sons, for good or for bad. That's just how it is."

Cassie hid her smile, musing about how Tom might be a father soon. But it was too early to tell him the good news based solely on the assessment of elderly witches. It's not like they were infallible. Natalie especially had been scatterbrained since the Witching Faire. And she always had an excuse whenever they invited her to the new place. It was hard to read her, but Cassie was pretty sure something was wonky in Natalieville; Nat never refused a hand of poker or a free meal or a free anything really, but she was doing all kinds of refusing lately. Gillian even said she'd caught her arguing with herself out loud at the shop when she thought Gillian was out of the room. But even if there was something wrong, Nat would never accept anyone's help. It wasn't in her to admit weakness.

"Yeah, I know," she said. "Robert's the best. He really is. It's hard to understand how such a good man got such a big fail at parenting." She clutched at her tummy protectively but caught herself, immediately moving her hand to her side. "Just...tell me about the room upstairs."

"I dunno...you might want to turn a few more lights on. It could get intense in here."

She leaned forward to slap him playfully on the shoulder, then lay back against the pillowed arm of the couch and put her bare feet in his lap. He rubbed them as he dropped into storyteller mode.

"The first body turned up right inside the tree line by the lake in Corey Woods. Not drowned. Strangled. They were all strangled."

"All?" Cassie asked. Her shoulders tensed.

"There were three of them that year. Each of them done in with a long length of rope that the killer left behind. And each of them was found with a plastic toy in their hand. And how did the Stanfords make their money? They owned a chain of upscale department stores in the Boston area. William had recently stepped into the job of buyer for the toy departments."

"Oh, that's why there are so many toys. It wasn't a kid's room, was it?"

"No. That was his room. I've checked. There are still undershirts lined up in the drawer with his name sewn into the tags. They must have been from when he was still in school. He was the younger of the two kids, but he was in his twenties when he disappeared. My mother gave my father a good tongue-lashing a couple of times for scaring me with stories about how William had a special toy in his room for me if I didn't behave...and let me tell you, even though I was in my teens, that was a much scarier threat than a lump of coal in my stocking had ever been."

Cassie pulled her feet out of his soothing grasp and sat up, leaning in to him. She settled a kiss on his cheek. "Poor thing." She pulled back and laughed. "Now finish the story! Don't get me all worked up just to leave me wanting more."

"Like there's any danger of that." Tom grinned, adding of pinch of bedroom eyes.

Cassie rolled her own eyes in response. And tingled a little. Not enough to want to interrupt the story. But maybe enough to want to hurry it up. "Just go on."

"It was an open and shut case. They found an identical rope in one of the outbuildings behind the house and all those toys in William's room. It wasn't hard to put it together. And he didn't have an alibi for any of the nights the bodies were found. His sister Letitia said he was here all night, but the servants sang another tune. He was out of the house each of the nights there was a murder."

"So, they left his room that way when he went to prison?"

"He didn't go to prison. He disappeared. There was never a trial. I bet he's still out there somewhere, picking off victims one by one." Tom leaned closer. "In fact, he could be out in that hallway right now." His voice dropped to a whisper. "Stalking us. Waiting until we've fallen asleep..."

Cassie breathed in with a small, sharp intake of breath. She forgot to breathe again when he continued.

"...dragging his toy train behind him on a string...ready to railroad us to hell on the end of a wet rope..."

"A wet rope?" she squeaked.

"Yeah. A wet rope. No one ever figured that one out." He moved his head quickly, cocking one ear toward the doorway. "Did you hear that?"

Cassie's eyes grew round. "Hear what?"

"It was like a...a wet rope dragging along the floor..."

Cassie hit him a little harder on the shoulder than she'd meant to. She didn't feel the least bit tingly anymore.

Rain sheeted down the plate glass windows of Cat's Magical Shoppe, shadowing the bottles of colored potions that lined the display window shelves. Despite the rain, the sun tried to shine through the clouds and made a dappled effect on the polished wooden floor. Cat leapt from one patch of light to the next, trying to catch the shimmering spot that always disappeared when he landed.

Natalie was glad of the weather. She hoped it would prevent marauding tourists from spoiling her plan to enlist her friends' help for a second day in a row.

"It isn't about young or old, being the Maid," she told Cassie. "It's about being open to the big world that's out there before your options close around a man and children."

Cassie looked at her sideways, her head askew at a disbelieving angle as she passed her hand over the charms she was preparing. "Still can't see how that's you, Nat. Other than avoiding the marriage and kids thing."

"Can't you? The Maid gathers the makings of life. She sees the dreams, the ideas, the wanting. But she's impatient. There's so much to learn and do. So she gets things started and moves on."

Cassie grinned. "Okay, I can see it now. The impatient part for sure."

Gillian opened the front door and stuck her head in before Natalie had time to fire back. Her yellow rain hat and slicker dripped onto the entryway floor. "Be there in a tick. This had better be important, Nat, to make me come in early when it's pouring down rain like this." Gillian propped the door open with her body as she shook off her wet things.

Cassie followed up with Natalie while they waited. "What does the Mother represent?"

Gillian butted in with the answer as she hustled in, her umbrella and yellow Mac now stowed away. "She bakes the bread, sweetheart. Quite literally. But figuratively as well. She has the strength to take all the things she's been handed and make something new from them. She completes things, then feeds and protects them."

"That sounds nice. Although bread-making is more Tom's department than mine. I think I'd like being the Mother, even if it turns out that I don't really have a bun in the oven."

"Oh ye of little faith," Gillian said, rolling her eyes.

"And the Crone?" Cassie asked.

Natalie snatched the lesson back while Gillian was still looking thoughtful, preparing her response. "The Crone's stories are about endings. She's accepted that all things will pass with time. She sees beyond the passing, helps others accept it, and comforts the ones who are left behind."

"But," Cassie looked at her, her brow crunched up, "you can manipulate the magic of the afterlife. Wouldn't that make you more Crone-like? Don't witches with death magic help people pass beyond if they get stuck?"

"Yes, they do," Natalie snapped. "But I don't. And my grand-mother would not be proud of me because of that." She took the basket of teas she'd been bagging and moved it roughly to the end of the counter, taking conspicuous care to rearrange its contents just so. "Things might have turned out differently. I'd have moved to the role of the Mother, then the Crone, in time." Her lips tight-ened, shriveling up around the words. "There's no point musing on it now. And anyone who disagrees can hold their tongue."

"Wow," Cassie said. "I wasn't going to object. Were you, Gilly?"

"Argue with Nat when she gets like this?" Gillian replied, shak-ing her head. "I don't think so."

Natalie jumped in with, "Good. Because it takes a Maid, a Moth-er, and a Crone to create a ward against ghosts."

She joined Cassie behind the counter and retrieved the white cardboard box, setting it up on the counter. The others looked on curiously until she unwrapped the tissue paper and brought the contents out.

"Cool, Nat!" Cassie said, "That bag looks exactly like your old one. I know how much you loved it. It's been weird to see you with-out it."

"I certainly paid a premium for it. And I'll need to spend anoth-er long evening cleansing it again before it's ready, thanks to the shop's curious kitten. While the ritual obviously doesn't require this particular bag, an effective ward to keep the dead away needs to be red. And, my dears, a woman must sometimes bow to style."

She hung the handbag on her arm. Yes, it completed her outfit nicely, providing a needed splash of color to the vintage black and gray wrap dress she'd chosen from her wardrobe that morning.

"Looks great," both Cassie and Gillian agreed.

"Yes, and now that I've got the appropriate anchor for the spell, the final element is a freshly dead body. Someone who was taken by surprise. The deceased can't be waiting for what's coming, so it won't be as simple as hanging around the old folk's home until nature runs its course on one of the residents. The ones who are ready to go zip through to the Summerlands far too fast for us to complete the ritual."

"Hang on, you're not going to like, ask us to steal somebody's soul or something?" Cassie questioned. "Because I love you, Nat, and I know it must be uncomfortable to see dead people all the time, but there's no way I would do something like that for you. That just sounds wrong."

"Don't be ridiculous!" Natalie crossed her arms over her narrow chest and tapped a foot clad in black pumps rhythmically on the wooden floor. "I need a piece of the afterlife. And to get one, there has to be an open portal. They're only available until the spirit crosses."

"Oh, okay," Cassie said, looking over to Gillian in relief. "I'll help with that if Gilly does."

Gillian looked thoughtful, her green eyes rising from her work to fix on Nat's meaningfully. "Personally, I think there are better ways to deal with one's ghosts than shoving them aside."

Natalie stopped tapping and stamped her foot petulantly. "I knew it! Always expecting everyone to do things your way. I don't know why I thought I could count on you."

Gillian waited for the storm to pass, her eyebrows raised. When it had, she said, "I wouldn't be a good friend if I told you anything but the truth. And if this is what you want, I'll help you. Of course I will. You shouldn't have to be in pain because you sacrificed your ward to save us from being pulled into the Summerlands when Anat tore the veil."

Natalie didn't exactly say thank you, but she uncrossed her arms and let herself relax. She was suddenly so tired that she was sure she'd fall down if she didn't sit down first. She pulled one of the tall stools behind the counter forward, turned, and scooched backward to sit. She motioned them in toward her. "Good. Here's what we'll need to prepare."

✳✳✳

Cassie was late for work at the gallery because she hadn't been willing to tear herself away from Natalie. The details of Natalie's request had been super fascinating from a witching perspective. There was no way she could have made herself duck out in the middle of it. As penance, she'd volunteered to dig into the inventory reconciliation paperwork she and Dash had both been avoiding for the last couple of months. He sat across from her at the small table near the sales counter, slowly cruising through his own stack of receipts while filling her in on the latest gossip.

They both looked up expectantly when the entry bell signaled the arrival of a possible buyer or, even better, a possible art lover. Cassie ditched the invoices she'd been surveying, and Dash tweaked his Dali mustache into an even finer upward point, releasing the scent of vanilla from the wax that warmed to his touch as he molded the ends into just the right position.

They both stood and put on their best company smiles, but immediately froze with their smiles in place as a middle-aged woman in a form-fitting skirt and low-cut blouse barreled toward them brandishing one of the gallery's gift bags at arm's length. "Who do I talk to about returning this? It's horrid. Years out of fashion. Is this what passes for art in this pothole in the road you people like to call a town? Well, is it?"

Cassie looked at Dash, whose nose was twitching like a rabbit's, forcing the ends of his mustache to keep time. It was losing its upward thrust.

Cassie realized she'd better get this one; the boss was terrified. "I'd be happy to help. You're Caroline Akers, right? The town's new publicist? You and your husband bought that gorgeous Frank Lloyd

Wright inspired house out on the boundary of the woods that butts up to the lake, didn't you?"

Dash dipped his eyes to her gratefully before making a beeline for the back.

Caroline didn't soften. "Yes, yes. If you like rustic. But this picture. Take it back. And I want the cash immediately."

"Sure. Give me a minute to check our copy of the receipt. I sold this to your husband only last week. It's by a local artist who went off to the big city and made a name for himself. And he's recently moved back to town. We're super thrilled to represent his work."

"This garbage? I wouldn't display it in my bathroom! Refund. Now."

Cassie took the picture and looked down at it, confused. "Really? But it's remarkable. If my husband brought this home…"

"Skip the sales talk and get me my refund. I have shopping to do."

Cassie punched the gift receipt information into the register. "It looks like he paid with a card. I'll have to refund it to that. Unless you'd like to exchange it for something you like better? If you want to look around…"

"As if there's anything worth having in this podunk gallery in this podunk town. No thank you. I'll leave your merchandise for the great unwashed. No one but uneducated housewives and my husband would think anything here qualifies as art. Put it back on the card." She held out her hand. "My receipt?"

Cassie waited for the receipt to print, then put it into the woman's outstretched palm. "Here you go. It may take a few days for the refund to show on your statement." Caroline's hand closed around it like a bear trap.

As she flounced out of the shop, Cassie muttered under her breath, "And please don't let the door hit you on the way out…"

"Omigoddess, Dash, she was the most unpleasant customer I've ever had to deal with," Cassie said when her boss peeked out from between the curtains that hid the backroom from the public.

He parted the curtains and stepped out, saying, "She'd have given your grandmother a run for her money even in her heyday." He raised his hands and shook them, fingers splayed open like a jazz dancer. "Spare me any more customers like that one. And saying something so awful about Lou Frank's work! I cannot understand what is wrong with that woman."

Cassie picked up the painting again and looked at it longingly as she carried it across the room to the empty space it had left when it was sold. "Me neither. I'd love to have this. It's amazing, isn't it? The way he glazes to build up the depth of color, and yet it's still so subtle and delicate...and the expression in her eyes. It's so passionate and yet somehow wrong, scary in a way. But it's fascinating. Beautiful."

Dash pursed his lips. "Hmmm...do I know a young lady who'll be using her employee discount soon?"

"I wish. Even with a discount, I can't afford to buy art right now. I made Tom agree that we'll keep the spending down to what we earn from the businesses—only until the attorneys sort out my Granny's assets and we find out exactly what we've got to work with after any debts are paid. The truth is that the house is eating our money up as soon as we get it. If it didn't, that painting would have come off the wall the minute you hung it up." She sighed, then placed it back on its hanger, backing up and giving it a lingering goodbye look.

Her attention was torn away by the sound of brakes squealing outside on the street, followed by the impact of metal on metal. They both rushed for the door. When bad things happened in a small town like Giles, they were bound to involve someone one of them knew or someone who knew somebody they knew. Or maybe just the friend of a friend who knew somebody who knew somebody.

A Mercedes had run right up on the bumper of a much older blue Ford in front of the diner, but there didn't appear to be anything very bad happening. Or at least, there wasn't until the unpleasant Caroline stepped out of the Mercedes and started shouting for the driver of the other car to get it out of her way.

A tall black kid in a ball cap, Celtics T-shirt, and jeans got out of the car in front and walked to the back to look at the damage.

Cassie cocked one ear toward where the two of them stood. She had to strain to hear the boy, who talked softly and looked upset more than angry. "I don't know what you're yelling about," he said. "I had my signal on and was already backing up."

Sure enough, there was an empty parking space next to Caroline's car. Parallel parking incidents happened all the time on the too-narrow downtown street. Nobody could have been going very fast, so the damage shouldn't be much more than a dent or a scratch. Cassie headed back to the shop to follow Dash, who had already gone inside. She stopped and turned back when she heard the sound of blows followed by the boy shouting, "Hey, hey, back off!"

The kid had his hands up to block the hits that Caroline rained down on him with her large leather bag. *Okay*, Cassie realized, *this might get ugly.* She pulled out her phone to put a call in to the police, but before she could dial, her friend Daria vaulted out of the passenger-side door of the kid's car and ran toward the fight. Cassie put the phone away; she didn't want to get a friend in trouble. But no...it wasn't Daria. Whoever she was, she had the same mahogany skin and long, curly black hair, but she was younger and smaller.

Caroline Akers was still screaming about how she was going to sue when the girl started smacking her with a clutch that definitely wouldn't have the same effect as the older woman's larger bag.

When the mini-Daria clone yelled for the woman to stop if she knew what was good for her, Cassie was sure that hysterical little voice could never come out of Daria.

Cassie rushed down the street as things appeared to be veering out of control. When she got closer, she noted that the girl also had the same generous mouth and big brown eyes as her friend. Whoever she was, she had to be a relative.

The boy had only defended himself so far, but when Caroline turned to the girl and lashed out at her, he reached out to stop her, grabbing the purse.

Caroline screamed anew. "You let go of that, you nasty little thief! It's not bad enough you back into my car, but now you're ripping me off in broad daylight?"

The boy let go of the bag and Caroline pulled it away, but as she did, it began to smoke. Then flames licked its sides.

Caroline stared at the bag for a moment before dropping it, glaring at it as if it was alive and had done her an injustice.

Cassie yelled, "I'll get help," and flew down the street as fast as her feet would move. She ran back with one of the gallery's red extinguishers. The kids' car was rolling away by the time she returned, and Caroline was stomping at her purse, trying to stamp out the flames.

Cassie put them out easily with a phffft from the canister.

Caroline didn't even bother thanking her. She just picked up what Cassie was pretty sure was an authentic Louis Vuitton bag, now irreparably damaged, and got in her car and sped off, narrowly missing another collision at the first corner as she did.

Cassie couldn't say for sure who'd run into who, but she knew who she'd put her money on if she had to bet. On the way back to the gallery, she dropped a text to Daria with an invitation to meet after work. She wanted to find out who Daria's little doppelganger was. And she hoped that she really was a relative rather than an actual, real-life doppelganger, because the town didn't need any more magical disruptions for a while.

✳✳✳

It was peaceful where Sean Harper parked in the shaded back row of the Corey Woods cabins parking lot, waiting for Caroline Akers, who was running late. She'd said she had a quick errand to run, and Sean was getting bored; he wasn't a fan of peaceful. He liked action. He needed to be moving, doing. Still, it was convenient that there was nobody around this time of year except the caretaker, who didn't mind Sean making use of the empty lot as long as he flipped him a twenty every so often.

"That woman sure keeps her own timetable, doesn't she?" he muttered to himself after getting bored scrolling through the latest videos in his phone's Facebook feed.

He drummed with both hands on the dashboard to a familiar song on the radio, which he'd tuned to the classic rock station Caroline always liked. When it was done, he glanced at his watch and then out the car windows again. If she didn't get here soon, he'd have to get back to the Frank place without an afternoon snack. He'd given up his opportunity for lunch to meet her, and his grumbling stomach wasn't going to let him forget it. Now he was hungry in all kinds of ways. He should take off and cruise by the downtown diner for something to go. He'd have to work late to make up the wasted time now.

Forget her, anyway. She was way too much work. Even if she'd shown up, he was done with her. She'd make it ugly when he tried to end it—she was that kind—but he knew how to keep her quiet if she went ballistic. He reached for the key to crank the van to life but was stopped by the sound of tapping on the passenger-side window.

Sean turned slowly to his right. Caroline was wearing a low-cut blouse that showed off her perfectly shaped breasts like ripe melons on a gilded tray. A more urgent sensation replaced his stomach rumble.

Okay, one last time.

He leaned across the seat and unlocked the passenger-side door. Once she was in, he led her by the hand into the back where he'd prepared a cozy nest with a small but soft mattress and a pile of throw pillows. He pulled the curtain shut that separated the back of the van from the two passenger seats up front; it made a soft swishing sound. Then he lit the candles he'd tucked in among the tools that hung from the walls. Give 'em a little romance, that's how he saw it. If a lady wanted to pretend emotion had something to do with the arrangement, who was he to deny the illusion?

∗∗∗

Seated in the Toadstone Tavern after work, Cassie took a tiny sip of wine before continuing her story of the day's excitement outside the gallery. She didn't want to have to explain to Daria why she wasn't drinking, but she didn't want to do any harm to the maybe-baby, either. From here on in, though, she'd just hang on to the stem of her glass like she was too busy talking to bother with it. "Okay, so, this girl is yelling at this woman, who is a real...well, let's say I'm not on her side on this. And the girl—I thought it was you at first. She looked so much like you. Until she smacked the woman back."

"Around one o'clock? Really?" Daria asked. "She was supposed to be at her first day of school. Mama registered her this morning. Instead she's already running around town with a boy. That girl is too much!"

"Girl who?"

Daria made a wry face. "My cousin Twink. I'm sure I've mentioned her. She used to be a good kid and, you know, you expect a teenager to do some stupid things once in a while, but she's been nothing but trouble since she hit her teens. At least that's how her mother tells it. Delia, that's my aunt, Twink's mother, wants Mama to whip her into shape, but my mama is too old and too mean to deal with another teenager. Especially a wild one."

"Wow. But if anyone can get her under control, your mama can."

"I know, right? Who wouldn't fall in line when the Terror of Giles is eyeballin' 'em? I sure did."

"The poor kid. Your mama will definitely hear about it if she hasn't already. That Caroline Akers, the accident woman—she's a piece of work. I'd bet she really did run into the boy's car when he was backing in to park with his turn signal on and everything, but she's just the kind of wench who won't let it go until she has both of them in court. Just, you know, if it happens…"

Daria dropped her forehead onto her hand. "I can't think how I'll stop mama losing it. And my place isn't big enough for me to take Twink in if mama tosses her out. There's no place left for her with her father out of the picture now. Maybe I can find a bigger place." Daria shook her head. "No, who am I kidding? I don't have the money. I'm still cobbling together contract jobs to make ends meet. And they say a college education is the key to a good job. Yeah, right."

"I might know a place," Cassie said. "For you and Twink both. I mean, if you really think she just needs a chance and you're willing to help her out?"

"I work from home with most of the contracts I get, so I'd be around to keep an eye on her. But not in an efficiency with one small bed, I couldn't."

"Nobody's staying in the living quarters at the shop right now. We use the kitchenette downstairs, but with the main kitchen upstairs, I could slap on a door at the end of the hall that leads into the parlor. It would be a nice place for the two of you. Furnished and everything."

"Seriously?"

"Sure. And cheap rent. Having somebody in the building instead of having it sit empty means less possibility of the shop being broken into. It's a good deal for both of us. I hope Twink isn't into shoplifting or knocking over convenience stores?"

"Not that I've heard of. But who knows?" Daria gave her friend a wry look, followed by a big smile. She lunged forward suddenly, grabbed Cassie, and engulfed her in an enormous hug.

Cassie barely kept her wine from ending up in her lap by holding the glass out away from the squeeze as Daria followed up with, "You're the best! This solves everything. I've got to go tell Twink right now. Call you later for the deets?"

Cassie didn't have time to reply before her friend was out the door and zipping along the sidewalk.

3

The next day, two cats prowled silently through the early morning woods. The new leaves above them barely stirred as they stalked the forest floor for small prey.

The black male watched the female calico's ears prick up as she shoved her petite nose into the air, sniffing. He raised his own nose and the scent hit him too. It was much more interesting than the damp smell of last year's fallen leaves turning into mulch beneath their feet, where the final, shaded pockets of snow were melting. His companion bolted in the direction his sensitive sniffer knew could only lead to trouble.

He blasted after her and poured on the speed to catch up. He jumped her before she got a bite of the enticing meat. Even newly dead, it smelled delicious. Fresh. Ready.

Human.

She clawed at him and hissed. He let go and backed off, not wanting to hurt her, but also knowing he had to draw her away, no matter how difficult she became.

He lured her on steadily, lunging and giving her a bite on the neck or the ear and then running away again. When the smell of her intended meal was far enough away and the calico stopped fighting and trying to go back, the black cat fell to the ground in a seizure. But the seizure soon became something else. From the jittering form that had been a cat, the jittering form of a man took shape.

The calico followed his lead and, in seconds, a dainty woman emerged from the yowling, morphing mass.

When she regained control of her body after the shift, Cassie threw her arms around her husband, shuddering. "Thank you. Oh, thank you. Sheba wouldn't let me go. She was so determined."

"I know. It's okay now." He rubbed her upper back gently, then folded his arms around her as she shivered against his chest. "When you have more experience controlling her, that won't happen. I promise. It's only been a couple of months, and I've had years and years of practice snatching back control when I'm with my animal."

"But omigoddess, if she'd...omigoddess."

Tom reached for the small, not-at-all-smart phone that dangled from the collar he wore around his neck and shrugged. "You don't need to tell me. I've been there. I'll put a call in to the police."

"Ummm. Let's hold off. I want to call Nat first. You remember how she needs a corpse for the ritual to make a new ward? This could be it. This could be what she needs."

Tom handed her the phone. "Sure. But tell her that it makes us square. I won't owe her a striptease at her birthday party."

Cassie grinned. "I think she'd be willing to let that go for this."

A few minutes later, Cassie said, "Nat and Gilly will be here in about half an hour. I asked Nat to bring us some clothes."

He wrapped his arms around her again. "Good idea. It's cold as a witch's tit out here." He brushed a thumb against the closest inspiration for his metaphor and Cassie giggled in spite of herself.

"We've got about half an hour, you said?" Tom turned her around to face him, pulling her close, skin to skin, and she began to heat up as he purred in her ear, "Baby, I can think of a way to keep warm until then, if we hurry."

✳✳✳

Cassie was focused on trying to control her shivers despite being wrapped in Tom's arms when she heard Gillian's "Yoohoo" through the trees.

"Over here," Cassie called.

The two older witches appeared soon enough. Natalie was dressed in muddy, knee-high boots, mechanic's coveralls, and had a hunter's red plaid hat on her head with the flaps pulled down to cover her hair. Her makeup was flawlessly executed, but Cassie guessed she hadn't had time to do her hair as well. Gillian slogged beside her in galoshes with her flowing flowery skirt pulled up between her knees and tucked in at the waist so that it didn't drag in the leaves and mud.

"Well, where is it?" Natalie asked while Gillian handed thick cotton robes to Cassie and Tom.

"It's this way. Or, she's this way, I mean. By the lake. She was definitely female." Cassie's smile faded.

They trudged back in a line the way the two cats had come, mostly silent. Cassie was still cold despite the robe, and tired, too, from her and Tom's brief but satisfying attempt to stay warm. Besides, there was really nothing to talk about in the presence of unexpected death.

Cassie pointed. "Over there."

Natalie walked to the body, put a hand on its topmost shoulder where it lay on its side and scanned the surrounding woods. Her eyes stopped as she looked to the north.

She spoke quietly, turning away from where whatever she'd seen had held her eyes. "This will work. She hasn't taken her portal. She's angry about the whole thing. Stridently angry about it, but I have no idea who she thinks she's yelling at. I can get what I need and then give her a little push on her way. At least, that's what a death witch is supposed to do. This will be good for both of us."

Gillian said, "So how do we help?"

"If I'm to get that ward to keep the spirits away, I first have to hold this one here long enough to coax a piece of the afterlife's essence out of her portal. That's not an easy thing to do. So, first we need to figure out who she is. I need a name to anchor her. I don't want to have to speak directly to her and give away that I can see her. That might be uncomfortable for both of us, and it might also distract her from taking her portal like a good little spirit when all of this is done."

Cassie asked, "Why not go through her pockets? She's got to have ID on her."

"No," Nat promptly replied. "Going through her pockets either physically or magically could leave traces that would foul the police investigation."

Gillian nodded her head. "We certainly don't want to interfere with either her passing successfully or the police finding who did this." She walked to the other side of the body where it lay face down near the low brush. "She looks familiar, but I can't quite place her. Oh, and she...this is definitely not a natural death. No wonder she's angry."

"What do you mean?" Cassie asked.

"She's been strangled. You can see her face from this side and there are bruises around her neck. But the rope still lying here is probably the biggest hint. Come take a look and see if you know her."

Cassie hung back, all too aware that she'd nearly allowed Sheba to have the unfortunate woman for dinner.

Nat walked to the other side of the body and shook her head, then said, "You, Tom? Take a gander."

He did as he was told. "No. Haven't even seen her around the diner."

Cassie didn't have a choice. She made a circuit around the body and looked into the corpse's wide-open eyes. She gasped. "It's that woman, Caroline. The publicist. She returned a picture to the gallery yesterday."

"Caroline it is," Natalie said. She waved Tom away with one hand. "Off home with you. Cassie will be along later. The ritual circle of the Triple Goddess should never be tainted with male essence. I won't allow anything to interfere with my having a ward to keep the specters of the dead away."

Tom handed his robe to Gillian and transformed back into a black cat. Cassie knew the shift would have been extra painful coming so soon on the heels of the last. As Kit, he brushed softly up against her legs before loping into the woods.

Natalie placed Cassie and Gillian equidistant around the body in a triangle, leaving the third corner for herself. She traced a circle around them with the coven's jeweled athame. Cassie wasn't an experienced witch yet, but she took it as a good sign when Nat didn't caution her not to break the circle until she'd used the athame again to cut it. She was one of them now, all the way. Knowing that Natalie trusted her warmed her nearly as much as Gillian's thick robe.

Natalie lit three purple candles. After handing one to each of them, she stepped confidently into her own place.

Holding the candle out from her body, she closed her eyes and stood still for a long time as the candle flame grew brighter and taller. Purple sparks leapt from the flame and hovered in the circle she had drawn around them, competing with the morning sun that slipped through the surrounding trees.

Cassie expected a soft, rhythmic chant, but when Natalie finally spoke, her voice was loud and pleading. "Dear Goddess who grants us magic, lend me your strength today. For I have been lost and..."

Natalie's plea ended abruptly, and her eyes opened wide, darting to the north. Her candle dropped into the wet carpet of forest mulch and extinguished. She pulled the athame out of the pocket of her coveralls and brandished it in the direction where she'd indicated the dead woman's portal had been. "You $@✳#! You @@$*#ing $@✳#$! How could you?"

Cassie had never heard Natalie swear before. Not a real swear, an angry swear. One that was nothing at all like "Great galloping golliwogs" or "Fluttering fairy goodfellows." She looked at Gillian across the body, confused. Gillian whispered, "I always knew it was only a matter of time before she lost her mind."

"I heard that!" Natalie said as she leaned over and cut the circle without breaking her stride as she moved purposefully forward. "You're going with her," she screamed, then broke into an awkward trot, her hands in front of her, palms up and open, ready to give something a shove. Whatever it was, it was something the others couldn't see. Something in the land of the dead.

Then, with a whimper, she stopped abruptly and slumped to her knees like a broken doll, all the fight gone out of her, her head hung low. "Why are you still haunting me?" she whispered. "What right do you have to keep me from getting what I need? I only want some peace..."

Cassie and Gillian both started toward her, but she looked up at their approach, fury building in her eyes, warning them away.

They stopped in their tracks. Gillian turned to Cassie and said, "Go on. Catch up with Tom. We'd never be able to explain why you were out here in a robe, and somebody has to call the murder in. It doesn't look like Nat's capable."

Cassie steeled herself against the pain as she shifted. When it was done, she bounded through the woods, distracted here and there by the activity of the other wild things, leaving messy human emotion behind.

* * *

It took only fifteen minutes from Gillian's call until the police arrived. The approaching sound of damply scuffling steps was accompanied by a male voice saying, "Natalie Taylor. Imagine you being smack in the middle of things when something suspicious happens."

Natalie adjusted her gaze to see Police Chief Karl Denton making his way toward her. She sighed. He was hardly who she wanted to deal with after today's disappointment. Dr. Don, the coroner, whose crisp black dress slacks and jacket over a starched white shirt contrasted sharply with the chief's lived-in uniform, followed. One of the town's patrolman completed the parade.

Dr. Don mouthed, "Drowning?" with a lift of his eyebrow from behind the chief's shoulder. The coroner was not himself one of the magic-using inhabitants of Giles, but he understood that his high-paying, underworked position as the full-time coroner of a small town depended on discretion. Mysterious deaths from unnatural causes, even if the body was found overhead in a tree, would often be determined to be the result of careless use of the nearby lake if the mayor or a select group of his friends said so.

Natalie knew he had an inkling of what the residents were up to, but he also knew not to talk about it. The witches of Giles weren't dangerous by intent, but there were accidents. Spells backfired. Demons possessed a resident or two and went out for a night on the town. That sort of thing.

Natalie met his eyes and shook her head nearly imperceptibly to indicate the death would not require a cover up, then answered the chief with, "We were out walking. Beautiful day for it, don't you think?"

"Sure it is. Neither of you will mind if I ask you to empty your pockets and bags while the doc here takes a look at the deceased?"

Gillian handed her crocheted shoulder bag to the young officer while Natalie turned her pockets inside out. Dr. Don moved to the body and began taking pictures from all angles as he began his initial physical investigation on site.

When Natalie pulled the athame out of the wide top of her boot, and the officer called, "Chief? You'll want to see this," Denton stalked toward them and held out his hand for the blade.

Natalie offered it to him, hilt first. "That's an antique. Treat it gently. My grandmother used it to gather willow bark like I planned to do today. There's a nice stand of pussy willow around here somewhere."

Chief Denton took the knife, inspecting its delicately etched blade and jeweled handle. When he was done, he raised his eyes to hers. "It looks clean, but I'll be taking it with me until we rule out it hasn't been used on the victim."

Natalie harrumphed. "Of course you will. Might as well harass little old ladies out to collect the ingredients for their headache powder while the real criminals laugh about how they got away with it. Perhaps you'd like to take off with Gillian's bag, too? She could easily beat someone to death with the thing, given the sheer volume of her daily essentials."

Gillian was busy repacking an assortment of hair accessories, cones of incense, candles, books, bags and bottles of herbs, and general flotsam back into her bag. "Natalie, leave him alone. The man is only doing his job."

"Fine," she replied. "Are you done with us now?"

He rocked on his heels for a moment, then said, "Let me..."

He was interrupted by a "What the heck?" as Dr. Don fell backward onto the seat of his previously spotless pants. One of the corpse's hands had fallen open, and a plastic set of chattering teeth clattered loudly as they jumped up and down in the dirt.

Dr. Don scrambled up, composed himself, and stood looking down at the body. When the clacking sound had stopped, he said, "That's odd. I wonder what that's about?"

Natalie's face froze.

Strangled.

Toy.

There was only one more piece.

"The rope. The rope that was used. Is it wet?" she asked.

"And an odd question added to the mix," the coroner said. "Let me check." He reached out to touch the rope that was still wrapped around the woman's neck. "It's damp." He next put a hand to the woman's blouse. "But her clothing isn't. There was no dew last night, and the rain had cleared up by yesterday morning. How did you know?"

But Natalie was already stalking away from him, her big boots kicking up last year's leaves as she went. "I'm done here. I'll come in tomorrow to make my statement. And I'll be needing my knife back sooner rather than later."

Gillian gently held out a hand to stay the young cop as he started toward Natalie. "Hang on a minute, Nat. Please?" she called.

Natalie stopped. But she tensed where she stood, ready to move again at any minute.

Gillian turned to the chief. "Robert wouldn't have a problem with you letting her go and talking to her tomorrow at the station. You know how she can be. You also know she's not involved with this. I was with her the whole time, so I can fill you in on everything we did before and after finding the body."

The chief nodded. "Ms. Winterforth, for the mayor's sake, I can accept an assurance from you that she'll be there. But after that bit of prognostication, she definitely has questions to answer."

Gillian looked at Nat, who dipped her eyes in subtle agreement. Gillian said, "She'll be there."

Natalie stomped away.

***

Sheba darted in through the newly installed kitty door and raced around the big living room, leaping with claws extended at particles of dust, looking for her playmate. But Kit was nowhere to be found.

She discovered her favorite wadded-up ball of aluminum foil under the couch. It made an irresistible scritching sound as it shot across the hardwood floors. It was fun to bat around, but it was too predictable to be fun forever. The spider she found crawling up one side of the fireplace was not only fun but also tasty. But it wasn't as tasty as the meal that had been stolen from her in the woods would have been.

She padded up the stairs and ran down the hall to the big bedroom and found Tom there instead of Kit. She mewled up at him, disappointed, but willing to accept an ear scratching if he could be convinced by her soft, seductive self. Still, if it was Tom instead of Kit lounging on the bed, playtime was over. When he didn't reach out to her, she curled up in a ball, her tail twitching at the tip, her green eyes glaring balefully into his. She was going to be pushed into the background now before she even had a proper nap.

Tom stood, stepping to the side of the bed so Cassie would have enough room to transform in the middle of the mattress. At least the bed was softer than the forest floor.

Cassie's eyes were still shut against the last of the pain when Tom lay down next to her, taking her in his arms and stroking her hair gently. She knew it meant a lot to him that she had chosen to share all parts of his life by joining with Sheba when he joined with Kit, and she had never once regretted it, but she often wished this part of their partnership didn't hurt so much.

When she opened her eyes and smiled, he kissed her on the forehead. "So how did it go? Did Natalie get what she needed?"

She frowned. "No. Something went wrong. I've never seen her so angry. You know how she is, always in control no matter what's simmering under the surface. She uses negative feelings to keep focused, you know? No way would she let them take her over and cloud her judgment. But today? She broke down. Literally broke down."

"Nat? Our Nat? Scary old Nat?"

"That's the one. Gillian sent me away while Natalie was still on her knees after she cut the circle and ran out of it, yelling at someone we couldn't see. I don't know what happened."

Tom's smooth brow wrinkled. "That can't be a good thing."

"Yep," she said. "If you can't depend on Nat to keep her feelings hidden, what can you depend on? Something big is up with her."

Her eyes jolted wide open, and she pushed his sheltering arms away so she could sit up. "Omigoddess! I need to get dressed and then I need to call Daria. I just realized that since her cousin was involved in a fight with Caroline the day before she turned up murdered, the police are going to need to know about it." She groaned.

"Why would they?"

"Caroline assaulted the boy that Daria's cousin was with, and then Twink—that's her cousin—went after Caroline. So the boy stepped in to protect her. And the woman those two kids had a big, screaming, public fight with has now turned up dead in the woods out by the lake." She groaned again, longer this time. "I mean, it looks bad. I don't have a choice. Somebody else is going to report it when they put two and two together. There were plenty of people downtown that day, and you know how everyone gossips around here. I need to get there first with the real scoop. Or, better yet, Twink should do it. Because as soon as word starts to spread about a murder, there will be plenty of people running in to have their say."

Cassie got dressed, then pulled up the contact for Daria on her cell as she headed through the house toward the garage. All she got was her friend's voicemail: "Leave a message. The usual drill."

This would be the worst time for Daria to start swiping left on her. On her second try, she left a message. "Daria, call me. Twink needs to go to the police about the accident. It's really important that I talk to you."

Tom moved up behind her and rubbed her shoulders. "You want me to go with you?"

"No, I'll be fine. But if Daria can't convince Twink to go in and tell the police what happened or tells me she'll hate me forever for talking to them myself, you can have a big batch of carbs ready for my dinner when I get home tonight. Baby will definitely need comfort food." She'd looked down as she said it, knowing Tom wouldn't think twice if she called herself baby because that's what he always called her. There wouldn't be a bump down there for ages yet, but she smiled a secret smile at it anyway. She could hardly wait until she was far enough along to do a pregnancy test that didn't rely on magic, just to be sure, and let Tom in on the secret, too. But her stealthy internet research told her she still had at least two weeks to go before she'd be ready for that kind of confirmation.

When they parted ways after Tom parked Eunice's old station wagon behind the Diner of Earthly Delights, she nearly forgot a goodbye kiss because of what she had to do. Kids needed to be protected; they should be allowed to make mistakes and not pay more for them than is due. If she let one of the local gossips report the accident, it would turn into robbery at gunpoint. Small-town people can have some really big-time imaginations.

Still, if what she was doing was right, why did it feel so wrong? She dialed the police station from in front of the gallery. The desk sergeant made an appointment for her to come in and report the incident the next morning. He told her the whole department was engaged today and unavailable for anything other than emergencies.

She didn't tell him she already knew why. The news probably wouldn't be around town yet. She made an appointment to go in to talk to the Chief early the next morning.

As soon as she hung up, her phone rang and Daria's pretty face smiled up at her from the screen. She steeled herself, then swiped right.

The day after the murder, Cassie dragged herself into the gallery, feeling drained from her early morning interview with the police. But if Cassie looked drained, Natalie, who had been sitting in the lobby when Cassie was on her way out, looked like she'd been drained and wrung out, drained again, and then hung out on the line as an afterthought. Their greeting had been brief—a "hi" from Cassie followed by raised eyebrows from Natalie.

Dash had known she might be late, and he and Jon were hovering around the counter, perusing a takeout menu from the Diner of Earthly Delights. They were discussing what sounded good, holding hands as they said, "mmmmm," or "no, too rich."

"It's *all* good, you know," Cassie told them. "Tom could make an old sneaker taste great. He's super excited about buying his grandfather's old family business and wants everyone to love it as much as he does. Anyway, sorry I'm late. You can go out now instead of bringing something in." Cassie had almost forgotten to put the part about Tom's grandfather, who was Tom himself, into the mix. But Dash and Jon knew nothing about Tom's past, and no matter how much she cared for them, that was how it had to stay. Tom had a birth certificate that said he was Tom Sanders III, and that's who everyone but the coven thought he was.

Dash said, "Obviously, work has to come second in a situation like this. It's terrible, just terrible. Do you think the police will want to talk to me too?"

"I don't know. I told them we both went out to see what happened, so they might contact you. I feel rotten about the whole thing—I wish I hadn't seen it. Those kids had nothing to do with the murder. I'm sure of it."

Dash leaned in across the counter, conspiratorial, and Jon followed his lead. "Did you get any details? Do they have any suspects yet?"

Cassie shrugged and shook her head. "I was there for them to ask me questions, not the other way around." She realized she felt uncomfortable now that her friends had adopted the gossip pose. They hadn't seen the body. Or nearly eaten it. "But look, if you guys want to go to lunch..."

"Actually," Dash, said, taking Jon's hand, "Lou Frank is coming in today, and I want Jon to meet him..."

Jon winked. "Dash has a crush on him. We may have to duke it out. He talks of nothing and no one else since the man offered his work to the gallery on consignment." He squeezed his partner's hand. "But I do enjoy his work." He looked toward the wall where the artist's paintings hung. "And we have to encourage our local celebrities if we want to put Giles on the map. Wasn't that the reason we hired that unfortunate woman?"

"Wait a minute, Lou Frank is coming here?" She reached into her purse for the vintage compact she'd kept from her grandmother's things. Lou Frank was such an amazing artist—there was no point in making a poor impression. The rhinestones on the lid sparkled as she opened the compact to check her makeup and decided she needed another layer of candy-pink lip gloss. The applicator was still sliding across her lips when the bell above the door sounded.

When she turned, she was surprised how handsome he was. She knew from his bio that Lou Frank was in his seventies, but a thick shock of white hair fell rakishly over his forehead in a mass of curls. She was pretty sure he'd had some work done too, because she knew he wasn't a client for the shop's Magical Masque, which kept Natalie looking at least ten years younger than she was. He would have been a lady killer when he was young.

Jon whispered to Dash behind her, "Put your tongue back in your mouth, dear."

Dash giggled. Then he rushed past her with his hand outstretched, gushing. "It's such a pleasure. This is Cassie, who's training to take over the gallery when I retire, and this is my partner, Jon. They're both huge fans."

Lou smiled at him indulgently and shook Jon's hand. After that, his gaze moved to Cassie. "Are you a fan, truly?"

"Oh, absolutely. Your work is so..."

"Then I have something for you. Because I won't sell a painting that's been returned. It has no value to me unless it goes to someone who will love it enough to make it worth something again. I'm withdrawing this despised painting from sale." He walked to the wall of watercolors and took down the portrait that Cassie had admired so much only yesterday.

After removing the price tag on the back, he handed it to her. "I hope you'll accept this as a gift from me. I have the perfect replacement for it, which I will return with soon. Perhaps we could meet for a glass of wine and discuss art, life, when I do? After all, aren't they the same?"

The question hung in the air as Cassie looked down at the beautiful artwork in her hands, stunned. Then she remembered herself. "I can't accept this, and..."

"I'm aware you're married. You wear a ring that proclaims that loudly. And you're too young for me even if you were available. But you know how this town is, don't you? Everyone is busy telling everybody they know about anyone else's business. The grapevine also tells me that you recently earned an art degree, so I can safely predict it won't bore me senseless to converse with you. You'd be surprised how few people really enjoy talking art. Particularly in Giles."

"Oh..." She blushed.

"Not that I wouldn't chase you around that counter if I were a younger man..."

She blushed even darker. "I still can't..."

"Of course you can. Otherwise I'll just throw it away. Please take it."

"I...well...you would really throw it away?"

"I would."

"I guess I have to take it, don't I?" She beamed at him. "You'll have to come for dinner. My husband is an amazing cook, and he wouldn't mind us talking art at all. We recently moved in to the old Stanford place."

There was a flicker of recognition mixed with something else, but it disappeared before she could latch onto it. He said, "I know it well, and I'll look forward to it. Now, please, let me relieve you of this for a moment," he said, taking the picture and placing it carefully on the counter, "so that I can bid you farewell."

Cassie felt like royalty when he bent at the waist and kissed her hand.

"Until we meet again." He turned and strode toward the door.

From behind her, Cassie heard Dash say, "Jon and I would also love to have you come for dinner if..."

The artist lifted his right hand, waving the suggestion off without even looking back.

✳✳✳

Natalie had chosen a no-nonsense black pantsuit for her interview that day, and her steel-gray bobbed hair was sprayed carefully in place so that no strays could distract her. She knew she'd need all of her wits about her to make sure that she got through it without losing her composure again.

She ignored Chief Denton's posturing as he leaned back in his chair, his shirt sleeves unbuttoned and pushed up over his ropey forearms. His hands made a steeple in front of his mouth while they waited for his assistant to return with files that had been stored in the basement for fifty years. Natalie had at least convinced him to send someone to look for them. That was something.

They had mistrusted each other since an unfortunate incident in the nineties when Denton had been a young officer and Natalie had been pulled in for questioning after an impromptu healing spell had gone wrong. In a moment of haste, she had missed it when her patient's spirit passed through to the Summerlands, going beyond anything healing could help. Her ritual, performed too enthusiastically and far too publicly, had blown the doors out at the emergency room and melted the wheels on the town's only ambulance. In the end, Robert, the long-time mayor of Giles and now Gillian's boyfriend, had smoothed the waters, convincing Denton that Natalie couldn't possibly have been responsible for an act of sabotage at the hospital given her excellent reputation as a nurse, but the damage had been done. For twenty years, they'd circled warily around each other like alpha wolves protecting their packs.

Finally, Denton moved his hands to the desk. "So, what makes you think this murder is like the ones from the—what was it? The Sanford murders?"

"Stanford. And there was never a trial. William Stanford wasn't convicted of any crime. He disappeared just before they named him as a suspect."

"If every kid in Giles grew up on the legend this could be a copycat killer, that's what you're saying? Or are you saying this Sanford fellow is back to finish what he started?"

"Stanford! The man's name was William Stanford. And he's not back. There's no doubt of that."

The chief looked her in the eyes, trying too hard to read something there, she thought. He asked, "And how would you know?"

"I have my ways."

"As in, you helped him escape the first time?"

She glared at him. "Are you going to take this seriously or not?"

A voice sounded from the door. "Karl, how's things?"

Natalie turned to see Robert standing in the doorway, dressed in mayor casual, with his dress shirt open at the top button and his tie loosened. His black shoes reflected the shine from the overhead lights only slightly more brightly than the shine from the top of his very bald head.

He nodded at her when she turned. "Nat. Good to see you. Gilly told me the two of you had gotten yourself into a situation in the woods. She asked me to check in when you stopped by today. I hope you don't mind."

"Ms. Taylor was just telling me that this killing looks a lot like one that happened in Giles a long time ago. The Sanford murders. Do you remember them?" Denton said.

Robert's eyes dropped to Natalie's quickly, and he held her gaze for a second longer than necessary. He'd known about them, about her and William. She pulled her eyes away. She didn't need his compassion.

Robert looked back up at the chief. "I never believed that William could do what he was accused of—and it's Stanford, not Sanford, by the way. He was a good man. If he hadn't disappeared during all of that mess, I'm sure he'd be sitting in the mayor's chair now instead of me. Everyone thought a lot of him, and his family did good things for this town before they withdrew from the community when William disappeared. They never recovered from any of it: the accusations, William going missing. It was too much for them."

Natalie glanced back at the chief as if to say, "See?"

She stood up to leave. She'd accomplished what she'd come here to do; the file would be plopped onto the chief's desk sometime soon. He might be annoying, but he was a persistent little cur, and he'd see in that file exactly what he was meant to see. If there was evidence linking these murders to the old ones, it could finally clear William's name.

But she wasn't going to sit around waiting for Denton to make headway. No, she had her own resources. No reason to twiddle her thumbs until the official results were in. Her own investigation would begin today, right after her shift at the shop ended.

∗

The last orange sliver of sunset still lit the sky when Gerald Akers opened the door, peeking around the door jamb at Natalie. She noted that his eyes were red-rimmed and his voice shaky, but she told herself he might simply be drunk and celebrating after a successful kill. You can never be sure about these things. Natalie had seen enough of both life and the afterlife to know that nothing was certain.

"Mr. Akers? I'm Natalie Taylor. The ladies in the choir want to extend their condolences." It wasn't from the choir, obviously. Although the members of Giles's "choir" would certainly agree that it had been if Akers thanked them for the casserole their high priestess had delivered. She held out the large casserole dish that held a repackaged store-bought lasagna. She was competent with herbal teas, but making edible dinners could not be considered one of her skills. It had been TV dinners all the way for Natalie since they'd first appeared on the market.

Gerald took a deep breath and opened the door wide. "You're so kind. Will you come in? If you'll write down the reheating instructions for me, I'd appreciate it. I can't seem to remember anything for more than a few minutes today."

"I'd be happy to," Natalie said, following him to the kitchen. She noted that Caroline's husband was quite a bit older than his wife's reported age of fifty-five. He appeared to be in his mid-to-late sixties. But then, grief can age a person overnight. She'd seen it happen often enough among her peers. But even on a happier day, he wouldn't be an attractive man. His red-rimmed eyes were small, his nose was large, and his cheeks were pitted and pockmarked. He was in good physical shape, though. His rolled-up sleeves revealed well-muscled forearms, and he moved like a younger man with none of the delicacy or stiffness of someone with aging joints.

As she wrote down instructions—she hoped they would result in a warmed meal rather than a burned one—she said, "You must miss her terribly."

He sighed another sigh that narrowly escaped turning into a sob when he pulled it back at the last minute.

"I'm a terrible husband. I didn't even report her missing. I assumed she'd spent the night in Boston with friends because she was unhappy with me. I didn't think anything of it until the police arrived this morning."

"Oh?" she prompted, extending a hand to pat his. It was an unnatural and uncomfortable gesture for her, and she pulled back almost immediately in disgust at her own duplicity. She needed to get out of here. It wasn't right to be snooping, not now. Not even to find out the truth for William's sake. But his next words made her stay.

"She'd gone shopping. Shopping! Shopping for a man who wasn't me, I'd bet. If she had been merrily spending my money in Boston like she said she was going to, she would have been perfectly safe..." He broke down, his head falling into a well made by his folded arms. His back rose and fell sharply, like he was sobbing silently.

The scent of ozone filled her nostrils, and a voice sounded in her ear. "Leave the poor man alone. I don't want your help if it causes this kind of pain."

William. The last thing she needed was him squatting on her shoulder like a good angel. But she couldn't respond to him. Not now.

Fortunately, her own resolve was sitting on her other shoulder to urge her on.

"Why do you think she was in Giles instead of Boston?" she asked as gently as she was capable of.

Gerald's breathing began to relax. He was clearly fighting to pull himself together. Good. Enough of his sloppy grief. She needed answers.

He raised his head and, despite his previous sobs, his eyes and cheeks were now dry. "I don't know. She seldom told me her full plans. She was out a lot, saying she was meeting with the town council about the publicity campaign or going to one of the businesses to gather information for social media teasers. I thought things were going well with her campaign and she was enjoying it. She always came home in a mellower mood. I'd hoped she was starting to like Giles, but maybe she only liked someone she'd found here."

William's voice in her ear said, "Come on Nat. He's had enough," but empathy had never been her strong suit.

She asked, "Was there anyone in particular you suspect she might have gone to see?"

His eyes and mouth tightened. "There was a handyman she hired. Sam or Shane. Something manly like that. I never met him. He was always gone before I got home. She said they had become friends. I was still tying things up with the business before we sold the condo and moved here full-time. He did a nice job with the kitchen cabinets." He looked away, although she couldn't tell if it was due to anger or grief, before turning back with a face drained of all emotion. "If there was something more between them...well, who could resist her? She was fearless, beautiful, intelligent. That she'd ever looked at a man like me..."

He went silent and Natalie patted his hand again. Best to give what support she could to keep him calm. She didn't want to get trapped giving comfort if he started crying before she could get away.

"Gerald, do you have anyone coming to stay with you? Children? Siblings?"

"No, nothing like that. Caroline and I married when we were older, and our work consumed us, I'm afraid. We were both only children. She had family in the west, distant cousins, but they weren't close. The funeral will be in Giles once they release..." he paused, his eyes far away, "her body. My Caroline's body. I'm sure that if they come in for it, they'll be staying in the city. I doubt I'll see them except at the funeral."

"Then may I ask a friend to stop by to check on you over the next few days? You shouldn't be constantly alone at a time like this. She'd be happy to check in. Have you met Gillian Winterforth, the mayor's girlfriend?"

He perked up considerably. "Robert Andrew's partner? We met at a council meeting where Caroline's work was discussed. She had kind eyes."

"Yes, she does," Natalie said. Not that she thought having a kind demeanor was necessarily a positive trait. "I'll let her know you're expecting her."

There. Gillian would be more than willing to deal with the man's pain. She was always in people's way, offering a chubby shoulder, even when one wasn't wanted.

As she dialed Gillian's number on her way out to the car, William asked, "Compassion? Or do you want to put a spy in his camp?"

"Hush," she replied. He knew her too well. "You're giving me a headache."

✳✳✳

Natalie hoped that the place where Caroline Aker's body was found had been vacated by the police. She walked purposefully through the woods, a flashlight gripped tightly in her hand to guide her when the twilight ran out. William's enthusiasm for the mission since they'd left the Akers place hadn't waned, but she wasn't tired enough yet of his chirpy optimism to send him on his way.

"Oh shush," Natalie said, refusing to even glance at him as his specter glided along beside her. "Some of us are too old to become giddy at the possibility that you might be exonerated. And the other of us are too dead for it to do them any good."

"That's one of the reasons I've always loved you. Because of the hope hidden beneath your grim practicality."

He loped along ahead of her, skipping at times, turning and walking backward, grinning like a fool. If her neck hadn't gone so stiff while visiting Akers, she could almost see herself getting caught up in his antics.

He looked so real that she shouted, "Watch out, you fool. There's a tree right behind you!" She felt like a fool herself when he passed right through, popping out none the worse for wear on the other side.

He walked up next to her and grinned. "You've forgiven me, haven't you, for helping that woman pass over? She wouldn't have made it if you'd held her there until you'd coaxed what you needed out of the portal. Would you really have sentenced her to be trapped here, wallowing in her anger?"

She pictured old Mrs. Olson, whose slowly fading specter still screamed her agony soundlessly every night in the window of the bakery. She'd been robbed and beaten by a passing hobo she'd taken in and fed during the Great Depression, long before Natalie was born. Natalie's grandmother had tried to help her pass many times, taking Natalie with her once, but the spirit had refused the portal, too trapped in that last moment of betrayal to move on. Eventually, the portal had stopped appearing when summoned. The old woman would continue fading and be entirely gone in perhaps another hundred years or so, never to know if the peace beyond the veil was real.

"I would have," she said quietly.

"Then you're not the Natalie I know. That Natalie wouldn't have let another soul suffer so she could get what she wanted," he said. "And I don't think that Natalie, *my* Natalie, has gone anywhere. And anyway, I'm only doing your job for you. You're the one who should be helping the lost spirits find their way. You couldn't do it, so I've been following in your mother's footsteps for you. I've been looking after the town's dead."

"You?" She looked at him appraisingly. "That's why I've not been overwhelmed by the spirits in Giles like I was before I got my ward. A few here and there, yes..." Her eyes narrowed. "You're very responsible for someone who still looks like he should be wearing short pants."

"Does my appearance bother you? I guess it would. Wait a minute. I can fix it, I think."

She continued walking. This was a ridiculous mission. What was the point of it? To clear the name of someone who'd been dead for fifty years? She was a fool. An old fool.

"Nat, I said wait, please? You don't have to be in such an all-fired hurry all the time, do you?" His voice sounded lower, more assured. No longer the voice of the happy toy buyer.

She turned, and her breath caught in a short gasp.

He looked exactly like she'd imagined he would if he'd grown old beside her the way they'd planned. Not bald, thank goodness, but gray-haired. His skin had settled lower, and he had jowls along with the creases around his mouth and eyes that had been cut deep by smiling. But his brown eyes hadn't aged; they were still William's gentle eyes, bright and full of fun.

It wasn't fair that he'd gone off and died before he could grow old with her. It wasn't fair that he'd left her to go her own way down the witch's path, too busy and too prickly to ever let anyone in again.

She closed her eyes. "Stop it. Go back to the way you were. We're almost there, anyway."

When she opened her eyes, he was young again, a tease of what he was, but at least no longer a tease of what might have been.

When they reached the spot where she'd drawn the circle around the corpse the day before, it was already dark, but Natalie didn't mind; she always felt comfortable in the dark. She set the heavy, un-lit flashlight aside while she worked. She placed fivecandles to make the pentagram and set a cone of homemade incense in the center. It smelled like bay leaf, a smell associated with soup, not magic. But bay leaf was exactly what she needed to draw sense memory from the surrounding woods. There was little chance the spell would work; it had been two days now and nature forgot things quickly. Still, she had to try.

Despite what William had said, he had been working toward his own ends as much as he had worked toward helping the unhappy spirit when he'd coaxed her across the threshold, she was sure of that. He knew she needed energy from the portal to build and charge a ward that would disperse any spirit that came too close to her; he'd been hanging around in the background when the first ward had been built. She pointed a finger at him, gesturing back toward the way they'd come.

"You need to back off. I won't have your energy confusing the casting." She glared at him, red sparks beginning to glow at her fingertips. "Way back. Out of the woods."

He dissolved into a milky glow, his smile fading last.

When he was gone, she lit the candles and began her incantation—softly, slowly. The red sparks grew until they turned into an aura that surrounded her, then expanded out from her body, rustling leaves and turning over loose piles of mulch as it rippled out away from her in waves, seeking the forest's memories.

She worked her way back slowly, feeling the forest things sense her striding through the woods, followed by William's glow, which was formless to the trees and mice and centipedes. Next, she felt the traces of the police investigation being pulled away, the body being bagged and removed.

She pushed, but the senses of the spiders and the toads had nothing else. She needed something bigger, something smarter—a raccoon, a stray dog. The red glow began to fade at its edge. The candles burned down close to the ground, but still she chanted. She didn't want to give up while the least spark of the spell remained. But it was getting colder in the dark woods, and the first candle sputtered out in a pool of wax, leaving only the barest stub.

She wasn't going to prove anything by dying of exposure and being the next corpse her furry friends found in the woods. When she tried to rise, she found she'd been sitting cross-legged so long on the damp, chill ground that her body fought her.

In the end, she had to roll and lift her backside into the air like a stink beetle to get her limbs working again so she could push herself into an upright position. What had she been thinking, coming out here like this to help find a murderer and clear an innocent man's name? She was stiff and sore, and she'd need to soak more than her feet tonight, but she had absolutely nothing to show for it.

It's just like they always say. No good deed goes unpunished.

∗∗∗

Cassie handed Tom a glass of wine and flopped onto the couch next to him with a fizzy water of her own. A leisurely dinner with mounds of garlic mashed potatoes slathered in butter had relaxed her. Glancing at the picture she'd set on the coffee table for Tom's approval, she said, "It's beautiful, isn't it?"

"It is. But I'm not sure how much I like other men giving you expensive presents."

"Technically, it's just a handmade gift."

"Mmmmhmmm," he said. "Like a ceramic ashtray from a kindergartner, right?"

She snuggled into him, smirking. "Exactly like that. I did say that we would love to have him to dinner sometime, but..."

He smirked and said, "You really think I'm cooking for your gentleman caller?"

"Yeah, well, now I'm not so sure you should. I mean, I really liked him, he's so...continental in an old-time movie kind of way. I have to admit I was flattered. And he's so talented. I mean, soooo talented..."

"But?"

"He was completely dismissive to Dash when Dash said he and Jon would love to have him over for dinner too. I mean, Dash can get pretty emotional and over the top sometimes, but that's just because he really feels things that strongly. So, he gushed. And Lou blew him off like he was a nothing, a nobody. I didn't like that. Dash is kind of remarkable, you know? Nobody is nicer or more forgiving than he is."

"I can live without this Lou Frank guy coming to dinner. Tell him that I'm a caveman who's so jealous I can't even allow you to be in a room with another man. And it would be true, too." To prove his point, he hopped off the couch and beat his chest with his fists, yodeling his best Tarzan yell.

While she giggled, he picked her up in his arms and raced off with her up the stairs. There would be no more talk of artists and gifts tonight.

5

The next morning, Natalie vied for a place next to Gillian in the doorway behind the counter in Cat's Magical Shoppe. They watched as a tank-top-clad, muscular young man in his prime finished hanging a new door at the other end of the hall.

Natalie spoke first. "Who is that man, and why is he putting up barriers? Who said there was a problem with the old door?"

Gillian nudged her with a shoulder. "Like it matters? I can think of a lot of things around here that could do with some fixing."

Cassie walked out of the kitchenette with a cup of tea, blocking their view. "Hi guys. Sorry. I figured he'd be done with the work before you got here. Oh, Sean," she said, "these are my friends and co-shopkeepers Natalie and Gillian." She turned back to them. "Cinnamon recommended him. He only started taking jobs in Giles a few months ago, but she said he did a great job refinishing her floors."

The man smiled broadly, flashing a set of movie-star teeth. He appeared to be in his thirties or so. "Yeah, Cin's a doll. Makes a mean cinnamon roll, too." He winked and turned back to his work.

Natalie wasn't quite sure what he meant by that, but she didn't ponder on it for too long. Gillian and Cassie were far too distracted by the young man, and she needed them to be sharp when she told them her news. She hadn't expected an outsider to be in the shop when she arrived. The delay made her testy.

"Why do we need a door, anyway?" she asked. "And is he almost done?" she continued to Cassie, who'd brought her tea into the shop and was blowing on it to cool it while she leaned on the wooden counter top.

"Finished now, ladies, since you're interested," came the reply from down the hall.

Natalie grimaced. Oh marvelous. He'd probably heard Gillian going on about him earlier, too.

Cassie straightened, set her tea down, and opened the till, counting out a stack of bills. "The old door was too lightweight. I'm renting out the house to my friend Daria and her cousin, so it needs a sturdier one that muffles sound, has locks, and keep us both out of each other's business."

She walked into the hallway and handed the bills to Sean, who rifled them quickly and then saluted Natalie and Gillian with the money still in his hand and a huge smile on his face. He said, "It was nice to meet you all," before heading for the back door. Cassie walked with him but was back quickly. She locked the new door on her way in, saying over her shoulder, "You know, if I didn't have Tom..."

Gillian laughed. "No one would blame you, sweetheart. Blimey-...I'm sure I felt faint for a moment. Warn us first the next time you plan on having one of the Chippendales stop by to entertain. I'll bring my smelling salts."

Natalie harrumphed. "Really, the two of you..."

"Lighten up, Nat," Cassie chided her. "Like you're not always perving on Tom to embarrass him. Just admit that the guy was hot."

"I don't have to admit anything of the kind. But if it will make you happy, yes, I noticed that he was an attractive man wearing tight, unnecessarily brief clothing. Fat lot of good it does me at my age." She turned to her right and spat out, "Don't be ridiculous. I told you to wait outside...no, don't rush me. I'll handle it in my own time."

When she turned back, Cassie and Gillian were staring at her with their mouths slightly open as if they wanted to speak but were mulling it over carefully before they did.

Natalie spoke for them. "No, I haven't gone around the bend. However, after my little tête-à-tête with Robert yesterday on my way out of the police station, it's apparent that's what my good friend Gillian thinks, isn't it?"

"I said nothing of the kind," Gillian replied, a little too quickly.

"You said that I seemed more distant than usual and that you'd caught me talking to myself several times. You also said I seemed unfocused and distracted."

Gillian didn't respond.

"Well? Did you or didn't you?"

Gillian sighed. "I'm worried about you, Nat. You know Robert and I both care for you. You haven't been yourself."

"I've been very much myself, thank you," Natalie snapped. "In fact, I've been more myself than either one of you have ever known me to be. Because without the ward that I gave up to protect this town, my world encompasses both the living and the dead. And the dead can be quite attention-seeking. It isn't myself I've been talking to."

Cassie said, "Why didn't you tell us that?"

Natalie hated the pitying look that Cassie probably thought came across as concern. "I had to wait until conditions were right, didn't

I? At least you and Tom haven't wasted any time. I could have approached one of the other witches in town who has had children, but there's no one else I trust to be in my business. And the stronger the individual witch's magic, the stronger the spell. I need a powerful spell. One that temporarily disperses any spirits within a wide range."

"Is it very bad, seeing the dead?" Gillian asked.

"Not always. But it's difficult sometimes sorting out what's real and what's Memorex, so to speak. The dead are mostly harmless, although the ones that have resisted passing for a very long time can manifest briefly and manipulate objects. That can become an annoyance." She turned to Cassie. "By the way, William is sorry about dropping the letter opener. Apparently there's a letter from his mother lying on his dresser top that he'd like to open. He has very limited ability to impact objects, and his attempt to carry it down the hall went wrong."

Cassie's mouth dropped open. "William? William Stanford? The serial killer William Stanford?"

"Yes. I mean no. He didn't commit those murders. And yes, William Stanford."

Cassie looked around the shop. "He's who you've been talking to?"

"Yes. He's the reason my mother, my grandmother, and I created my first ward fifty years ago. He never gave me a minute of peace, insisting he still loved me and that he had to clear his name because he hadn't killed anyone. Not that I thought he had. But it was difficult for me with him always nearby."

"You and he," Gillian said, "you were?"

"We planned to marry. But it was a secret from most. After my grandfather's attempt to raise my grandmother from the dead by sacrificing his second wife, my family's reputation was ruined. Non-magicals saw him as a murderer and corpse-defiler. The coven knew him as something much worse—a necromancer who abused his magic in a way that could have destroyed us all. And although William knew nothing of my family's magical history until after he was dead, a family like the Stanfords wouldn't have allowed its favored son to date someone from a family like mine, much less marry her, no matter how much old man Stanford depended on my mother to keep him organized. She was his secretary, one of 'the help,' in addition to being the daughter of a murderer. You see the problem."

"Oh Nat, that must have been so hard on you..." Cassie's mouth turned down at the corners.

"It was a long time ago. Few people even remember the story about my grandfather anymore. But until everyone started scaring their kids with the story of William Stanford, the story they told to keep them in line was how Josiah Taylor killed his second wife and dug up his first."

"And William is here right now?" Cassie's eyes darted around the shop again.

"He's outside as instructed. I got tired of his jabbering. He did always like to talk." She looked out the big picture window where William was peering back in at her, smiling. He nodded expectantly. He would have looked dapper if he'd died in something other than that horrid sweater vest. "I thought you should meet him. We need your help."

"What kind of help?" Cassie and Gillian spoke at the same time, darted their eyes to each other, then looked back at Nat.

"To solve these new murders. I'm sure they were committed by the same person who committed the original ones. It's possible that once his name is cleared, William can finally find the peace he needs to go on to his afterlife. Of course, this depends on also solving the mystery of how he died. I've always assumed the two were linked."

Cassie's eyes widened. "He doesn't know how he died?"

"They often don't, dear. Particularly the ones who refuse to run along to the Summerlands when their time is up. Maybe it's too final for them. Not that I have all the answers, mind you. There are still plenty of mysteries about death, even for a witch with knowledge of death magic. You never really know until you take that portal to the other side, do you?" She handed each of them a bottle full of thick, greenish liquid. "Prepare yourselves, please. We'll need to up your supply of adrenaline for a moment to intensify the spell. You'll only have a couple of minutes, so talk fast if you plan on having a conversation. Ignore the sweater. I never could get him to stop wearing it."

She watched them drink their potions approvingly, then called, "William? They're ready," as both of them flushed bright pink. Gillian fanned at her face with both hands while Natalie blew a fine powder toward them from her open palm.

＊＊＊

When Twink found Daria waiting at the house after school with instructions to pack, she didn't roll her eyes even once. Daria knew that she would never hear the end of it from Mama, but maybe she could at least shelter Twink from Mama's anger. For now, her mama wouldn't know where they'd gone and she wasn't the kind to ask around for them. Mama Barton didn't want anyone up in her personal business.

When she parked behind Cat's Magical Shoppe, Daria asked Twink to stay in the car for a minute while she reached under the mat for the key. The metal was cool between her fingers. At least something was going right. She got her first set of boxes out of the car and set them inside the door. She motioned for Twink to follow.

Nothing much had changed in the parlor since the last time she'd visited Cassie there during summer vacations. When Daria went back for her packages, Twink stood in the doorway, her lone bag in her hand, her hoodie pulled up around her curls, hiding her face.

"Come on. Don't stand there looking like you've just lost your last friend. Things will get better. We'll get the rest of my stuff from the car and then we'll sort out who gets what room. I've never been upstairs because Cassie's grandmother didn't like kids much, but I bet it's nice. The old lady had some serious cash."

Daria hustled upstairs with Twink's slower steps sounding behind her. Her shoulders clenched involuntarily when she pictured the fury that had glowed in Mama's eyes when she'd said, "You got no idea what you're gettin' yourself into. She's the spittin' image of your grandmother in more ways than one. You'll be back wishin' you didn't never take her in. You mark those words, girl."

Daria knew that Mama hadn't gotten along with her own mother, but the old woman had died by the time Daria was born, and no one talked about her much. It was worth more than you wanted to pay if Mama heard her mother's name mentioned.

"Come on, Twink," she said as she walked into the bedroom on the left, taking it all in. "This room is wild, isn't it?" She ran her hand across the silky surface of the shiny, red, embroidered bedspread. "Wow, that's satin, the old expensive stuff like in the vintage stores. This room is cool. Feminine, that's for sure. A real lady's 'boudoir,' like in some old movie."

"Awfully red, isn't it? Like the whole room is wearing some skank's lipstick." Twink walked to the bed and ran her hand along the satin spread while looking around at the matching wall hangings and curtains with the pink tassel pulls. She walked to the vanity and sat on the metal stool with the scrolled backrest while she looked at herself in the big mirror with the faceted insets around the outside. When she was done, she walked to the window and pulled the curtains aside to look out into the downtown street below. "It's maybe cool, though."

Twink didn't turn back to face her cousin, but Daria could hear the hint of suppressed desire in her voice when Twink asked her,

"You want this one?"

"No," Daria replied. "Too fancy for me. You take it. I'll see what else we've got."

She waited while Twink took off her hoodie, folded it, and put it down gently on the velvet bedside chair, leaving her mark.

✳✳✳

After Natalie had left for the day, Cassie poured boiling water from the kettle into Gillian's cup and then moved to fill her own. "That was odd, wasn't it? Seeing a ghost?" she said as she watched the steaming liquid fill the cup, scenting the kitchenette with mint and lavender.

"Can you imagine, though?" Gillian replied. "No wonder she's such a misery guts. Spending years clinging on to that purse so that her dead lover—no, that's not right, if she's a 'maid' as she says she is—her secret boyfriend then, who everyone says killed three people, doesn't keep showing up mooning around her, reminding her that he isn't really gone. How could anyone move on from something like that?"

"I'm kinda glad that he stopped Nat from making another ward, aren't you? He seemed nice."

"That's fortunate since he's your tenant." Gillian smiled.

Cassie tugged her lip absently and said, "Yeah, I'm not sure how I feel about having a ghost around the place. It's a little creepy, isn't it? Especially if it turns out Natalie's got it all wrong. I mean, there's no real proof that he didn't do what he was suspected of. When Tom was telling me about it, it sounded like they'd found a lot of evidence that pointed right at him."

"I don't know about any of that. I didn't move to the States until later. But how could anyone look as innocent as he did and be guilty of anything? No, I'm with Natalie. Let's see what we can do about solving the mystery of this murder and putting things right."

"Sure. And maybe Nat will let William move in with her while we work on that." Cassie hoped she hadn't sounded too pushy. It might not be a great idea having a ghost hanging around the house with a baby on the way, even if he did look like a refugee from reruns of *Leave It to Beaver*." She smiled as she said, "It might even perk her up a little if she had a man around the house. Look how much happier you are now that Robert is in the picture."

Gillian reached over and patted her hand. "Yes. But I'd like to keep Robert alive, thank you."

"Oh yeah, sorry...I didn't mean it like that." She grabbed a set of dirty tea cups and washed them under a streamed of running water at the sink, setting them on the draining board when she was done. "If you don't mind closing up, I think I heard Daria come in earlier, and I want to welcome her and her cousin to their new home."

"No bother at all, dear." Gillian winked. "I've been meaning to have a good clear-out and reorganize when Natalie wasn't around to stick her nose in it. Now seems like the perfect time!"

∗∗∗

"Look, I'm really sorry that I had to go to the police about the accident. I didn't want to," Cassie said, but Twink wasn't interested. As far as she was concerned, her new landlord should have gone home after work instead of stopping by for a visit.

She crossed her arms, defiant. "I haven't done anything wrong. Marcus didn't do anything wrong. That wench was crazy. I shouldn't have to talk to the cops. That's why I didn't go talk to them when you put your nose all up in it in the first place."

She also didn't want to hear about it from Daria again, but Daria jumped in anyway. "Look, Twink, nobody thinks you did anything wrong. You were just one of the last people to see that woman before they found her. So they have to ask you questions. They'll want to know who the boy is and where he went afterward. Cassie was right about that."

"They think Marcus did it? Marcus would never do anything to hurt anyone. He was protecting me. I'd be more likely to kill someone than he ever would."

Cassie sat down next to her on the couch and tried to pat her shoulder, but Twink flinched away. Cassie's voice was quiet, friendly, like she was on Twink's side, but Twink knew better. And she certainly didn't want anyone talking to her like she was a stupid kid. Cassie said, "I believe you. Except you might not want to put it exactly that way, know what I mean? All the police want is answers about what happened to that woman after the accident. No one is accusing you guys. They just need to talk to you so they can rule you out."

Daria added, "And Cassie is really, really helping us out by renting this place to us, so you should thank her for that. You know I'm right. This is lots better than both of us trying to squeeze into my old place."

Twink's eyes narrowed, and she uncrossed her arms to point a finger at her cousin. "You don't need to double-team me. You're worse than my mother!" Thinking about her mother took all the fight out of her. "Just leave me alone. I'll talk to them. It's not like I have a choice anymore, is it?"

She stormed upstairs and slammed the door to the big, red room. The impact rattled all the windows in the house.

The next day, Cinnamon Brown glided in to Cat's Magical Shoppe a few minutes before opening time, her long gypsy skirt kissing the floor, her gold-painted nails and eyelids glinting against her dark skin. She carried a large bag across her shoulder and a folded card table grasped in one hand.

"Thanks for letting me drop this off, Gilly-girl. I know the shop isn't open yet, but Sean is taking my car away for repairs tomorrow and I can't carry this table all the way from home without it. I don't want to have to cancel."

"Nor do we want you to," Gillian said, moving aside a tall stand of pussy willow branches so that Cinnamon had easier access to the small storeroom where she gave her readings. "It's nice when we can bring Salem people to Giles instead of the other way around. I know Cassie would be happy to make your readings a permanent offering so you could leave your things. The store does well on the days you're here."

Cinnamon acknowledged the compliment with a dip of her chin as she bent to open the table legs.

"Nothing serious with your car, I hope?"

"No, no...but Sean says it needs basic maintenance or it will end up serious. He's a player, that one, but he's a handy friend to have if a woman has enough sense not to get her heart tangled up with him."

"Handyman Sean? He just put up a door here." Gillian raised an eyebrow. "Oh, that's right, he mentioned you."

Cinnamon took a folded cloth out of her large shoulder bag and unfolded it. "Let me guess—he said I make a mean cinnamon roll?" Gillian nodded, so she continued. "The man sure thinks he's clever, and he can't resist trying to make people believe he's planting seeds in everyone's patch."

She shook the cloth out into the air and it settled gently across the top of the table. She straightened it just so. "But a grown woman, she ought to know better, and I am well grown. You warn young Cassie, though. That one doesn't care if a woman has commitments."

Finally, she took a pack of tarot cards out of her purse and set it on the table.

Gillian grinned. "Oh, Cassie's fine. But if I were thirty years younger and Robert wasn't in the picture..."

Cinnamon laid out a row of runes on the table as she talked. They were from a nice set, carved from jadeite, and they looked good against the maroon tablecloth. "Girl, let me tell you, it doesn't need to be thirty years. The man is seriously experimental. You know that woman who got herself killed out by the lake in Corey Woods a couple days ago?"

If Gillian had drifted off to an image of male pulchritude earlier, all of her attention was on the conversation now.

"Caroline Akers? What about her?"

"What do you think—early fifties, maybe? At least ten years older than me, so she had to be twenty years older than Sean. Well, they were meeting up together out in those woods in the parking lot by the cabins. He says she had a thing for getting busy in places where she might get caught. He seems pretty spooked about her turning up dead, though. Especially since he was with her the day before they found her."

"Oh my. Do you think the police know about this?" Gillian asked.

"What? You think Sean had something to do with it? No, not that man..."

"Or if her husband knew about the affair, that would give him a motive, wouldn't it?"

Cinnamon looked thoughtful. "There you go makin' too much sense. You think I should give Sean a push to go in to the cops? 'Cause he didn't do it, that's for sure. But it's not like he's discreet. The husband could have found out easy enough."

"If he was my friend, I'd encourage him. It'll be a lot better for him than if the police find out about the affair on their own."

"I'll talk to him when he picks up the car later today," Cinnamon said. "I like him. I don't want to see him in trouble." She headed for the door, but Gillian followed, stopping her with a hand on her arm.

Gillian asked, "Do you think he'd be willing to let Natalie ask him some questions? She has a special interest in this. I'd like to tell her about it with your permission."

Cinnamon shrugged. "Don't see why not. She's female, isn't she?" she said as she glided out, laughing. "I'd like to see Sean try to charm that one."

7

Sean was surprised to find one of the women from Cat's Magical Shoppe standing outside his door so early in the morning. Maybe the beefcake show he'd put on while working there had been a little over the top.

Based on his in-depth experience with women, he realized that his visitor was probably older than she looked. Not that it mattered much, since she looked like she was in her early sixties, putting her out of his range of interest. If she was looking for a booty call, she was out of luck. But no, that was not what she wanted. Her severe expression made it clear she expected something but had no plan to make it pleasant for him.

After she introduced herself as Natalie Taylor, he let her in at her request for a private conversation. Could be she had a job for him. Working on the old houses in Giles was turning out to be lucrative.

There was nothing particularly physically imposing about her; she was thin, with brown-verging-toward-black eyes and a chin-length, tidy, and still thick head of gray hair. That she looked like someone's grandmother didn't matter. It was the way she sat squarely on the couch in her black pantsuit with those dark eyes never leaving his face that told him what he needed to know about her; Sean thought she was the most commanding female he'd ever faced. Even tougher than Caroline, who he'd been careful to approach with kid gloves to avoid the outbursts. He decided quickly that he would need to handle Natalie with something softer than kid gloves—fluffy pillows wrapped in marshmallows maybe? Because if she decided to bite, those slightly graying teeth—her own, he was sure, despite her age—would sink in deep.

He was surprised when she said, "Cinnamon Brown says you knew Caroline Akers. Tell me about your relationship with the deceased."

"Look, I already told the cops everything I know about it when I stopped into the cop shop yesterday. I don't mean to be rude to such a lovely lady as yourself, but why do I need to tell you about it too?"

Natalie sighed, and her expression softened a little, but he didn't think it was in response to his flattery. *Maybe not such a dragon lady after all*, he thought.

She replied, "I have a personal interest in this investigation. What happened to Mrs. Akers mirrors a series of murders that happened a long time ago. Murders that were blamed on someone I knew."

"You knew William Stanford? The strangler guy? I mean, you were close? That's who you're talking about, right?"

She pursed her lips, parting them a moment later with a dry, clucking sound. "You've put a foot in it if you thought you couldn't be accused of being a copycat. You obviously know the stories." She jotted down something in the notebook that had somehow appeared in her hand.

"Who doesn't? It's the first thing any of the townies ever gossip about with out-of-towners, although not the last, that's for sure.

Giles is pretty dull as far as I can tell from the rest of what they've got to gossip about. Not much to do. But I gotta say, the town did put on a mean show at the last Witching Faire. That was kick-butt. If you do that every year, you could really draw some crowds."

Her back stiffened. Dig up the demon Anat, who currently resides inside Natalie's much-loved original red purse within a block of concrete, so that she can tear a hole in the veil between life and death for the amusement of the masses? Over Natalie's very dead body.

Between gritted teeth, she responded, "Hmmm...I don't think the town has the resources or the energy to put on another show like the last one. You attended?"

"I was sanding Cinnamon Brown's floors that week, heard about it, and thought it could be fun. Brought my nephews. They had a blast. Those costumed folks walking around, like the one with her head under her arm? Creepy."

"Yes, but here we are in Salem, so why are you in Giles so often if you don't live there? Not much to do around town, like you say."

"I met Cin when she was doing readings at one of the witch trial tourist spots here last summer, and I gave her my card. Not for a job, but oh well, that's what I got out of it. She told me she hadn't been able to find any general handymen in the area, so I found a few places that would let me post flyers. I did some work for Caroline and her husband last month, and I'm up at the Frank place now doing some plastering, painting, general rehab stuff. It's in pretty good shape. Just needs a touch up."

"Fascinating," Natalie said, drawing out the word in a way that made it clear it wasn't. "So you met this Caroline when you worked for her?" Natalie looked down as she started jotting again.

"Yeah. Not really my type. I like strong women, don't get me wrong, but she was beyond aggressive in her approach to things. She came on to me, and I was like, why not?"

"Even though she was married?"

He shrugged. "Like I said, she came on to me. If it wasn't me, it woulda been some other guy. It's not like we were out in the woods making a love connection, you know what I mean? It was just harmless fun."

"Until she turned up dead out in those same woods, you mean," Natalie said.

"I didn't have anything to do with that."

"Then who else knew about you and her?"

He shrugged. "I may have told a few people. I don't worry much about gossip."

Natalie blew out air between closed lips. "Phht. You like to brag about your conquests, you mean."

He cocked an eyebrow and smirked. "Maybe."

"Did you tell anyone who would tell her husband?"

"Don't think so: Cinnamon, a couple of the dudes I hang with around here, Lou Frank, the artist I'm doing the work for—he just moved to Giles from New York. He's one for the ladies, maybe as bad as I am. Can't see him interfering. He's never said he knew her."

Natalie sat silent, nodding slightly. "That's it, then? No one else?"

"That's it. It's not like I took out a billboard on the interstate."

Natalie reached down to pick up the red bag she had earlier parked at her feet, opened it, and put her notebook away after tearing out a leaf and handing it to him. "That's my phone number. If you think of anything, please give me a call."

"Seriously? And why would I want to do that?"

She looked at him piercingly. "Unless you want the kind of show that happened in Giles at the Witching Faire to happen in your apartment, you'll take my request seriously."

As she held his eyes, he saw things swirling in her pupils that shouldn't have been there. When he looked away, he couldn't remember exactly what had scared the cockiness right out of him, but the sense of what he'd seen lingered. He got to his feet when she rose from her chair to leave.

"Ms. Taylor," he said, "I will always take any request from you seriously."

***

Natalie was so absorbed in her thoughts when she left the young man's apartment that she hadn't noticed the specter until it was right in front of her.

"Hippity hopping hangnails!" She stopped short and looked into the filmy eyes of a woman who would have been in her midthirties when she'd died. Maybe a little younger. She looked hard done by in any case. This one carried a lot of baggage with her into death.

The spirit put icy hands on her shoulders, "Ooooh, tell him to stop. Please. Please. Make him stop." The wailing was so loud that Natalie covered her ears, breaking through the ghostly arms with flailing elbows. The cold made her shiver. She knew she was the only one who could hear or see what was happening, but she looked around just the same. No one in the hall.

If Sean had killed the woman in Giles, was this another of his?

"Who?" she asked the ghost. "Stop who?"

The specter look surprised. Her voice dropped to a girlish whisper as her eyes focused on Natalie's now, realizing Natalie could see her. "My husband. Terrance. My sweet, sweet Terrance. He's hurting me." A tear rolled out of a puffy, blackened eye. "Can you make him stop?"

Sean wasn't responsible for this one, then. Natalie looked around for a portal. Nothing. Without grave dirt and a brush-up on what her grandmother had taught her, she couldn't bring a skipped doorway back. She stepped to the side and went around the lost spirit. It forgot about her once Natalie was no longer directly in its path and drifted slowly down the hall, moaning.

She looked down at the red purse that hung on her arm, disapproving. It looked exactly like the last one, but this one was only good for ferrying around essentials. She sighed. The purse was stylish but useless without the spell three generations of her family had placed on the last one. She deeply missed her ward at times like this.

At least William couldn't follow her this far out of town. He'd want her to help the woman who was trapped in the corridor by her trauma; if he knew about it, she'd never hear the end of it until she did. But she'd need to brush up with her grandmother's notes to help the poor creature. And he was probably right about her; fifty years ago she would have done it without prompting.

She turned back to watch the specter make its mindless way along the corridor. After a while, her chest felt tight and she turned away. No one deserved to spend their afterlife like that. What harm would it do to take a peek at grandmother's grimoire?

***

Natalie swung the door shut. The bell above the door tinkled merrily, causing that blasted kitten to come running out, expecting fun.

She pushed it aside with her foot, then stomped a warning when Cat lifted a paw to give the hem of her black pantsuit a bat. It ran off, keeping a wary eye on her from the safety of its basket.

"That's right," Natalie warned. "Not every witch enjoys the company of cats. You can wait right there until Gillian gets here to feed you."

She headed for the counter, noticing that the nearest set of shelves looked wrong. Rearranged? Hmmph. Gillian's work, she assumed. And right when she'd gotten it exactly the way she liked it. What was that woman thinking putting the Ouija boards in easy reach like that? They were far too dangerous in the hands of the gifted but uneducated. She wished the shop didn't carry them at all. She started toward the shelf, but changed direction when she heard muffled voices coming down the hall from behind the counter. She wondered why Gillian hadn't left the door unlocked when she'd come in. She headed for the back, ready to part with a loud and sharp piece of her mind, and peered into the small kitchenette. No one there.

She tried the hallway door. It was locked. Of course—Cassie's friend was scheduled to move in. Still, that wasn't a female voice. In fact, that big bass voice could only be Chief Denton, even though it was the wrong kind of voice to come out of such a scrawny man. Natalie cocked an ear and put it closer to the door.

She didn't think that a teenage girl would have what it takes to do what had been done to Caroline, but it wouldn't hurt to listen in. It might save time if she didn't have to question the girl herself. That was, of course, assuming Denton had got it right.

Natalie had her doubts. Hopefully he'd read the files she'd pointed him toward and knew to ask the right questions. At the moment, he was just making conversation, trying to get on the girl's good side, trying to make her feel like he was a friend.

Natalie preferred a more direct route. Had anyone ever been fooled by the "good cop" routine?

"Oh, so you two met in Spanish class? You interested in languages?" the chief's voice boomed.

"Not so much. But you have to have one to get into a lot of colleges," came the girl's reply.

"Yeah? What about your boyfriend? Marcus, right? He interested in languages? Got a couple on the go?"

"No. But he's got a lot better shot of getting into a good college than I will, at least if a scholarship comes through." Natalie heard the pride in the girl's voice.

"That right? Basketball player or something?"

"Sure. 'Cause that's the only way a black kid gets himself a scholarship, right? No, he's not a baller. He's got top scores in all of his classes. Including Spanish." Natalie smirked. She would have liked to have seen Denton's face when the girl called him out.

"Fair enough," Denton said. "I see where I assumed too much. I apologize." Natalie couldn't tell through the door if he was being sincere or not. The man was hard to read in the best of circumstances.

He continued: "Let's just talk about what happened the other day, if we could. Had you ever seen Caroline Akers before the accident?"

"No." Twink had a girly voice, but the response was firm.

"So tell me about it. What caused it?"

"We were hungry and there's not a single fast food place in town, so we were going to get something at the diner. Marcus had his signal on, and he was backing into a parallel parking space—which, by the way, he's great at—and this woman pulls out of another space with her head buried in her phone and plows right into us."

"Hmmmm...'zat so?" Denton said. "And then what did your boyfriend do?"

"Same thing anyone would do. He got out of the car to see if she was okay and to look at the damage."

"And was she okay?"

"If you call being crazy okay. She ran right up to him and started smacking him with that expensive bag of hers. He would never get in a fight with a woman. He let her hit him. So I got out of the car to help."

"And did what?" the chief asked when she didn't continue.

"Told her to leave him alone. And then she started hitting me instead."

"And Marcus let her do it? Not much of a boyfriend."

The girl's reply was vehement. "'Course not! He tried to take the bag away from her. She stopped hitting me after he grabbed it."

"What happened next?"

"She snatched it away like it was precious and she hadn't just been using it to beat us up. And she accused him of trying to rip her off. Then the bag, it started smoking. Like she'd dropped a cigarette or something into it before she got out of her car. She was drunk, that's what I think."

"Anything else after that?"

"That bag lit up. I mean, flames and everything, so she dropped it and started trying to stamp out the fire. Marcus and me got in the car and took off. It would have been stupid to hang around."

"Where'd you go?"

"He dropped me off at Daria's mama's house, where I was staying," the girl replied.

"What time was that?"

"I don't know. About the time school would have got out if we'd gone to school," she said.

"So he would have had plenty of time to go back and take care of business with the crazy lady." Denton's voice sounded cocky.

"Sure," she said. "If he hadn't parked the car around the corner and come back to the house so I could let him in at my window." Her voice went soft and low. Natalie stopped breathing, straining to hear. "He didn't leave until real late, you know what I mean? I'll bet he made it back to the place where he stays in Boston before sunrise, but it couldn't have been much before that."

The chief didn't sound quite so full of himself when he responded, "'Zat so? That's all I need, then. Thank you for your cooperation."

Denton took his leave. Afterward, an older, but still young, female voice said, "Twink, so help me...if mama ever finds out you had that boy spend the night in her house...you and I, we're both going to have to move out of state. Maybe all the way out of the country."

"Whatever," Twink said. Natalie heard the sound of rapid footsteps pounding up the stairs.

But Natalie hadn't been convinced by the girl's performance. It was clear from what she'd heard through the door that this young lady was smart, way too smart to pull something as likely to doom her as sneaking a boy into Ella Barton's home. No, she'd given the boy an alibi, that was what she'd done; Natalie was sure he had been nowhere near Twink's bedroom that night.

The real question was, was there a reason the boy needed the alibi she had been so quick to give him?

✳✳✳

Sean finished taping off the ceilings at the Frank place that he'd painted a few days before. He was doing the walls today, and he wanted a crisp seam between them. He was careful not to shake the rickety wooden ladder his employer had supplied for reaching the top of the vaulted bedroom. He didn't think any more of the choice of black for the bedroom walls than he did of Lou Frank's choice in ladders, but he wasn't the artist, and the artist said that when the bronzes and the watercolors in their wide white frames were placed, it would turn the room into a showpiece.

He grinned to himself. As he stepped carefully down to the next rung, he wondered if the man would be asking women in to see his etchings. Seemed like the kind of thing the snobby old sleaze would get up to.

There was a sudden crack and Sean lurched downward. He yelled something his mother would still wash his mouth out for as he fell backward, pulling the ladder with him as he smashed into the mystery pile of furnishings hidden beneath the drop cloth he'd moved everything under the day before.

Wow, his head hurt. But the ceiling looked great. A clean, smooth white that really would contrast nicely with the black walls he'd be painting today.

So long as he didn't have a concussion.

He rubbed his skull where a bump was just starting to rise before getting up and pulling up the drop cloth to view the damage underneath it.

It was easy to tell what he'd clobbered—one of Lou Frank's precious bronzes was missing a limb. He was lucky the thing hadn't gone right into his brain; the hand still attached to the broken arm was definitely pointy enough. Although everyone always said he could be hardheaded, this was the first time he'd realized it could be useful.

He knew his jerk of an employer was going to blame him for the damage, even though it was his own deathtrap of a ladder that caused the problem. And he hadn't made a dime on the job yet. The advance had gone for the materials. If his employer found out about this, he wasn't going to end up with anything for his labor.

Yeah, well, he better not find out about it then, Sean told himself. He went out to the truck and dug around through his tool boxes for a tube of epoxy. That should do it. The crack might show, but with luck, the old goat wouldn't ever look at it close enough to see it until Sean had the money for the job in his pocket and was long gone.

***

When Cassie arrived at the gallery for her afternoon shift, she was surprised to find her boss, all smiles, talking to Lou Frank, who she had to admit looked very dashing in a much-older-man way in khakis and a white button-up shirt with a colorful fringed scarf wrapped loosely around his neck. The swooping shock of white curls really finished the look. She got why Dash had such a crush on him.

Dash turned to her. "Cassie! Lou brought us another painting to replace the one he gave to you. It's..."

Lou turned to face her directly, interrupting. "I didn't come just because of the painting. I owe Dash an apology. I was completely inside my own head when I left here the other day. I'm afraid I may have appeared rude, and I had to make it up to him."

"Oh, wow, that's really nice of you."

"And presents!" Dash said, holding up a bottle of wine. "Such a nice vintage," he added, looking down at the label. "Lou, if this is how you make up after a fight, you can be rude to me any time."

"Never again, Dash. It was thoughtless of me. Thoughtless." He patted Dash's hand and her boss beamed.

"So gracious. But you must show her the painting!"

It was only about six inches by six inches, but it was clear who the subject was. It was her. Her own face peered back at her in the luminescent tones characteristic of Lou's work. But instead of eyelashes, her eyes were ringed with flower petals and her hands were clasped over her mouth as if she was keeping a secret.

She had no idea what it meant, but it was remarkable. She blushed a deep-down blush.

The artist set the painting on the counter and rushed toward her, taking her hand. "I'm truly sorry if I've embarrassed you. But you have a beauty that I had to paint. It's what distracted me as I was leaving the other day. I have an excellent memory for visuals, and I was concentrating so hard to keep your face fresh in my memory until I could complete a reference sketch that I forgot to be civil, and I didn't realize until later how it must have appeared."

Cassie stopped blushing when she realized that her face would be hanging in a stranger's home and that no one had asked her if she was okay with that. "The painting is amazing, but...I don't know how I feel about you having painted me, I...I didn't know that I would be a painter's model. I'm not sure my husband would want... and until Granny's inheritance is released, I can't afford..."

Dash stopped her. "It's okay. I've bought it for the gallery's permanent collection. It will come to you when you buy me out many years from now when I'm too decrepit to make it in to work anymore. Tom doesn't have to share you with anyone."

Cassie sighed, relieved. "Dash, you're the best boss ever!" She threw her arms around him, glad she didn't have to explain to Tom how her face had ended up for sale. He wouldn't have made a big thing out of it, but she knew it would have bothered him.

"Well, the sale is *almost* complete..." Dash said when she let him go. "I had to promise I'd let you go for lunch on company time with our favorite artist to sweeten the deal."

With her excellent boss pleading with his eyes like that and Lou Frank having turned out to be not at all the creep she thought he was, she couldn't say no. She owed him. "Sure. How could I not?"

Lou offered her the crook of his arm. "I have a picnic waiting. It's a lovely day if you like your weather cool. We can enjoy our meal in the town center by the gazebo, if that suits you?"

Cassie felt relieved again, although she didn't let on. But a public place would work really well. She was sure Lou was just a harmless old flirt, but it was reassuring to know that he definitely couldn't try anything weird on such a nice sunny day with half of Giles out on the streets.

✳✳✳

Cassie wasn't exactly hanging on Lou's every word, but she did find the man interesting, and he really was an engaging conversational-ist. If he could tone down the flirting a little, Tom might even like him; judging from the contents of the picnic basket, Lou Frank knew and appreciated good food and wine.

She had refused the wine, but she recognized the label. Lou put it away immediately and brought out a bottle of sparkling water instead.

The wild mushroom pasta, still warm thanks to an insulated serving dish, was beyond amazing. The freshly baked bread, also still warm and brushed in butter with the smallest hint of garlic, was crisp on the outside and perfectly fluffy on the inside. She wouldn't normally allow herself to take in that many carbs in one sitting, but, well...there might be another whole being inside her now who needed feeding, right?

And the dessert? Yep. She committed at least two of the deadly sins while savoring her own portion, plus a little extra.

The biggest pleasure of the meal, besides the carb coma that Lou countered with steaming hot shots of espresso from a silver flask, was his never-ending store of the latest arts talk from New York. In a place like Giles, despite Dash's enthusiasm, you didn't get the latest version of anything. But Lou was tied in. In big ways. With big galleries that represented big artists.

Who was she kidding? Tom would hate him. And he would probably be right. The artist said all the right things, got the food and wine right, and dropped all the right names. He was exactly the kind of pompous jerk Tom would accuse him of being. He would hate it that she was having a great time listening to his stories.

"Are you comfortable enough?" he asked. "Now that the shade is skimming along here, it's getting cooler."

Cassie hadn't noticed. She'd been completely absorbed in the story he'd been telling about the old days of The Factory. The man had known Warhol! "I'm good, but we've been here for..." Cassie looked at her watch. It was two-thirty in the afternoon already. "I've left Dash alone for almost three hours! I need to go." She jumped up.

"Give me a minute to pack up and grant me the pleasure of walk ing you back?"

"Sure," she said, pulling her cardigan around her.

They walked back briskly once she'd helped him put the leftovers back into the basket. "What brought you back to Giles, anyway?" she asked him as they headed toward the gallery. "You're too sophisticated for such a small town."

He smiled at her and raised an eyebrow, flirting again. "There are *some* things in Giles that are worthy of my notice. But, truthfully, I hadn't thought much about Giles for years. Then I heard that that fellow—" he pointed to the statue of Giles Corey, the town's namesake and hero to many local witches, which stood on pedestal farther down the street—"was damaged in a freak storm during the Witching Faire. Since I'm the artist behind the statue, I felt that I should be the one to repair it. It's made of hammered brass—I don't know what I was thinking, really. Lost wax casting would have been easier in the end, if more expensive, but it was my first major work. I suppose I wanted the hands-on experience. Of course, now the repairs are all tied up in the city council. I'm quite concerned the small crack will become a bigger one while they wrangle over what they can and can't afford." His words sounded clipped by the end. He obviously wasn't happy about the situation. "Anyway, that got me to thinking about how the pace of New York is starting to wear on me after all these years, and I didn't have a tenant for my parent's home, so setting up housekeeping seemed like a good idea."

"I'm sorry to hear that the repairs are being held up. It sounds like you're attached to our statue."

"It was my last project in Giles before I decided to leave town. At the time, it was a..." He paused as if looking for the right word,

"...significant moment for me. I wouldn't want the statue ruined by cheaper, shoddy work."

"Absolutely. I had no idea. I'm friends with Robert Andrews, the mayor. Maybe I can put in a good word."

"Would you? I'd appreciate that. I know Robert superficially from my youth here, as you do in a small town, but the word of a close friend couldn't hurt." He patted the hand that was still wrapped around the crook of his arm.

"Did you know that the body they found in the woods this week might be the victim of a copycat killer? Like the murders that happened in the sixties. Did you still live here when those happened?

My friend Natalie is sort of investigating them—although don't tell the police that, of course. I don't think they'd like it much. She was close with the man who was accused of the murders and would like to see his name cleared. A number of my friends and I are going to the funeral tonight. We didn't know Caroline well, but..."

"Is your friend Natalie Taylor?" he interrupted.

"Yep. That's Nat. You know her?"

"Like I said, Giles is a small town, and it was even smaller when I lived here."

As they walked by Cat's Magical Shoppe on the other side of the street, Cassie noticed an older black car driving slowly past, the driver looking up to the upper windows. She looked up, too. Twink was in the window, her hand raised to the driver of the car, but she closed the shades when her eyes drifted to Cassie. Cassie ducked down to look at the driver through the passenger window as the car passed.

It was Twink's boyfriend, or at least, he was wearing the boyfriend's black hoodie and red ball cap. She couldn't get a good look because the car sped up and was gone as soon as Twink disappeared.

He was probably in town to talk to the cops. Those poor kids. What a mess they'd gotten pulled into.

8

"Thank you for coming," Gerald said as he shook Robert's hand after the brief ceremony at the crematorium that night. Gillian couldn't help but see how overwhelmed he was. His pocked skin was pale, and he looked barely able to stand. The smell of the lilies that filled the hall took her back to her own Martin's funeral for a moment, and she nearly had to sit down herself. Even years later, with Robert standing by her, thinking of Martin's death could make her feel alone.

Robert frowned. "We're both very sorry about your loss." He put his arm around Gillian and pulled her tight to his side. "It's a terrible thing to lose a wife or a partner, especially when it happens before her time."

Gillian exchanged a glance with him and added, "We both know exactly how difficult it is. I don't want to seem like I'm fussing, but do you have someone to drive you home?" Her eyes scanned the room behind him, but there was no family, no one she didn't know.

Only locals, who had known Caroline briefly, had shown up.

Gerald's eyes followed hers. "I held the ceremony at night, hoping that her friends and clients from Boston would be able to attend," he said, "but Giles must just be too far for them to travel on a weeknight. Maybe I should have scheduled for the weekend, but I..." He shook his head.

Having met Caroline, Gillian wondered if the lack of attendance was more about who Caroline had been than where the ceremony was held, and she immediately felt terrible about having thought it. She couldn't judge the woman on only a few brief council meetings, could she?

She said, "Gerald, I don't think Robert will mind if he has to find his own ride back to City Hall. I'd like to see you home safely tonight."

"I can't inconvenience either of you that way."

Robert intervened. "No inconvenience at all. I insist. I'll flag down Cassie before she finishes talking to that young man over there. I'll be fine."

Gillian followed his gaze, finding Cassie just inside the door, talking to Sean, the handyman she'd hired and who Gillian now knew had been Caroline's lover. She'd been surprised to see him in the reception area, and even more surprised when he'd gone, hand out, to offer his condolences to Caroline's grieving husband before the ceremony.

She hugged and released Robert, then turned to Gerald. "I'll make myself scarce until you're ready. Please don't rush on my account." She patted his suited shoulder soothingly, then moved away toward the food table as the funeral officiant approached him.

✳✳✳

Twink kept her voice low and her mouth close to the phone. Even though Daria had let her stay out of school all day because the cops were going to interview her, her cousin now seemed as convinced that Marcus was trouble as her own mother had been. It had been tough to get a call out to him after the interview with Daria looming over her, offering to make her hot chocolate or a sandwich or a bowl of ice cream. She'd had to eat an entire bowl of rocky road just to get her off her back.

Twink had to admit she'd kind of fanned the flame by saying she and Marcus had spent the night together. Didn't matter. It wasn't the cops' business where he'd been that night. She whispered into the phone, "How did it go with the cops?"

Marcus's quiet voice made her feel better. "Not bad. He didn't keep me long. It was just the police chief. But I didn't like making him think I'd climbed in your window. I don't want people believing that about you."

"Like I care. It's what my mother thinks we've been doing anyway, so we might as well let the cops think it too if they leave you alone because of it."

"But baby, once people think something of you, it's hard to make them change their mind," he crooned.

"Tell me about it. Sometimes I think Daria is on my side, and then she goes and lets her friend turn me in to the police for something I had nothing to do with. I've had it with everybody, you know? Everybody but you."

"I hear ya. But just stay cool. Don't make a bigger mess. If I don't come around for a while, maybe it'll all die down."

Twink heard Daria's footsteps on the stairs and whispered urgently, "I gotta go, but you remember that you were with me all night just like you told the cops, right? You have to stick to that."

***

Natalie attached herself to Cassie as soon as Sean left the crematorium. "I hope you paid close attention to everything that young man said."

Cassie hissed, "Are you serious, Nat? This is a funeral, show a little respect."

Robert joined them before Natalie had a chance to hiss back. She supposed she should store up the verbal venom for a more deserving victim—Cassie was right, after all. It could wait until they were in the car.

"Robert." Natalie dipped her head slightly in greeting as he approached. Cassie echoed her.

Robert nodded to Natalie. "Cass, could you drop me at City Hall on your way home? Gillian's driving Gerald, and I'd like to check in on how the investigation is going. Denton's in overdrive. I'll catch a ride with him the rest of the way home. It may be the only way I can convince him to leave the building."

"No problem," Cassie said, "I've got Nat tonight so the more the merrier. We were just heading out since Nat can't manage to behave herself."

Nat's mouth tightened, but she fell in behind Cassie and Robert as they exited through the short hall to the parking lot.

As soon as she was inside the car, she asked, "What did that Sean fellow say?"

Cassie buckled up and put the key in the ignition. "Oh, I forgot about that...yep, he said he killed Caroline and that he was going to go after you next if you didn't leave him alone."

Robert coughed in the back seat, but it sounded suspiciously like a smothered chuckle.

✳✳✳

Gillian heard the click of Gerald's seatbelt. If she'd known she would end up driving, she'd have insisted on taking her own smaller and easier to maneuver sedan. Although she'd stopped by and introduced herself at Natalie's suggestion two days before, bearing baked goods and soothing words, it had never occurred to her that Gerald would be alone on the day. After Martin died, the members of the coven and her yoga classes hadn't left her to herself for weeks. Her life had been an unending round of casseroles, herbal teas, and friendly shoulders of varying quality.

"She didn't want to move here, you know. Did I tell you that?" Gerald said as Gillian looked left, then right, and made a wide left-hand turn at the edge of Corey Woods, heading for the narrow street that ran along the outline of the lake for a few miles. Most of the homes along its path were the newer and more expensive ones in Giles, built in the seventies on generous acreage. The trees between each house were thick, blocking them from the watchful eyes of prying neighbors.

"No, I didn't know that." Her tone was meant to encourage. She was there for him if he wanted to talk. Robert wouldn't mind if she showed up at home a little late.

"She never liked a relaxed pace of life. She'd rather be a minnow in a big pond than a frog in a small one. But I always liked it here. I always wanted to come back and be a part of the community, even though we were just summer people."

Gillian reached over, after darting a glance away from the dimly lit road to make sure she was aiming correctly, and gave his hand a pat. "I'm sure you'll fit in fine when you're ready to get out and meet people. We have a lot of opportunities to volunteer for community events. Everyone's welcome to join in. Did your family rent one of the cabins, or did they own a place here?"

"We rented. But we had the cabin for the whole summer. The summer kids whose folks owned a second home here looked down on us. You know how things are. And, of course, my parents looked down on the 'townie' kids I met. There weren't that many families here they considered to be up to their standards. I never really made many friends, but there were a few boys I met who made time for me until…"

He went silent.

She glanced over to him, but he was looking out the window into the darkness.

Finally, he said. "It was years ago. Kid stuff. And here I am with the mayor's partner driving me home. I really am accepted in Giles now, aren't I?"

How curious that fitting in was so important to him. Most men in their sixties had stopped seeking acceptance from their peers years ago, but Gerald seemed to need it. Perhaps it was only a protective reaction to grief. She didn't mind. She could help.

"Of course you are. And Robert and I would love to have you to dinner as soon as you're up to it. You can call me any time to arrange it. I'll stop by to make sure you don't need anything over the next few days?"

She could see him nodding his agreement from the corner of her eye.

"The driveway is coming up on the right. Just past the reflector," he said. "The mayor wouldn't mind me coming to dinner?"

"He suggested it," she said, looking to the right as she turned into the drive, which was well-illuminated by path lights along the borders.

Gerald's happy smile seemed out of place on a day like today.

✳✳✳

Gillian shrugged off her clothes and slipped under the thick down comforter next to Robert. He'd waited up for her, reading something ancient, judging by the age-worn leather binding. He didn't use magic often, but his knowledge of it was broad and deep, spanning back centuries to when people still believed the work of demons accompanied every spell. Like Natalie, he could call on enormous natural forces at will, but his power was quieter, more inward.

He often chided her for overusing her magic for the day-to-day things of life, but she couldn't possibly remember where her keys were all the time, and a pie was always better with a little healing and peace baked in.

When she slid across the big bed and snuggled against him, he placed the book on the bedside table carefully before laying his reading glasses beside it. His arm moved around her shoulders to pull her close. She rested her head on his chest.

"How is he?" he asked.

"I'm not sure. Probably just the stress of it, but he positively lit up when I told him you'd invited him to dinner. And he seems...I don't know. Trapped in the past somehow. You said you'd met him a few times when he used to summer here—did something happen to him? He hinted at some unpleasant experience."

He was silent for a while before he answered. "I'm not sure it's my place to tell you. I hadn't thought about it for years, but when I realized who he was...but yes, Gerald was the victim of a very poor joke among the summer set that, unfortunately, became so notorious that his family stopped coming to Giles. The parents were snobs, both of them, and the older children were as bad. Gerald was the youngest, fifteen or sixteen. Before they stopped summering here, he tried to impress me, I suppose. Of course, I was older, in my twenties, and he was a kid to me. I wasn't mean, but he was too young to be interesting. I was already plotting and planning for my future."

"So," she nudged. "What happened?"

"Oh. Yes. The incident. Thinking back on it, it must have been terrible for him. Things always seem worse when you're young. It started with his interest in one of the local girls, I believe. I would have been mortified if it had happened to me."

She listened and, as Robert talked, her heart broke for the young boy Gerald had been. No wonder the man he was now didn't want to talk about it; children could be so cruel. She was determined to make his life here easier in any way she could. Perhaps he'd get lucky and heal the old wounds along with the new.

✳

Natalie had refused to acknowledge Robert when he'd disembarked at the city hall before her stop, and she wasn't any less frosty when Cassie dropped her off at home. Cassie refused to accept the same treatment. She rolled her window down and chirped, "I said goodnight, Nat! And I hope you're in a better mood tomorrow..."

"Yes. Fine. Goodnight." She was tired, that was all. Feeling her age. And she had work to do before she could tuck her old body into bed.

She changed into coveralls and grabbed a flashlight. On the way to Salem, she stopped at a darkened graveyard and carefully cut away a sod of earth from the center of the nearest grave. Working quickly, she scooped several handfuls of earth into a waiting jar and tamped the sod back down in place, leaving the grave the way she found it. She'd have a better chance of success if she knew where the woman's body was buried, but she wanted to get it over with. If it didn't work, she'd do the research, but if it did, then it would be off of her to-do list and she could get back to the more important business of investigating the murder.

After entering the stairwell to the second floor where the unhappy specter roamed the hall, she made a small gesture with her left hand which was still in her pocket. All of the lights along the hallway extinguished at once, leaving the zzzzzt of bulbs burning out to hang briefly in the sudden dark. She stopped for a moment to let her eyes adjust. It wasn't really necessary. The sheen of ectoplasm that lit the spirit was more than enough for her to see by.

A glance at her wristwatch told her that it was nearing midnight, the witching hour, the moment when the barrier is thinnest between this world and the next. She walked on, pulling the jar full of dirt out of her bag. She hoped that none of the residents were late-nighters; it wouldn't do to have one of them stumble through the ritual. It was a thing to be done in the dark and alone.

The specter bobbed up and down in the center of the hall, moaning the refrain that had stuck her to this place: "Make him stop, make him stop, make him stop." Natalie approached her, unscrewing the lid of the jar as she went. The sound of the metal rasping against glass was loud in the empty hallway.

She made a circuit around the ghost, sprinkling the earth liberally in a wide circle. It made a dark line as it piled up. As she went, she whispered the spell she'd memorized earlier that day. When the circle was complete, the air inside sucked at the specter's sheen, expanding it to fill the circle.

Natalie picked up her pace, continuing to sprinkle the earth to ring the unfortunate ghost again, more urgently now. The specter was confused, screaming "Make him stop, make him stop!" louder than before. It hurt her ears, but Natalie continued.

The portal opened above the circle, illuminating the specter in the bright, white glow. For a moment, she resisted, then she stopped screaming, her eyes drifting toward the ceiling. She smiled when they finally looked toward the light. Her body floated upward, the mists of ectoplasm curling into the opening, drawn by the force that Natalie had made irresistible.

When the portal closed, Natalie used the toe of her shoe to break the circle of mounded earth and release the spent spell. No one would thank her. No one ever thanked the witch who made doors for the dead, and she couldn't blame them. Who wasn't afraid of passing through that door no matter what they believed was beyond it?

9

Natalie drummed her fingers on the counter with a steady tappa tappa tappa tappa, repeat, repeat, repeat. No one had come into the shop to browse in at least an hour.

"It's dead in here. I'm going for my constitutional," she announced, walking into the hallway and taking her jacket off the hook. "Try not to give the shop away while I'm gone."

Gillian looked up from where she was sitting on a low stool with her long, colorful cotton skirt pooling around her. She dangled a string in front of Cat, who eagerly chased it and grabbed for it each time she pulled it out of reach. "You mean your daily nosey-parkering around town? I think I can manage the shop without you for a while."

Natalie tried to leave through the back, remembering it wasn't an option only when she turned the knob and walked right into the unmoving door. She turned around and went out the front, ignoring Gillian's smirk as she passed by, then cut through the side yard

106 THE INNOCENT DEAD

between the shops into the back parking space where William was waiting. No matter how dead it was inside, it was deader outside, she thought.

At least he'd been keeping his promise to leave her alone while she worked.

"Anything new in the investigation? It's put color in your cheeks being out there in the world poking around, hasn't it? You look so alive. I'll be waiting years and years for you still. But you're worth it."

She rolled her eyes. His niceness seemed even more unrelenting in death than it had in life. If she didn't know better, she'd think he was honing it specifically to irritate her. "Nothing certain, although I'm not ruling anything out at this point. Except that girl they call Teak or Blink or some other nonsense. She's tiny. I don't see how she could take that angry woman down. She's protecting her boyfriend though, telling a lie to give him an alibi, but I hope that's just loyalty. No one ever wants to believe that—"

"The person they love could be capable of something so horrendous?" he said, his transparent mouth turning down at the corners, his barely there eyes drooping like a basset hound's.

Something stirred in her. She tried to push it down, but it forced its way out, and as she walked, eyes straight ahead, she said, "I never for one minute believed you hurt anyone, William. That's not why I made the ward. Nor is it why I pushed you away."

She turned to him, her sweet, lost William, and reached out a hand to brush his cheek, then stopped when she remembered all she would feel there was emptiness. She started forward down the alley again. Even as she stalked along, she was running out of steam.

"People didn't just think I was crazy, catching me talking to someone who wasn't there. I was *going* crazy. Slowly. And my mother knew it. She forced the ward on me. Made me say goodbye to you. And she was right about it. It saved me."

She shook her head and sighed. "You didn't do me a favor, William, waiting for me. It doesn't matter what you did or didn't do. It's taken all my focus my entire life to keep going, knowing you were just outside that barrier, waiting. And all I had to do to be with you was to die. Do you know how hard it was for me those first few years? How hard it was not to die?"

She felt old suddenly, a feeling she seldom experienced. Her shoulders stooped forward, her limbs felt heavy. She forced herself to straighten up and to keep walking to the end of the alley.

When she turned to look at him again, he'd gone. She was alone.

The rope passed by her eyes so quickly she didn't have time to process what it was until it bit into her neck.

*** *** ***

William spun away, drifting swiftly down the alley, dispersing as he went, not sure where he was going. Why go anywhere at all? It's not like a ghost has a calendar full of social engagements. But Natalie didn't want him around, that was clear.

He thought about what he'd just learned: he'd hurt her when all he wanted to do was love her. Why hadn't he ever taken the time to consider her side? It was just selfishness that had kept him here all these years, he realized, hanging on to a shadow life.

As the realization swept through him, the pull of the Summerlands beckoned, like a welcoming friend. If Nat truly didn't want him, he could go. He *would* go as soon as he found someone who was passing, he told himself. He'd share their portal.

The sound of strangled cries brought his dispersing spirit back.

Natalie. A rope around her neck. Behind her, a man in a black hooded sweatshirt choking the life out of her.

He rushed toward them, becoming more and more solid as he went. This wasn't some letter opener he wanted to carry up the stairs. This was the life of the woman he had always loved, and no one was going to take that life away before she was done with it. Nearly solid now, he rushed forward and seized the arm that pulled the rope tight.

The man looked up, his face covered by a stocking under the sweatshirt hood, and William heard his sharp gasp. Whoever he was, he'd seen William, which meant William's ability to coalesce had grown to match his need. William's hand hadn't gone through the man's arm; it had a grip on his sweatshirt. He tightened it. If he could hold him and pull the mask away, he might finally know who'd set him up for the murders.

But the attacker tore away easily as William's grip began to evaporate. He tried to cradle Natalie as she went down, unconscious now, but the effort he'd expended chasing away her attacker was tearing his essence apart. She slid through his arms to the ground. Her head hit the gravel. He tried to hold himself together, but it was no good. He was fading away.

His final thought before he slipped out of the visible world was of her. If the predator came back, no one would be there to help her.

＊＊＊

Natalie surfaced to pain. The side of her head ached and something sharp dug into her cheek. Her neck felt like it had been in a vise; there was something wrapped around it. She raised a hand to it weakly.

It was wet. Wet rope. And as she remembered what had happened, she couldn't understand how William had accomplished it, but she was sure she was only alive because of him.

She sat up slowly, pulling herself to her feet. She took one step, accidentally kicking something that skipped forward a foot in front of her. It cut through the silence with the sound of plastic scraping against gravel. She stooped to pick it up. Bad idea. She nearly blacked out again, but managed to straighten up and push the blackness away.

A fake nose attached to a pair of glasses? She would have had to wear them into the Summerlands if the killer had placed them on her as she died; they would have been part of her wardrobe forever. She was now more determined than ever to catch the killer. Whoever he was, he had made it personal.

She pulled herself up, shoulders back, the rope still trailing across them like a scarf, but she was moving now, back the way she'd come, one foot forward, then the other. The sound of her heart pounded in her ears. A concussion? She struggled around the side of the shop, her hand up against the wooden siding.

She made it in the front door, where Gillian turned to look at her in horror as Natalie sank to the floor. "Whoever that mangy murdering maggot is," she croaked, "he underestimated Natalie Taylor! Nobody comes after the people I care about! And nobody comes after me..." Her voice started to fade, but she forced her eyes open. "When I regain consciousness, I'm going to..."

She didn't have time to finish the thought.

The kitten that had approached her when she went to her knees skittered away as Natalie slumped forward. Her face hit the hard floor with a thwack.

10

"Just give her some air, ladies and gents!" Natalie heard as she surfaced. Was she drowning? Had she drowned?

If not, why was the neck of her blouse damp? Why was she laying on her back looking up into the eyes of...Denton? Of all people!

"Slap me with a mackerel and call me a macaroon!" she cried out after she sucked down a big gulp of air.

She recognized quite a few of the shoes that gathered around her. Lots of black ones next to boxes of equipment that could only belong to EMTs. Gillian's vintage earth shoes that had the heel lower than the toe. Tom's zip-up ankle boots. Cassie's black work flats with the tiny pink bow at the back.

But no barely there penny loafers with a real Indian head penny in the slot. No William.

Where was he? Why wasn't he here? And why had someone called Emergency Services when they had all the supplies for healing most emergencies right here in the shop?

Well, something had happened that the EMTs could not have done. The pounding in her head was gone. Gillian's work, most likely.

"Take it easy, ma'am. I'll help you sit," came a young voice. Then a strong arm in a white uniform supported her back as she rose. The entire thing was certainly undignified, but she was glad she'd worn a pantsuit today instead of a skirt.

William. How had he done it? The dead should never be so alive. But he'd been right there. Solid. He'd grabbed the man who had held her. Forced the hands that gripped the rope to slack it. She'd seen it happen before she passed out.

But it never should have happened. Spirits don't have that kind of power.

She barked, "The show's over. The shop is closed. Everyone out." She looked down at the blood pressure cuff still wrapped around her arm. "And get this off me."

"Ma'am, you—"

"Except for a sore throat, I'm fine. You can go."

"In a strangulation incident, we really need to take you in for an X-ray to make sure your hyoid bone isn't broken."

"It's not, and if it is, I'm quite sure it won't be tomorrow. Go on. You're no longer needed," she rasped.

She turned her head to look up at Chief Denton as she crossed her legs loosely. "I'll give you a statement as quickly as possible and then you can run along too."

She had little to say to him. The man had come from behind. And yes, she felt sure the attacker was a man. He'd been over six feet tall, based on the feel of his hot breath on the crown of her head as he'd pulled the rope tight.

"You need to find out where that Sean Harper and that young Marcus were when this was happening," she said, pointing a finger at Denton.

He leaned back against the counter and crossed his arms. "Ms. Taylor, may I remind you who's conducting this investigation and who's supposed to be the victim? If you let me ask the questions, we'll get through this quickly."

"Ask away. It's not like I could stop you." That wasn't strictly true. She could stop him. But it would be an abuse of her powers, so she refrained. And anyway, her head ached too much for the required focus.

"Did the attacker say anything? Did he have any distinguishing vocal characteristics? An accent maybe?"

"Like, for instance, being a pipsqueak with the voice of a much more imposing man?" Although he must have known this was a dig at him, the chief didn't flinch. "It would be hard to put a finger on an accent when the only real exchange was his grunting and my trying to scream."

"Details of clothing or shoes?"

"Black sweatshirt with bands at the cuffs. Hood. Black gloves. But I didn't get a look at his face. The sweatshirt could have been a pullover. Could have been a zip up too. Couldn't tell you what age, race, or creed he was, and I'm not going to guess."

"Wouldn't want you to guess. It wouldn't be helpful. But what you've given me is." Now that she'd stopped taking her frustration out on him, the chief was all business. "Shoes? Anything you noticed there?"

Natalie paused and closed her eyes. She shook her head. "No. Nothing."

Gillian appeared from the direction of the kitchenette with the teapot and four cups. Enough for the trio of witches and Tom. She said, "Karl, I'm sure Nat is exhausted from the attack and the excitement."

The police chief nodded. "I'll be telling the mayor about this development. You may want to get to him first so that he doesn't worry."

Gillian nodded. "Yes, I don't want him flying down here to protect me when there's no reason to suspect I'm in danger. I'll call him right away."

When the police chief left, Gillian pulled out her phone and made a call while Cassie turned the open sign on the door to closed and locked it.

Tom helped Natalie to her feet, steadying her with an arm around her waist. As she leaned in to him, she said, "It's such a shame you and your lithe body won't be performing at my upcoming birthday party now that your debt is cleared. I may have to cancel the event all together."

Gillian winked at Tom as she finished up her call with Robert. "Yes, I'll tell her. But she seems fine now. Right back to her old self. In fact, she'll likely be getting a bollocking from Tom if she's not careful."

When she hung up the phone, Gillian smiled at Natalie. "Robert's glad to hear you're okay. He's going to make sure the force stays on this around the clock if they have to."

"Phfftt," Natalie responded. "I know more than the force does at this point, I'm sure. You could say I've been a busy bee. I'll have this investigation wrapped up in a jiffy."

Cassie made a shooing gesture. "Everyone in the kitchenette now. I don't think Natalie has been filling us in completely on what she's been up to." She held out a finger as Natalie started to protest. "You're a terrible liar because you never bother telling the little white ones to make other people feel better. That means you don't get any practice for the big ones. Plus, Gillian is giving you another going over with some exploratory magic before you even think about stepping outside this door. I can't believe you refused to go the hospital!"

"I was a nurse for longer than you've been alive, young lady. I can tell when I'm damaged and when I'm not."

Cassie's face said she meant business. "You know what, Nat? I just don't care. You'd be the first one ordering people to sit down to get checked out if it was anyone else who got hurt, no matter how much healing any of us had thrown at an injury. We're witches, not doctors, remember?"

✳✳✳

Cassie boiled water for tea while Gillian ran her hands gently down Natalie's neck, over her head, and finally over her shoulders, her fingers feeling for places where Natalie's aura felt disrupted.

When Cassie came to the table with the tea tray, Gillian said, "She's right. No permanent damage. Clean bill of health."

She took the seat next to Natalie as Natalie added, "Exactly as you had already been advised."

"Good," Cassie said, sitting next to Tom after pouring the boiling water from the pot over the cups. Mint, jasmine, rose, and lavender scents filled the air. "Now I don't feel so bad about pressing you for the details of what you've been up to. This guy came after you for a reason, didn't he? And you didn't tell Chief Denton everything, I'd bet."

"You know he doesn't want to know anything about the choir or our 'music.'" Natalie said, making quotes with her fingers. "He is intentionally and happily tone-deaf. Where do you think I'd be right now if I'd told him that my attacker was chased off by the ghost of the man who was supposed to have committed the original crimes?"

"Fair point," said Gillian. "Despite his loyalty to Robert, Denton makes sure not to know what Robert does in his off-work hours on the ritual grounds. However, I certainly want more details."

Natalie leaned in to the table, her left hand to her mouth, then took it away and said, "I don't know how it's even possible. I've never seen a spirit do what he did before. William was solid. Solid as you or I. He grabbed the arm that held the rope and forced that arm to move. Everything I know about the separation between the worlds says that cannot happen."

Gillian shrugged. "Stranger things have happened in this town. The dead that walked through from the Summerlands when Anat created the rift between the worlds sure looked solid to me. But we were all a little too occupied to check that one out."

Natalie nodded, pensive. "It's true. The shades I saw that day didn't have the sheen of ectoplasm. But it's not the same. There's no rift here now to mix things up. I'd feel it. Without my ward, it would prickle like heat rash."

Gillian inclined her head and raised her shoulders in a small shrug. "The goddess works in mysterious ways. Maybe she owes you one."

Anyone else would have looked grateful, but Natalie was unmoved. "Given what this town's been through because of the goddess's relatives, I'd say she owes all of us. Although I'm sure you'll happily defend her." She looked at Gillian pointedly.

Cassie caught Tom's eye, shaking her head. "Are you two ever going to get over your stupid rivalry? We're united now, right? Maid, Mother, and Crone. Three strong witches working together. So let's act like it."

Gillian smiled at her fondly. "The wisdom of the Mother."

At that, Tom's head went to the side and one eyebrow came down. He looked at Cassie. "The wisdom of the Mother?"

Cassie looked back at him, her face a picture of innocence, like she'd just been caught sneaking a cookie. "Ummmm...Natalie and Gillian think that, you know..."

"We're pregnant?" His shoulders stiffened and his eyes widened.

Cassie nodded her head. "At least that's what these two say. But I was waiting to tell you until I could take an actual medical test. It's really early—"

"Pish toddle!" Natalie interrupted. "I know what I know. You're having a baby in something less than nine months."

Cassie waited for Tom to say something, but he just looked blank.

"Tom?" she asked, in a small, cautious voice, "Is it...are you..."

All at once, his face broke into a massive smile, and he completed her sentence with, "...having the grooviest day of my life? Yes. Yes, I am."

He stood, then stooped to pick Cassie up from her chair, swinging her legs up and capturing her in the basket of his arms. It was a neat trick to accomplish in the small space around them. She protested weakly as he said, "Sorry, ladies, you'll have to battle on alone. I'm taking my wife and my child-to-be home for a celebration."

"Tom!" Cassie squealed. "I'm as happy as you are, but let's wait until Natalie tells us the rest of what she's learned about the murders."

"Not today. There will never be another today. I reserve my right to be a caveman just this once. Good night, ladies."

He swept out with her into the hall, and she settled against his chest, all her objections gone.

✳✳✳

Tom moved Cassie's long brown hair out of the way and raised himself up on his elbows to look down into her face. She beamed back at him, tired, relaxed, and happy.

His hands held her head gently on each side, his eyes met hers. Contentment. That's what she read there. He was going to make an amazing father. Amazing.

"If I'd known what my reward was going to be for being pregnant, I'd have told you about it right away."

He moved to the side and lay his hand protectively over her stomach. "Just wait until you get your punishment for letting me be the last one to know. Although it will probably be an awful lot like your reward."

She turned over to face him and ran a finger down his chest. It glided smoothly over the rise of his pectoral muscle, then circled a nipple until she snuggled her head against him.

"I'm sorry I didn't tell you right away. But I wasn't even the first to know! You know what Natalie's like. She just burst out with it, and then Gillian's all feeling me up with her magic hands." Cassie wiggled the fingers of her free hand in the air while she made a goofy face.

He pulled her tight and his chest vibrated with his laughter. "That sounds about right. Those two...I'm sorry I ever got you involved with them."

"No you're not! And I'm not, either. Plus, I knew Gillian long before I knew you. I think it's wonderful that with both of our mothers gone, this baby is still going to be blessed with two of the most devoted grandmothers any kid has ever had."

She could feel his head nodding in agreement above hers. "And that also sounds about right," he said as sat up and turned, swinging his legs over the edge of the bed. "I've worked up an appetite. How about you?"

"I could eat."

"I warn you, it will have to be something healthy. No bacon for you. Not anymore. Beet and ricotta grilled cheese? You'll like it. It's a lot better than it sounds."

Cassie grimaced. "It would have to be."

"Did I mention it also involves honey?"

"Bring it on." Cassie grinned. "I'll be here."

Tom pulled on a pair of pajama pants, then planted a kiss on her forehead. "You better be. Then again, I can't remember you ever refusing a meal."

She giggled.

When he was gone, she got out of bed and moved a few knick-

knacks from the round table next to the bed up to the fireplace man-
tle to make room for dinner dishes. As she did, she couldn't help
admiring the picture that had pride of place there. She was glad
that Lou Frank had turned out not to be a jerk after all. She still
couldn't believe that the amazing watercolor belonged to her. She
picked it up for a moment, peering into the frame. Wiggling back
down beneath the bed's warm covers, she felt sure that she must be
the happiest woman in the world.

11

Sean slid the chain lock back and opened the door. Natalie stood there, wearing a large, colorful silk scarf draped high around her neck and shoulders. It wasn't a great look for her. Against her pale skin, it was overpowering.

He smiled, although he hoped her early morning visits weren't going to become a regular thing. "You should have let me know you were coming."

"So you could prepare a rope?"

"Say what?" His head pitched to the side while he held her gaze from the corners of his eyes. He stepped to the side of the door so she could enter.

"You heard me. I won't be coming in. We can talk through the door. In fact, why don't you step out here?" She raised her keychain. "This red thingamajig here was forced on me by a well-meaning friend. I'll be keeping my finger on the panic button while we talk. I understand that when the alarm sounds, it's piercing. You wouldn't want to upset the neighbors."

"Sure." He shrugged, stepping into the hall. "But why do you think you need it?"

"Where were you and your hooded sweatshirt yesterday afternoon around 3 p.m.?" she asked.

"I was at the Frank house most of the day, but I guess I left there around two to go downtown. I put in a set of shelves at that new vintage boutique that's going in. Nice stuff. You should check it out. I bet some of their gear would be right up your alley."

Natalie mapped the downtown quickly in her head. The only spot that had been empty was on Bishop street, close to where she'd been attacked. She moved back from him reflexively in a swaying motion. Maybe this had not been her best idea this week.

He noticed the sway and said, "You okay?" He looked genuinely concerned.

"Did anyone see you there?"

"Sure. What's his name, the gallery guy? He was dishing with Ling Li, the owner. I was in his sights the whole time, if you know what I mean. Just so you know, though—I go a little older, but I'm not interested in crossing the gender divide. You can check with them if you want."

Natalie remembered Sean's tank-topped display while working at the shop. She expected the scene would have been every bit as entrancing for Dash.

"You can be sure that I will."

"So, why do you want to know this?" he asked.

"Haven't the police been here to talk to you? I was attacked yesterday."

"Wow. No, I didn't know. Is everything all right? Were you hurt?" He seemed genuinely concerned again.

She would have thought he'd ask about the police, not about her health. "I'm fine." She realized if it hadn't been him, perhaps he'd told someone else that she'd been investigating. "One more thing. Did you tell anyone that I'd been here asking questions?"

"Cinnamon, but that's it."

"And what did Ms. Brown have to say about it?"

He looked sincere when he said, "Ms. Taylor, I respect you too much to tell you what Ms. Brown might or might not have said about you."

Natalie gave him a last glare before she walked away.

She only put the alarm button back in her pocket when she was safely back in her car.

✳✳✳

When Cassie arrived at the gallery, a huge display of flowers nearly hid the counter. They were gorgeous. Dash hurried out from the back when he heard her enter.

"Those are nice," Cassie said, inclining her heard toward the flowers in the crimson vase. "A gift from Jon?"

"I wish they had my name on them, but sadly, they're for you."

"Really? Omigoddess, I can't believe he did this!"

"Special occasion?" Dash asked as Cassie picked up the card tucked into the foliage.

She beamed. "Yeah. Very." She slipped the card out of the tiny white envelope and was surprised when she didn't recognize the writing. It was cursive, big, and full of flourishes—a far cry from Tom's round, right-leaning block letters. Her eyes dropped to the signature.

"This is from Lou Frank, not Tom. Congratulating me on—oh, you might as well know since apparently everyone does now. I'm pregnant!"

Dash made forgive-me eyes when he said, "I know! Lou told me when he dropped them off. I'm so excited for you! How long have you known?" He hugged her, then pushed her away, scolding, "And more important, why did you tell Lou before you told me?"

"I didn't—even Tom only found out yesterday." She set the card back into the flowers. "Is it okay if I leave these in the shop? That way everyone can enjoy them."

"And your husband can't find out that Mr. Frank has taken a special interest in you?" Dash replied, rearranging a few of the flowers, then stepping back to view his improvements. "They really are lovely."

"My husband can find out whatever he wants. Like he has anything to be jealous about! I just don't want to encourage anything. I mean, I like Lou and all, but even if I wasn't married, I'm into guys who are a little earthier, you know?" She was thinking about Kit and Sheba's romp through the forest after dinner last night, and she couldn't imagine how anyone could be earthier than Tom was.

She couldn't get mad at Dash when he immediately picked up the phone to pass the news on to Jon, but the opportunity to make announcements to good friends should have been hers and Tom's—it bothered her a little that Nat or Gillian had put the news about the baby out into the community, even though she couldn't imagine either one of them doing it on purpose.

With Cat's Magical Shoppe closed on Mondays, Natalie took some of her day off to catch up with the details of life. Between working and investigating, she'd let things go around the house.

She plopped the wicker laundry basket on top of the dryer, started the water filling, and poured a carefully measured amount of detergent in. While she waited for the basket to fill, she went through pockets to make sure she wouldn't be adding unwanted ingredients to the mix. Not that she could accidentally turn her underthings into toads and her overthings into princes, but she didn't want her laundry to dye itself green and smell minty fresh.

Nothing harmful was revealed: a particularly smooth, round stone she thought might eventually find a use for, the angelica root she'd been carrying for protection since the attack, and a folded piece of paper from the pocket of the pantsuit she'd been wearing on the day it had happened. That was odd. She didn't recall tucking away any notes that day.

She opened it up and smoothed it out. In a fancy hand, embellished but scrupulously legible, someone had written "impicciona." She had no idea why she would have picked the thing up or what it meant. It went into the small wastebasket next to the dryer.

She scooped up the angelica root and whispered to it to strengthen the protection spell it carried and tucked it into her bra when she realized she didn't have a pocket in her slacks or lavishly beaded, black vintage sweater set. It can never hurt to be prepared, she thought, as she remembered how William had come to her aid. Especially when one's guardian angel is no longer waiting in the wings.

She meant to harrumph at herself for the thought—she could most certainly protect herself—but she found herself sighing instead. "Oh William..." she muttered, "where have you gone?"

✳✳✳

The bus that delivered the Giles high school students back from Salem would be dropping Twink off at the end of the street any minute now. That, thought Natalie, would explain the presence of the black teen in the old Ford across the street from Cat's Magical Shoppe.

She tapped on the window and he reached across to roll it down.

"Are you Marcus Wilkerson?" Natalie asked.

"Yeah. That's me."

"Twink Johnson's friend."

"That's me again."

Natalie sized him up. Black hoodie, sensitive brown eyes. He certainly didn't look like a threat. He also had that look that said he wasn't done growing up yet; his hands and feet looked too big for his thin build. But he was tall, and he might be strong despite his size—Chief Denton was certainly no slouch in the take-a-man-down department despite being slight.

"Do you know who I am?"

He shook his head. "No ma'am."

And polite, too, she thought. "My name is Natalie Taylor. I'm looking into the murder of a local woman you and your girlfriend came into contact with a few days ago."

"Are you with the police? Because they already talked to me." He didn't look like he thought she could be with the police. Probably just being polite again. "I was with Twink all night that night, just like I told them."

It looks like Twink had gotten to him before anyone else had. She laughed as she opened the car door and sat on the passenger side, closing the door behind her. "Bees in a blender! Of course you weren't. Not by a long shot."

He looked surprised. Not just sensitive, this one, but an inexperienced liar as well.

"I was!" His voice went up high and made him sound much younger. "You don't know nothin'."

"I know your friend Twink was covering for you. Now I want to know why. Where were you really on the night that Caroline Akers was killed?"

"You leave Twink out of it. I don't need to answer any questions from you." He looked straight ahead, avoiding her eyes.

She said, "I know what you're worried about. You think Twink started the fire in that woman's purse, don't you?"

He turned back to her, his eyes narrowed. "Like the girl could start a fire with her mind."

"Some girls can." Natalie held a hand out toward him and a yellow-orange flame shot up for a second and, just as quickly, extinguished. She hadn't exactly done it with her mind, although that was certainly involved, but the description was as good as any.

Marcus gaped.

"I can help her," Natalie said quickly. "I understand how trouble can follow an innocent person around. But I need to sort this out before I'll even think about it."

"You can help her, for real?"

"Oh for the goddess's sake, how old are you anyway? Do I have to cross my heart and hope to die or double-pinky swear or something?"

"Yeah, no...just that nobody believes she didn't do all that stuff her mother said she did. I've been real worried about her. I mean, maybe she did it, but maybe she didn't know she did it."

"I'll believe her, and my friends will too. And one of them is good friends with Twink's cousin Daria. But I need to know that she isn't covering up for a murderer. Because I'm not helping her if that's the kind of person she is. Is that why she lied to give you an alibi?"

"I'm no murderer. I can't even go fishing because I don't like to kill the fish." He looked down at his hands fidgeting on the steering wheel. Then he said, "I was visiting my mother. My foster parents and my social worker wouldn't like that—they'd rather think I was with Twink. They could pull me out of the home if you tell where I was. My mom's got problems...she's like...she drinks a lot and maybe does some drugs. But she's still my mother. It's not right not to let me see her." He didn't meet her eye.

The kid was telling the truth, Natalie knew. She felt it all the way down to her bones. But she'd still have to put in a visit to his mother to verify. No slacking on her part. She wouldn't be fooled by a child.

"Start the car, young man," she ordered.

***

What Natalie really wanted after a long day of putting her house in order and driving around Boston with a teenager was to put her feet up over a steaming herbal concoction and relax while her Cat's Magical Masque worked its miracle on her appearance. She could even do with a little light reading.

Instead, she watched Gillian kiss Robert on the cheek before they parted ways at the front of the conference room at City Hall.

She still sometimes felt prickly about those two ending up together, although she knew it would be difficult to separate that feeling from her normal, daily prickliness.

But what had she really wanted from him? Not to die a maid, that was all. She was curious what all the fuss was about. She'd waited too long and time had run out on her romantic chances. By the time she'd realized that, Robert had simply been the last man standing, the only potential age-appropriate partner whose address wasn't a pine box.

It annoyed her to admit it, but Robert and Gillian were good together. They both had a happy glow about them these days, at a time in life when the glow usually went out. She should probably try to be more generous about it.

Phfft. She'd prickle if she felt like it.

Robert took his place at the council table while Gillian wended her way down the aisle between the tidy rows of metal folding chairs and took the empty seat to Natalie's left. She wiggled her fingertips at Tom and Cassie who sat to Natalie's right.

The room was only about a quarter full. The townspeople of Giles tended to leave the governing to their elected officials unless there was something that piqued their individual self-interests or sounded like a hot topic for gossip. It didn't appear there was anything like that on the agenda tonight.

"I don't see why we have to continue attending these meetings every week," Natalie said. "I'm sure the council can manage without us."

Gillian tsked. "You know that Robert enjoys having us all here, his friends. Truthfully, I don't think he's going to run for reelection in the fall. It's begun to drag on him. He just likes to see some friendly faces in the seats."

"Fine. Council meetings every Thursday, it is. I'll wear my friendly face. Oh wait...I haven't got one. I'll just assume this one will be fine." After a beat, she added. "How is that Gerald fellow doing?"

Gillian's eyebrows drew together, and she clasped her hands in her tie-dye skirted lap. "He's gutted. I know his wife wasn't a very nice woman, but he obviously doted on her. As it turns out, he and Robert met when Gerald was a teenager. Robert was quite a bit older, in his twenties at that point. But Gerald told me he had a very positive impression of Robert. My partner was apparently a skilled politician even then."

"Yes, I'm afraid he was. Which is why he and I stopped seeing eye to eye after a childhood spent roaming the woods together. It would never do for him to be seen spending time with my type."

"Really? The way he tells it, you were the one who pulled away from the friendship as the two of you got older."

"Yes, yes. Take his side, dear."

Cassie turned and leaned in toward them from her place next to Natalie and said, "Could you two stop fighting for five minutes? The meeting is starting. Robert is staring the two of you down and everyone can hear you."

Natalie's eyes flew to the front of the room, where Robert was looking directly at them with that infuriatingly patient expression of his. How embarrassing.

With a final, "think what you like" look at Gillian, Natalie settled in to listen to the council consider the insignificant tasks of governing the town in excruciating detail. As the first order of business, the council took a moment to review the sad passing of its new publicist, Caroline Akers. There were quiet acknowledgments, but no wet eyes. It had become clear to Natalie through her investigation that Caroline was not the kind of woman who would inspire a sense of loss in anyone but her husband. Out of respect, the discussion of the town's tourist trade was tabled for another day.

The council moved on to its general agenda. Budgets. Easements. Noise complaints. *All very stirring stuff,* Natalie thought.

She didn't bother to stifle her yawn.

She closed her eyes and considered taking a nap until Gillian's elbow rammed into her ribs. Muttering under her breath, she opened her eyes and tuned back in to the discussion at the front of the room.

The council had taken bids over the past two months to repair the statue of Giles Corey that had been damaged during the "freak high winds" that had occurred during the "live entertainment" at the town's last Witching Faire. Natalie had been there when the council had discussed the damage to the statue at length, and now they discussed it again. The damage was described again in detail for some of the councilors who had not been present at the original meeting, and Robert explained in a way that most of them would understand—not as art but as a legal issue; the town would be liable if the damage progressed and someone was injured by a falling limb. The discussion would be much more interesting if he could add that the statue had been damaged by a demon goddess who had tried to suck the entire town into the afterlife because she was jealous that Cassie had taken her pet tomcat away.

She looked over at Tom, who had been the cause of all the trouble. Natalie found him handsome, as any reasonable woman would, but she couldn't imagine being so jealous over any man that she'd imprison him in the body of a cat for decades or try to destroy the world. Accidentally spill a cup of tea into her competitor's lap, maybe, but rend the fabric of reality out of petty jealousy? Probably not.

At least with the repairs now being attended to, Robert explained, the statue wouldn't end up falling on some poor passerby and hand them the same fate that old Giles Corey had himself endured when he was pressed to death during the Salem witch trials. Natalie thought, not for the first time, that the town should have picked a better patron saint.

The side door to the council hall clattered open and a tall, older man with a white, curly shock of hair that fell over one eye walked confidently to the front row of seats. He planted himself there, directly in the council's view.

Natalie almost didn't catch Cassie's whisper to Tom. "That's Lou Frank. The guy who did the painting." Tom's reaction was interesting. If he'd been attending the meeting as a cat, Kit's tail would have been bushed out to maximum effect. She remembered Cassie saying something about an artist who had been flirting with her. She decided to keep an eye on Tom; this could get interesting.

The most recent attendee spread his arms across the backs of the empty chairs beside him. He was the very model of a modern artist: all show. His legs were spread in that masculine way, saying, "I could run with the bulls at Pamplona," and the sweep of curls at his forehead and the scarf he wrapped rakishly around his neck said, "and I would make even the bulls weep for the beauty of my artistry." He looked vaguely familiar, but she couldn't place him.

"And finally," Robert announced, "we've finished reviewing the bids to repair the Corey statue, and..." Robert nodded his head apologetically to the man in the front row, "unfortunately, we received a lower bid from an arts restoration firm out of Boston. Lou, I know you were expecting the job, but we have to go with the lowest bid."

The man leaned forward, suddenly tense, all the pose gone out of him. "I'll bid lower."

Robert replied, "I'm afraid the bidding is closed." There were disappointed noises from the other council members, but no one disagreed.

Natalie smirked when Tom said, loud enough for everyone near them to hear, "Looks like someone is wishing he could go back in time and adjust his rates."

Even from the back, she could tell that Lou Frank had heard it too. There was an almost imperceptible shift in his posture. The gauntlet had been thrown down, and with his next words, he picked it up.

"I'll do it for free! I'll contribute the materials and my work to the community for the sake of art." He turned his head and smiled smugly back at Tom, appearing to know exactly where the comment had come from.

Hmmmm...as far as Natalie knew, Tom and Cassie's elderly suitor had never met, so how had he known to look at Tom? There were at least two other men scattered in the seats nearby who could have been the heckler.

"It's unusual," said Robert, "but I think we can readjust our decision based on this offer. We can't accept additional bids, but there's nothing to stop us from canceling the offer since we haven't contracted with the winning bidder yet." He looked to the other members of the council. "All in favor?"

There was a solid round of *ayes*.

"All opposed?"

The room was silent except for the sound of papers and feet shuffling restlessly.

Robert got up and walked around the table. The man, Lou, rose to meet him, and the two shook hands.

Natalie watched Lou's eyes drift to Cassie. Was he really trying to impress her when her sexy, young husband was right there in the room? *Some men just don't know when to quit*, Natalie thought.

13

Natalie sipped her tea mechanically, watching the spring rain bead on the display windows from the counter. The tea was the shop's newest mix; it smelled and tasted strongly of cardamom and maple sugar, although Cassie had repeatedly sworn she hadn't put in a single grain of the stuff. Natalie would normally have savored it as a treat, but this morning she barely knew she was drinking it. With every hint of movement in her peripheral vision, her head twitched, searching for a specter, but there was never anyone there.

It had been two days already, and William still hadn't shown up at home or at the shop. That wasn't like him. He might be gone for good.

She simply wasn't having it. She looked at her watch. It would be a full hour before Gillian came in. She walked purposefully to the front door and reversed the sign from Open to Closed. Satisfied, she marauded through the shelves, picking up the items she required: lavender candles, toadstool, moonflower, and one of the larger incense burners. Once she had what she needed, she mixed a selection of herbs: gardenia, camphor, jasmine, myrrh, sandalwood, and willow at the counter.

It was too light for her purposes in the shop despite the rain, so she poked her head into the small storeroom. Cinnamon's table was still set up. It would be the perfect place. She lit the candles and pulled the door closed.

The small pile of dried herbs at the bottom of the incense burner caught easily. As it burned, she fed in small pieces of the toadstool and moonflower as offerings to the dead. With her eyes closed, she could sense the spirit world around her open up. She focused and spoke softly, rhythmically, then reached around her own neck to undo the clasp of the silver necklace she had worn there for over fifty years. She opened the locket and there they were, the both of them in their separate frames, just as they had been when William had first given it to her.

Had she ever been that young?

She placed the locket in front of the candles and started talking, quietly, commandingly. "William Sanders, if you be this side of the veil, come take back your gift to me."

She waited, but nothing stirred. It should have worked. Calling a spirit is easiest when you have something that is personal to them, something charged with emotion.

She picked the locket up and carefully opened the compartment behind his picture, where a lock of his hair was stored. Her heart ached—she'd carried this piece of him for so long. And still she did it. She separated half of the hair from the strand and pulled it away, then dropped it into the burning pile of herbs.

"William Sanders, you must come to my call, for I remember you today with this small piece of the man you were."

And still, nothing.

So he was gone. She'd barged into something that had never

been her business, and it had ended up costing William his afterlife. And what good would it have done him if she had cleared his name? He'd be no less dead.

She cleaned up the storeroom, blew out her candles, and went to the kitchenette. She made another pot of tea before she flipped the sign back to Open.

As she sighed into her cup, steam rose into her eyes, joining the moisture that was already there. She blinked it away. And had to blink it away again.

Enough. William should have gone on to the Summerlands when he'd still had the chance. If he had, none of this would have happened. She would have forgotten him years ago, she was sure of it, if she hadn't known he was always there, waiting outside the boundary of the ward to come charging back to her if it ever failed.

She straightened her shoulders and composed herself. No point dwelling on his absence now. He'd been dead for most of the time she'd known him.

Of course, there was still the little matter of her not being any closer to solving the mystery. Her forehead crunched up at the thought—there, now she felt more like herself.

So, where did her investigation stand? She reviewed her mental notes as she cleaned up the residue from her ritual. There was no suspect that seemed to have the means, motive, and opportunity.

After talking to Marcus's mother, with a little help from a harmless truthing potion she'd slipped unnoticed into the woman's beer, she'd been sure that Marcus had been visiting her as he said he had when the original murder occurred. And just look at him, anyway—he was as ridiculous a suspect in a murder investigation as William had been. Some people were simply born with gentle souls—there was nothing that could be done about it.

The only suspects left now were the husband and that handyman, Sean. It was difficult to see either of them as potential murderers; the husband was a milksop, and the handyman was an uncomplicated womanizer. She couldn't picture either of them stalking anyone with a rope in hand.

Maybe it had been accidentally done in a fit of passion and the killer had later moved the body and dressed the scene to copycat the old murders? Accidental strangulation, perhaps. A romantic game gone wrong.

And romance pointed back to Sean. Why hadn't Denton brought him in yet? What was he waiting for? She imagined him sitting there with his feet propped on his desk, head back and eyes closed, having an afternoon snooze, completely unconcerned that there had been a murder on his turf.

Natalie already had her coat on when Gillian came through the front door.

"I'm on an errand. Fend for yourself," she said, brushing past on her way out, brandishing her umbrella, ready to enter into battle.

✳✳✳

"Denton, I deserve answers," Natalie barked as she barged into his office, having already pushed past the young patrolman who had tried to bar her way while politely telling her to stop.

The police chief sat taller in his seat and waved the officer out, saying, "Go ahead and close the door, Rogers."

Natalie stood to the side of the desk, declining the chair that he waved her to. "I'll stand, thank you."

"Suit yourself," he replied, picking up a mug. "Coffee?"

"No. I don't anticipate being here long. I've come to find out where you are in the investigation of my attack."

"We're still following up some leads." He leaned in and set his elbows on the desk, bringing his fingertips together in a fleshy steeple. "This is a complex investigation. Your insistence on opening the old files made us take a close look at the history of the case. Unfortunately, most of these old cases weren't as well documented as they are today. There's an indication that the murders had something else in common other than the use of a wet rope and the presence of the toys left at the scene. Unfortunately, it appears that whatever it was wasn't written down, at least not in the official records. I'm hoping we can find something to fill in the blanks. We've found something interesting on the body, and I want to confirm a link to the previous killings."

"And what does that mean, exactly?"

"I'm trying to get in contact with any of the officers who might have worked here at the time. As you can imagine, the older members of the force are no longer with us, and I'm having difficulty locating the two officers from that time period who might still be around."

"Which two?"

"Bill Charcross and Jeffrey Ames."

"I can't help you out with Jeffrey, but I know where Bill is."

He looked at her, waiting. When she looked at him in return, mute, he said, "Do we have to play these games? Ms. Taylor, I would appreciate any information you have about the location of Bill Charcross."

She didn't change her expression.

He looked like he was sucking a lemon when he added, "Please."

"Since you've asked so nicely, you can find him in the cemetery. Out by the shell of the Episcopal church that burned down in the nineties."

"I'd say that pretty much rules him out as a source of additional information."

Natalie smirked when she replied, "Not necessarily," as she flipped the edge of her black-and-white fleur-de-lis silk scarf back over her shoulder. "Good day to you, Denton. It's been educational."

✳✳✳

Natalie wasn't sure if the smell of spring coming through her open window as she drove was a positive or negative. On the one hand, the damp earth smelled of renewal as new growth pushed up through the mulch of last year's bounty. On the other hand, all of the dead things that had been preserved by the snow had begun to decay in earnest. Sometimes, on the first warm day after a particularly bitter winter, Corey Woods smelled like a slaughter house.

Fortunately, everything in the old Episcopalian cemetery had been dead for a long time. It smelled green. The graveyard had been mostly left to the vines, weeds, and the young trees after it had been closed to new burials. Some of the townspeople complained it had become an eyesore, but Natalie liked it that way—well, except when she was looking for a particular gravestone like she was today.

"Gillian, just look over there," she said irritably, waving her toward the back fence. If they didn't find it soon, they'd have to search in the dark. "I know he was buried here, but I don't know where. I may never have known. It was thirty years ago."

"Here it is, I think," Gillian called.

Natalie turned to see her pulling last year's vines away from the front of a stone. "William Charcross. Is that him?" Gillian said.

"Yes. Start clearing the ground above the grave. I'll be there in a moment. Who am I to miss a chance to harvest a few ivy saplings from the grave plantings?" She bent to her work with a spade, placing a few small vines into a plastic bag that she tucked into her red purse. When she was done, the spade went into a larger baggie and disappeared inside the purse as well.

Gillian was clapping her hands together, knocking chunks of mud from her heavy gardening gloves when Natalie joined her at the officer's grave.

Natalie surveyed Gillian's work. She had pulled out or trimmed the grass and weeds at the grave site to a uniform level, leaving enough space to do the work they'd come here for. "Yes, this will do."

"Do you think it's in your vocabulary to ever, just once, say thank you?" Gillian asked, shaking her head.

A young voice carried to them from behind. "Fighting already?"

The two women turned to see Cassie picking her way toward them through the rows of tilting gravestones.

"Of course we are, sweetheart. It's what we do," said Gillian, smiling.

"You're late," Natalie added. "Did you bring it?"

Cassie looked down to the box she was carrying, then back up to Natalie. "Um...yeah. You see the pet carrier at the end of my arm, don't you?"

"I was merely verifying its contents. You needn't be so testy," Natalie said.

Cassie's eyes rolled. "Really Nat, I don't know about you sometimes. Maybe Gillian's right. Maybe you've finally lost it."

"Just put it down here," Natalie said. Gillian bent down to the kitten, a finger extending through the bars to give it a scratch behind one of its small, midnight-black ears, but Natalie stopped her, saying, "And don't play with it! It's got a job to do here the same as the rest of us."

"Talk about testy," Gillian said. "Someone's on tenterhooks about this ritual, I'd say. Are you sure you want to go through with it? The last time someone in Giles messed with power beyond the veil..."

"Yes. Yes, I do. I need to protect myself now that I'm a target, but more than that, I believe William is gone, dissolved, and it's my fault. Mine and mine alone. He didn't deserve to lose his chance for a peaceful afterlife because of me. I have to clear his name now. I owe it to him. I won't have people talking about him that way again."

Cassie gave her a one-armed hug, at which Natalie stiffened. "I don't need pity. I simply need your help to make sure that there's enough magic to hold the spirit here until we have some answers. Calling one back from beyond the veil is more difficult and much more dangerous to pull off than calling one that never made it to the other side. Without the proper balance of the elements, the results can be explosive."

Cassie drew away with a sigh. "You got it, Nat, but when are you just going to let people care about you?"

Natalie didn't answer. She was already putting on the long black robe she'd retrieved from her purse. Cassie and Gillian looked at each other and shrugged before pulling on their matching robes as Natalie placed candles at five points around the grave. When she was appropriately attired, Gillian rubbed the tip of a taper in between her thumb and forefinger until it started to flame. She followed Natalie around the circle, lighting the candles.

Gillian placed the long taper at the center after the other candles were lit, about a foot in front of the headstone. The bright flame emphasized the gathering dusk around them. Natalie sunk to the damp ground in front of it. The morning's rain was gone, but it was not forgotten. She crossed her legs and cupped her hands on her knees. The others didn't need to know that it was only to warm them because they ached in the chill spring air.

She heard the soft groan behind her, and the whispered, "Oh no, the ground is far too wet for this."

"You don't need to sit, Gillian. Just keep watch from outside the circle and pull me out if anything goes wrong. And keep up the chant until I've finished with the specter. Even if the elements are properly balanced, it can be risky, depending on the strength of the spirit. Of course, he may not answer the call if he's been to the Summerlands or if he's moved through to be reborn." She looked over her shoulder and held out a hand. "I'll need the cat."

Cassie bent down and undid the carrier door, reaching in for Cat, who batted playfully at her hand. "He's safe, right? Nothing you do will hurt him?"

"He's safe. He's just an amplifier. Cats, ones that aren't carrying around a human on the inside," she said, nodding to Cassie, "are like death witches. They often see the dead. With the two of us, it will be easier to 'tune in' a spirit, so to speak."

Cassie gave the kitten a quick cuddle and handed it over. Natalie sat it in her lap and the kitten promptly curled up there, shoved its head up tight into the crook of Natalie's left leg, and went to sleep.

Once it was settled, she opened her red purse and took out an ornate metal plate, followed by the high priestess's athame; several packets of herbs; and half a dozen small, colorful bottles of liquids. Natalie heard Cassie whisper to Gillian, "Looks like the new purse is bigger on the inside, too."

"Silence," Natalie barked. She began to chant as she sprinkled herbs onto the plate, counting the drops as she added various potions, then lit the result with the taper. It burned with a blue flame, sparks leaping off into the twilight like living things, brightly at first and then dimming as they aged. Cassie and Gillian picked up the chant behind her, saying the syllables low and soft until they ran together in a stream of layered sound.

When Natalie felt the ritual space shift toward the ethereal, she began, speaking loudly above the droning chant of the other two: "Bill Charcross, you know me. You came to me to cure your warts. And I did. The poultice I gave you made them all drop off before that dance you worried so much about, remember? And now, Bill, even though you have passed beyond the veil, I need you to come to me again."

Nothing happened. The flame still burned. There was no breeze to make it waver.

"I call you, Bill. Bill Charcross! I helped you once. Will you help me? Will you do your job one more time, will you bring a criminal to justice? Will you catch a murderer you failed to catch in life?"

The flame flickered suddenly, burning outward, showering sparks. Natalie woke the kitten and set it in front of the flame. It backed away and hissed.

"I know you're here, Bill. The warmth of the flame is yours if you want it."

Natalie had only seen the ritual once, when her mother had performed it, and she was as surprised this time as she'd been the last when the small flame burst outward into thousands of glowing embers. She startled backward, catching herself on the heels of her hands to prevent tipping over, then quickly regained control and lifted her head toward the coalescing spirit within the sparks that were now concentrating around him like electrons around the nucleus of an atom.

"I remember you," he said. His voice sounded distant. Only a small part of his spirit would have traveled here from the Summerlands; he wasn't a proper ghost, not like William. But this piece of his spirit should have the answers she needed.

Cat tired of spitting at the new arrival and backed into Natalie's lap, snuggling into the hollow made by her crossed legs, but not coiling for sleep.

"Thank you, Bill. I appreciate you coming. I won't keep you long. Do you remember the case they called the Stanford murders?"

"Of course I do. Who could forget it? It's still hard to believe that William Stanford had it in him to do those terrible things."

"It is, and I don't believe it. Never have. It seems the real murderer may have returned, but some of the information from the original investigation didn't make it into the files. Do you know what I'm talking about?"

"Dunno. It wasn't my direct investigation, although it was me and Jeff who found the third victim, just by accident, back behind the Stanford place. We were out fishing." The specter shook its head. "A reporter from Boston, they said. The chief figured he'd been poking around where he shouldn't have. And him being found right out by the Stanford's dock? Just made William Stanford look that much more guilty once they found the matching rope in the boathouse."

"It had all the same characteristics as the other bodies? All of them?"

"Far as I remember. All killed with the same kind of rope, and it had always been wetted down beforehand. Might have made it easier to hang on to while he strangled them for all I know. And all of the bodies had some kind of toy left behind with them—plastic, you know. Not the good wood or metal ones. The cheap, new-fangled stuff."

Natalie realized that the sparks holding the man's spirit to the world had begun to dim. Her time with him was growing short.

"I know those things. But there was something else. What was it? What didn't get into the newspapers?"

Sparks danced in the spirit's eyes. He was quiet for a moment. "Well, there was the word. The Italian one. Writ down on the piece of paper that was found on each of the corpses. I don't know if it was the same every time, but the one that was on our victim—it was tucked under his shoelaces—meant slanderer or something. Like the murderer thought the guy was telling lies."

Natalie remembered the paper she'd found in her own pocket after a brush with the killer.

"Was it 'impicciona?'" she asked, stumbling over the unfamiliar language and holding her breath.

"Nah, nothin' like that. It was *cala* something. Calamine, maybe? I didn't know what it was exactly. Didn't seem as important as the murder weapon—" The spirit's mouth froze in place. There was a sudden flurry of sparks, and flecks of light blew upward and outward, roaring higher and wider, bursting out toward the witches like a swarm of angry blue bees. All three of the women jerked backward. When the sparks cleared, the specter was gone.

"Bury me in burlap!" Natalie roared. "I wasn't done." She tried to stand and got a claw in the thigh for her efforts. She settled back down and unfastened the kitten from her robe before plopping it unceremoniously to the side. "And keep this cat off of me!"

She thought back to the conversation during which Denton had asked about the languages the kids were studying in school, and she realized he'd already had the language link on his radar. The man was maddening. He could easily have let her know about whatever it was he'd found.

Cassie put the kitten back in its carrier while Gillian gave her a hand up along with some advice. "You need to tell Denton about this."

"Do I? And what do I say to good Chief 'Don't Ask, Don't Tell' Denton? By the way, Karl, while I was out at the graveyard conjuring up a spirit, I got some useful information that might assist your investigation?"

"True, that might be a difficult conversation." Gillian bit her lip and squinted, then said, "I could have Robert tell him! I can't see Denton pressing him for a source. That would work."

"Fine. Robert can tell him. I still don't understand how the chief has been loyal as a dog to the coven's high priest for all these years and still has no clue what goes on in this town."

"As Robert has explained," Gillian said, "some people don't allow themselves to know things that don't fit their world view. They'd rather cling to 'alternative facts' when faced with something that doesn't fit. I still don't know what Robert did to earn that kind of loyalty. All I know is that I'd rather face a hungry bear than Karl Denton if he ever got it through his head that I was a threat to my partner."

Natalie nodded agreement. "You tell Robert I need tit for tat though for that information. I think Denton has an Italian word he found on the Akers woman. I thought he was just asking that girl Twink questions to get her warmed up for the real interview when he asked about the languages she and her boyfriend take in school, but I underestimated him." Natalie made a face. That wasn't something she was happy to admit. "I want to know what that word was."

"I'll see what I can do. But you know Robert won't be likely to pass that information along unless there's proof the murders were committed magically. And I know you don't think they were."

Natalie dismissed her with a "phfft," then set her purse on top of her car as she unlocked the door. "Cassie, do you have that fancy phone with you? Can you look up a word for me? It was on a scrap of paper in my pocket after the attack. I don't know if the attacker put it there or if I saw it and stowed it away as I was coming to. Oh, and when we get back to the shop, we need to have a talk about that girl, Daria's cousin. I made a promise to someone."

Cassie was unlocking her own door, and said, "There's something about Twink? Yeah, we can talk about it. Just a minute and I'll do the word thing." After she stowed Cat's carrier safely on the floor of the backseat, she pulled out her phone, her thumbs poised. "Okay, what am I looking up?"

"It's Italian, probably. Impicciona." She spelled it out.

Cassie swiped, typed, and smirked.

"Well?" Natalie asked, tapping a foot, hands crossed over her chest.

"It means 'busybody.'"

The other two were still giggling when Natalie stomped on the gas, spinning the tires so fast it threw up a spray of dirt and gravel as she headed back to town.

✳✳✳

Natalie sipped her tea to make sure it was cool enough, then took a big gulp. It slid down spicy and sweet.

She turned to Cassie. "Do you remember when you told me that the Akers women's purse caught fire after the accident?" she said, her voice low. She glanced at the new door beyond the kitchenette.

"Yep, it was weird, but she had to be drunk or something. I figure she dropped a cigarette in there accidentally."

"No, it couldn't have been that. I'm learning more about their relationship than I probably should when I stop by, but it helps him to talk, I'm sure," Gillian said. "According to her husband, she didn't smoke. He quit for her when they were dating."

"Oh," Cassie said. She turned back to Natalie. "What do you think happened, then?"

"I didn't think about it at all until I saw Marcus's face when I asked him about his girlfriend. He's not a natural liar, but he would say anything to protect her, I expect, the same as she would say anything to protect him. But he suspects something that he's afraid to say. Something the girl doesn't even know."

Gillian leaned in. "I think I know where you're going with this..."

"I don't," Cassie said.

"That's because even though you didn't know you were a witch when you were her age, Eunice was training you, channeling those energies at the shop."

Cassie's eyebrows arched. "Twink's a witch? But Daria never..."

Natalie interrupted. "I'd bet Daria doesn't know it runs in the family. Ella Barton and her sister don't have magic. But Ella's mother, she was a voodoo woman, just like her mother before her. If you think I'm a cranky, bitter old woman, then you don't know bitter. After Henriette found out neither of her daughters would be able to work the family magic, she made their lives unbearable. When they were old enough, they left home without looking back. Ella, the oldest, married young. That didn't work out so well, and she found herself scratching out a living as a cleaner to support her children after her husband left her. She had a good reputation with the families she worked for though. Too holier than thou to ever walk off with a single paper napkin. Daria is the youngest of Ella's brood, a gift from the second husband, but he got tired of Ella's moods before Daria was even born."

"I never knew any of this—I know her brother and sister are a lot older than she is, though. But being a witch skips generations like that?" Cassie asked.

"It does, sweetheart. Think about your father. Has he ever shown any sign of magical talent?"

"I never really thought about it. But no, he hasn't, and he doesn't like Giles or the shop much. Says that if the old biddies in town want to play at being witches, he doesn't need to be around it. I haven't been able to get him to come for a visit since the wedding. It seemed to open up some old, bad memories for him."

Gillian laid a hand on her shoulder, rubbing it gently. "Yes, it's too bad about your father. With Anat standing in for his mother, he can't have had much fun growing up." Her lips pressed together briefly. "Although he could refrain from the 'old biddy' comments."

Cassie shrugged. "What can I do? He's my dad. But he's so against the very idea of Giles that I've never been able to tell him the mother he knew wasn't really his mother. That his mother loved him but couldn't tell him."

Gillian gave her a sad smile. "Yes, I think if you want to keep that relationship, you don't want to tell him things that make him think you're being influenced by the crazy biddies of Giles. But it's good you understand what he went through. Maybe that will help you understand Daria's mother better, too."

Cassie raised her hand to her mouth. "I didn't even think about that! But it makes sense, I guess, why she would try to keep her daughter away from all the magical stuff. But she has to suspect what's happening with Twink, don't you think?"

Natalie hmphed loudly and put a weathered hand on her hip. "I have no doubt that she knows what's happening with the girl, even if she denies it. Adolescence is a particularly difficult time for witches if they don't know how to channel their developing magic. Unbalanced hormones and magic are not a good mix."

She flashed a knowing look at Gillian, who fiddled with her rings. "Oh dear, yes. Things just rage out of control at adolescence and then later on in life, too. It's a miracle any of us survive menopause!"

"Like how difficult?" Cassie's brow drew down.

"All kinds of damage I'm afraid," Natalie said. "What non-magicals in the house often think of as poltergeist activity if they know where their children are when it's happening, or bad behavior and lies on their children's part if they don't. Fires. Property damage. Objects flying across the room of their own accord."

"But not strangulation with wet ropes."

Natalie huffed. "Most certainly not. Neither of those young people had a hand in that business. But if the shop burns down overnight...well, that's another matter."

Cassie took a deep breath and her mouth formed a tiny, perfectly round O. Before she could speak, Natalie said, "But don't worry about it, dear. It's easy to get under control once you know what it is. She doesn't even have to be aware she's being trained, if that's what you think is best. Just hire her for the shop and we'll teach her all the things Eunice taught you when you were a teenager."

Gillian smiled at Nat, one eyebrow raised. "Who would have thought you'd be so sensitive to the situation? But yes, I agree for once. If you want to, you can even do it without letting on to her sister."

"I didn't say it was the *best* option not to tell her," Natalie said, jumped in again. "Personally, I think you should. It's what I would do. After her training, the coven would be happy to have her if she'd have us. Without a few youngsters, it will soon die out."

"I really have to think about it," Cassie said. "Not about hiring her—that would give the two of you someone else to boss around instead of constantly trying to one-up each other, so that's a win already. But it doesn't feel right to me not to tell Daria and Twink what's really going on." Cassie tugged her lip, her eyes tightening at the corners. "Yep, it's going to take a little thought."

Gillian lay a hand on her shoulder. "I wouldn't wait too long, sweetie. Just for the safety of the girl and everyone around her."

Cassie nodded. "Decision by morning it is. I'll talk to Tom tonight. He usually has a pretty good perspective on stuff and he won't have any ulterior motives about bringing new blood into the choir." She looked pointedly at Nat.

Natalie's lips vibrated as she exhaled, her head moving backward in feigned surprise. "The things you suspect me of."

"And speaking of people making choices and keeping secrets," Cassie started, then hesitated before continuing, "I really didn't appreciate that one of you spilled the beans about my pregnancy to the rest of the town."

The two older witches looked at each other with confused expressions, then back at Cassie.

"I didn't," said Gillian. "I wouldn't. It was only yours to tell, sweetheart."

"What she said," Natalie agreed. "I've been silent as a corpse on the subject."

"Oh, then..." Cassie's hand covered her mouth and her eyes went to the ceiling as she tried to figure it out. "Well, I didn't tell anybody, and Tom didn't have time to tell anyone, so how did people find out the day after Tom did?"

Natalie raised a finger as if to punctuate her observation. "Another mystery to add to the pile, it seems."

14

The next morning, Cassie knocked lightly on the back door of the shop after Twink had left for school. She and Tom had talked about the Twink situation, and it seemed like the best way to handle it would be to introduce the topic to Daria first.

Cassie wasn't looking forward to the conversation. "By the way, D, that whole witch vibe Giles has going on? All true. Oh, and my homegirl witches need to start training Twink in magic so she doesn't burn the house down. You don't have a problem with that, do you?"

She'd spent most of the time she should have been sleeping running over the conversation in her head a hundred different ways, and she hadn't thought of a single way to say it that wouldn't sound nutty.

She closed her eyes. "Omigoddess. Omigoddess. Omigoddess."

She opened them when she heard the door swing away in front of her.

"Cass!" Daria folded her in a big hug. "I love this place. I love it. You're amazing for making it possible for us. I think Twink is even starting to relax a little." She grabbed Cassie's hand. "Come in!"

She pulled Cassie along to the big couch in the parlor. "Is it too early for wine?" She glanced at the clock and pouted. "It is, isn't it? You want coffee?"

Cassie caught her arm as she headed to the sink. "Just wait...I... there's something I need to tell you. Something about Twink."

A loud, rapid knock sounded at the back door followed by a deep female voice shouting, "Daria, you open up right this minute. And if you even think about sassin' me, girl..."

They couldn't see her through the curtains that covered the back door window, but those tones of retribution could only belong to one woman. The friends looked at each other, their eyes wide with fear. "Mama," Daria squeaked.

They stood frozen for a minute.

Daria unfroze first and broke the silence as the pounding continued. Her voice sounded small above the onslaught. "I have to answer that, don't I?"

Cassie shook her head yes, realizing at the same time that she felt a little unsteady on her feet.

This could end up being way worse than she'd imagined.

＊＊＊

"Did you think I wouldn't find where you were staying?" Ella Barton's voice rung out as soon as Daria opened the door.

She wore a patterned cotton dress covered in big, bright flowers and carried a black handbag over her arm. A petite black hat sat atop her salt and pepper hair, and its netting drifted down over her forehead. She should have looked like someone's granny on the way to church, but Mama Barton was a physically imposing woman. Cassie always thought she looked more like someone's burly linebacker brother in drag.

When Mama turned to her, Cassie covered her stomach reflexively. *Mama wouldn't harm a pregnant woman, would she? Big bark, not that much bite,* that's what Daria always said.

Mama's eyes bored into hers.

She dropped her own to make it stop. It didn't make a difference. She was in the crosshairs now.

"I told my daughter to stay away from you and your sinful grandmother years ago, and where do I find her? Right in the nest of vipers. What kind of spell have you worked on her?"

"Mama Barton, I..."

Cassie didn't need to continue. The elder Barton had turned back to her daughter.

"And you—I just found out you ran off with Twink to protect her from me because she kept a boy in her room overnight. I didn't raise you to take part in that kind of wickedness." Mama's pointing finger trembled.

"Mama! She's just a kid. And I knew how you would react. You can't raise her any more than Delia could. Kids need room to make mistakes, and a lot of attention—the good kind, not the threatening kind."

"Don't you dare talk back to me," Mama replied quietly. Cassie thought that somehow sounded even more dangerous than the shouting. "You gather up Twink's things. We're taking her out of school and delivering her right back to her no-good mama. We don't need any more of her kind ruining our family's good reputation."

Any more of her kind. The words smacked Cassie in the middle of the forehead. Nat was so right! Mama Barton knew exactly what was happening with Twink. Cassie pulled from her small well of courage by picturing herself standing with Tom, Gillian, and Natalie when they'd faced Anat and won. Mama might be imposing, but she was as friendly and playful as Cat when you pictured her next to a demon.

"Mrs. Barton, I think you'll want to join us in the parlor." Cassie swept a hand out to usher her toward the couch. "Because I know why you want to deliver Twink far away from here. Natalie Taylor told me about your mother. The big voodoo lady, right? So, if you want to talk about ruined reputations, I'm sure there's some juicy stories there I could resurrect."

Mama glared at her, her black eyes burning with terrible intent. Cassie swallowed, trying to keep her lip from shaking. If looks could kill...Ella Barton better not be a witch, because if she was, Cassie would be the recipient of some very ugly conjuring.

All at once, the woman deflated like a punctured balloon. Cassie exhaled slowly as Mrs. Barton walked quietly past her to the couch.

Marcus dug around in his backpack for his sunglasses. He hadn't been able to find them before he'd walked home from school, and he'd had to squint the whole way. He'd definitely want them before he had to go to work tomorrow morning—what if it was sunny again? They were good shades, and he didn't like driving without them.

What if he'd lost them? Or if they'd been stolen? And they were good shades. He'd hate it if they were lost. Or stolen. He'd forgotten his backpack in the car last night when he'd come home from work and the car door hadn't been locked this morning when he'd gone out to look for it. He guessed it served him right if someone had taken them, forgetting to lock up like that. Except he was sure he had locked it, and Twink held his second key for him. There was no way she'd come into Boston overnight and got into his car. I mean, how would she even get into the city?

At least he'd had his phone in his back pocket. Losing that would have really hurt. Twink and his mother wouldn't be able to reach him if that went missing.

It wasn't like you got to hang on to much when you were a foster kid. The other kids were always getting into his stuff, taking what they wanted. At least it was better with a foster family than it had been at the group home. They'd let him get a car as long as he kept up with the insurance. But with the Starrs fostering two other boys too, he still had to keep things he didn't want to see disappear close. At least they never narced him out for slipping out to see his mom.

He went about making sure he hadn't missed his glasses in an organized way. First, he pulled out his notebooks and stacked them up on his small twin bed. Next, he pulled out the stuff in the pockets: an extra pair of socks, a ballpoint pen, a pencil with a chewed-up eraser, his shirt for work, and a couple of scraps of paper he didn't recognize. It wasn't even his writing. In fact, it wasn't even English, as far as he could tell.

The doorbell rang, and he heard his foster mother coming up the stairs as he went through the outside pockets one more time, but his glasses weren't there.

When she got to his door, she didn't look happy. Giles's chief of police was standing behind her. This was the second time the chief had come around, and if his foster mother found out that he'd stayed late at Twink's, or at least what she thought was Twink's, she'd ground him for at least a month. Which he'd probably deserve if that's what he'd done.

If she knew where he'd really been, she'd kick him out and he'd be right back at the group home, where the door was locked at ten and the windows had bars on them.

"Marcus," said Mrs. Starr, "Chief Denton would like to talk to you. You and I will talk about this later."

He figured that was a fancy way of saying, "Whatever you did, here's a month on extra chores for embarrassing us with the neighbors by having the cops out again."

Denton leaned against the side of the door frame, his eyes moving over the pile of stuff on the bed. "I've got a few more questions for you," he said, then walked casually over to the bed and picked up one of Marcus's notebooks, leafing through it.

"This is rough stuff. Physics, right? I never had much of a head for it."

"Physics is OK. I do all right at it," Marcus replied, cleaning up the mess as he talked. He wadded up his work shirt and managed a layup into the clothes basket by the bunk beds that took up most of the rest of the room. He scooped up the crumpled scraps of paper and set up for another score, this time into the wastebasket, when the chief held out his hand. "Mind if I take a look at those?"

Marcus shrugged. "Sure." Ms. Taylor had said she wasn't going to rat him out about not being at Twink's that night, but you never knew what people were really going to do. All he had to do was cooperate. They couldn't arrest him for seeing his mother. But he never wanted to go back to that group home.

Denton studied the scraps of paper, first sounding out what was written on one, then switching it out with the other and looking real intently at that one too. He finally looked up at Marcus. "How do you know Italian?"

"I don't. Found those in my backpack when I was looking for my shades. They're missing. I really like those shades."

"Pretty good shades, are they?"

"Just knock-offs. Twink saw Russell Westbrook wearing a pair like them in a magazine. Just a black frame. Nothin' special."

Denton nodded and gestured with the hand holding the scraps of paper. "And where did these come from?"

Marcus shrugged. "Dunno."

"Well, kid, I don't think those shades are going to do you much good where you're going. I'll need to take you back to Giles with me for a longer talk."

Marcus zipped his backpack. He was surprised, but not that surprised. The old woman had probably blown his alibi after all. You can't really trust anybody, he knew that. He said, "Yeah. Can I bring my stuff? I don't like leaving it around here. It could disappear."

Denton stood back to let him lead the way into the hall. "I think that's a good idea, son."

***

Dash's mustache quivered as he slammed the stapler into the wad of receipts on the gallery counter. "You should have heard him. The things he said!"

Cassie's hands spread wide, palms up, to encourage him to keep talking about the disastrous dinner party with Lou Frank. Talking always helped him calm down when he was upset. "So, yeah...what did he say?"

"He said the gallery was good enough to satisfy the art needs of the bourgeois housewife, but that advertising in Boston was a ridiculous idea. He actually had the gall to say that except for his work, the art we carry simply isn't up to snuff for a more sophisticated clientele. That's outrageous, and just plain rude!" Dash slammed his palm down hard on the top of the stapler again.

Cassie's mouth turned down at the corners as she gently took the stapler. "Why don't you organize the receipts, and I'll do the stapling? And I'm sorry he said something terrible like that. He's like night and day."

"Oh, it gets better." Dash shuddered, then leaned in to her. "When I was out of the room getting dessert, he told my sweet Jon—my patient, kind, handsome partner—that it was a good thing we had decided not to get married even though Massachusetts has allowed gay marriage for over ten years. Because obviously, a relationship like ours could only end in divorce. What would *he* know about it?"

Dash's face was turning dangerously red. "It's not like we decided not to marry because we're not committed to each other...we've been together for twenty years. It's hardly a passing fancy. It's just that John's children have never really accepted me, and well...he's afraid he won't be able to see his grandchildren if we tie the knot. His children wouldn't be able to pretend I don't exist after that. It's a very difficult position for him."

Cassie went to her boss and hugged him. She could tell when he started crying from the jerky gasps against her shoulder. She patted his back gently. "Dash, you know that Jon worships you! How could you let that pompous, arrogant, mean-spirited Lou Frank upset you so much? I'm never talking to him again. He's the most two-faced jerk I've ever met. And I had finally talked Tom around to having him to dinner. That will never happen now. Never."

"No, you're right, I...well, I need to get myself together, don't I? This is the last time I'll be taken in by Luigi Franconi."

"Who?" Cassie asked.

"When he was just an unknown kid from Giles, Lou Frank was Luigi Franconi. His parents were immigrants. His mother worked for the Stanford family as a maid. He changed his name after his work was accepted in a New York gallery and, well...you know how it went from there. I think if you look at the signature on the Giles Corey bronze, it says Franconi, not Frank."

That was interesting. She'd have to look for the signature now.

Dash stood, his eyes red and blotchy. "I'm giving myself a time-out downstairs. A small meditation would do me good."

The thick curtains that hid the back room swished closed behind him. She heard the sound of the trap door, which was hidden by an oriental rug, being opened and then closed again. She had never been in the secret room, although Tom had. She could only guess what was in there that helped to calm him. Tom was sworn to secrecy, and so far, he'd kept his promise.

About an hour later, the bell over the door tinkled gaily. The sound was completely out of sync with her emotions. Dash still hadn't returned from downstairs. She turned from her dusting, her business smile in place, hoping it was someone with some good news. Her smile faded.

"How could you possibly think you're welcome here?" she growled as Lou Frank entered.

"I know, I know," he said, clasping his hands together against his chest pleadingly. "I'm sure he told you, as well he should—I was terrible to dear Dash and Jon at dinner last night. But I just...well, something awful happened that day, and I was losing my temper with everyone. I brought some of my best small bronzes with me instead of placing them in a gallery in New York, and one of them has been badly damaged by the careless handyman I hired. Not only that, but he tried to hide it from me with a bad epoxy job. I can re-pair it, but like the Giles Corey bronze, it will never be the same." He slid the large leather bag off of his shoulder and took out a cylindri-cal package wrapped in silver and gold paper and decorated with a gigantic bow. "So, please, if Dash is here..."

"He's not. Go away. Why do you always think that you can be a jerk and then get away with it by giving people presents? Just go..."

She heard the curtain part behind her. Nuts. She'd hoped she could spare Dash any contact with the guy, but that wasn't going to happen now. And when Dash said, "It's okay. Let the man speak," she knew that he was going to forgive him. Dash was like that. He couldn't hold a grudge even if his fingers were glued to it.

Lou walked to him quickly and took Dash's hands in his. "You must believe me when I tell you that I'm ashamed of how I behaved last night. You know how New Yorkers are; we're so rude to each other we forget that most people don't act that way. I haven't quite adapted to being back in Giles, although I think having friends like you, Jon, and Cassie is exactly what I need to help me develop kinder, gentler ways."

Dash's face split into a smile. "Well, you're here now, and apologizing too. That's certainly not the New York attitude." Dash's moustache seemed to perk up a little above his winsome smile.

"No it's not, my friend. I've brought you something I hope you and Jon will enjoy. But I fear you may never be able to forgive the terrible things I said, and I'm truly sorry. I didn't mean any of it. I was captured by my anger, which had nothing to do with you." He motioned to the package on the table. "Please accept it?"

Dash looked at Cassie. She gave him a neutral look, but it wasn't easy. It really was up to him if he wanted to give the guy the benefit of the doubt, but no matter what Dash decided about Lou, she was done with him.

She couldn't help but wince when Dash gave a little squee after opening the gift and finding a bottle of champagne. "Cristal! Oh, how marvelous. How...really, it's not necessary, it's..."

She winced again when Lou put his hand on Dash's shoulder. "You and Jon deserve only the best. That's probably why you have each other."

Dash was eating it up. Then again, hadn't she forgiven him the first time he'd been so awful? She couldn't blame Dash. If Jon was right, he'd been nursing a secret crush-from-afar on the guy for years.

Lou removed his hand from Dash's shoulder and flipped his white cascade of curls back dramatically. Yep. Dash was a goner again. He smiled up at the man, then back at his expensive bottle of champagne.

✳✳✳

"Who?" Natalie groused into her landline when Denton called. "Are you telling me that you seriously believe that polite young man attacked me? And what motivation would he have?" There was a pause. "No, no I'm coming down there. Do you think there are two copycats, do you? No, I didn't think so. That young man was nowhere near Giles when the Akers woman was murdered."

Natalie held the phone away from her ear and looked at it like it must be an idiot. Then she pulled it back to her mouth. "Of course I can prove it. Why else would I say it? I'm coming down there. And you treat that young man respectfully, or you'll have me to answer to!" She slammed the phone down in its cradle.

She gathered up her essentials: red purse, car keys, scarf. Maybe she should take the athame just in case the police chief needed some ritual convincing.

Pah! Too risky. She would have to make him see sense with her personal charm alone, which, she acknowledged, was bad news for Marcus. If all he had standing between him and incarceration was her engaging personality, that young man was going straight to prison.

16

Natalie put her purse on the roof of the car and unlocked the door for the trip to the police station. As she did, she heard a faint sound, as if someone was calling her name from very far away. Just "Natalie" and really only "Natal..." She turned, but there was no one there.

She collected her purse from the roof and was opening the car door when the voice sounded again. "Nuh..." was all she heard this time before it trailed off.

Once more, she turned.

This time, she picked up the barest whiff of ozone and a faint ghostly sheen that flickered in and out a few feet away. Nothing much recognizable there except that mouth. She knew those lips. She had never forgotten how they'd felt on hers. William!

He wasn't gone. For a moment, she thought her heart would explode as joy marauded forcefully through her body.

Then, his eyes were there, his nose, and his terrible, horrible, beautiful sweater. His specter was gauzy and insubstantial, but it was unmistakably William.

Soundlessly, he mouthed, "Follow me." He turned toward the house and went around the side to the backyard where it backed up to Giles Woods. Moving swiftly, his form began to disperse even as he moved. She rushed after him as fast as her old knees allowed. They were about a mile into the woods, coming right up on the edge of the lake, when he stopped and turned back to her before the trees ended and the stony lakeshore began. He disappeared again, his sweet mouth going last like the Cheshire cat's, except that William was not grinning.

She picked her way through the brush toward where he'd stopped and nearly fell over the body. It was a man—that was easy enough to tell from his broad, tank-top clad shoulders and short hair.

He was face down with a rope around his neck. She reached down to touch it. It was damp.

It looked like Denton would be coming to her instead of the other way around.

***

"Oh, of course, let me tell you the truth, shall I?" Natalie switched gears. "So, here's what happened...I lured the handsome young handyman Sean into the woods for immoral purposes and then knocked him off after I'd had my wicked way with him."

She stared Denton down. He didn't respond. *An unexpected display of wisdom,* Natalie thought.

"Just for the giggles, obviously," Natalie added. She had both hands planted firmly on her hips. "And don't give me that Columbo-on-the-case look. If you spent your time productively instead of harassing helpless old women and high school boys, there wouldn't be another body in the woods."

Denton's hand twitched where it rested on his gun belt. "Ms.

Taylor, I'm merely requesting that you account for your activities today so I can remove you from the suspect pool."

"Up at six. Coffee and the paper until seven. Brief shower followed by an hour working in the herb garden." She pointed back toward her house. "The one I asked you all not to tramp through when I led you here? Largely ignored, I might add. And then you called to tell me you'd brought in that young man Marcus and wanted me to see if I could identify him as my attacker. Afterward, I took a walk to compose myself before I went to the station. When I found the dead man, I changed my plans."

"And what about last night?" He turned to where the coroner and an officer were working near the body. "What would you say on time, Doc?"

"The presence of rigor says sometime between 10 p.m. and 4 a.m. Probably more like 2 a.m. since it's a cool night, assuming he was killed outside. Definitely less than twenty-four hours, in any case."

Denton turned back to Natalie until Dr. Don called, "But chief?" and continued, "This may be staged. I don't know that he was killed outside. The body may have been moved from somewhere else. Either that, or someone turned him after he'd been dead for a while. The blood that settled into his back indicates he was lying face up after he died. He was turned to his stomach a few hours later."

Denton looked at Natalie. "You're free to go, but don't make any trips out of the country."

"Great grimacing gobstoppers! As if I'm going to become a globetrotter at my age. Are you going to let that boy Marcus go now?"

"No. Not that it's your business."

"And why not? He wouldn't have done this any more than he would have attacked me. No motive at all. And he was your overnight guest last night, wasn't he? On some trumped-up evidence. So you don't have any cause to keep him. I'll slip by the station and give him a ride home."

Denton glowered, his hand snaking out to grab her firmly by the elbow, his voice low but packed with promise. "You'll stay away from him for now." He held up a pair of black sunglasses. "I found these near the body. He may not be involved, but I have a feeling these are going to show up with our prisoner's fingerprints all over them, and I don't want whoever dropped them near the body to know we didn't take the bait. So stop rocking the boat."

Natalie was silent for a moment. "Fine. I'm due at the shop, anyway." She shook off his hand and began the trek back toward the house. It was easy enough to find her way along the trail of broken underbrush that now extended through her garden. She didn't bother going around—there was no point. Most of the plot of tiny seedlings she'd planted last week were crushed beyond hope.

She knew she shouldn't be feeling good about anything right now, not with a new victim that had been set up to frame someone. And who was he framing? Marcus? Her? Whoever this killer was, he was disorganized. Perhaps that would work in their favor. He was bound to make a critical mistake sooner or later.

In any case, Marcus was most likely disqualified as a suspect since he couldn't have left his sunglasses with the body, so she didn't have to break her promise to him. She wouldn't have liked doing that, but she would have liked it a lot less if that nice young man was charged for a crime he hadn't committed.

✳✳✳

Natalie barreled through the front door of Cat's Magical Shoppe and started talking before looking around to see who was there. She headed straight for Cassie and Gillian, who were working at the counter.

"He's struck again! This time he's murdered that Sean, the handyman. And tried to—what is it they say in those detective shows—stitch me up for it. Dumped the body right behind my house."

A gasp came from the storage room. Cinnamon stood in the doorway, her deck of tarot cards dropping from a limp hand as her skin went gray and she looked like she might faint. Cassie hurried over to her.

"Cin, I'm so sorry." Cassie supported her while Gillian ducked around her into the storeroom and scooted a chair under her. As soon as she was sitting, she collapsed over her knees.

Cassie rounded on Natalie. "How could you be so insensitive?"

"I didn't know she was here. How could I?"

"It's Thursday, Nat. We always have 'Readings by Cinnamon Brown' on Thursdays." Cassie turned away from Natalie again. "You okay, Cin? Can I get you anything? Water? Or..."

Cinnamon was sitting up straight now. She took her hand away from over her eyes to wave Cassie away weakly. "No. I just don't...I don't believe it. He was trying to get up under my skirt just yesterday. He was such a player; he couldn't help himself. But a good friend. He was a friend..."

Cassie and Gillian exchanged a glance, and Gillian hustled Natalie into the kitchenette.

Natalie kept her mouth shut until the kitchenette door closed behind them. "I don't see why you're both so upset. Would you rather she heard it on the nightly news?"

"Don't act like that, Nat. You know why we're upset. And you can stay in here until we get Cinnamon home because there is simply no way she should have to put on a bright face for the punters."

Natalie put on the kettle and sat down by herself, frowning. It wasn't even the new murder she wanted to tell them about—it was William. William wasn't gone. There could be a dozen murders today and it wouldn't kill her mood. She wanted to be sorry she felt that way, but she couldn't.

She heard light footsteps coming down the hall. Cassie appeared in the doorway. "Gillian's taken Cinnamon home. I'm going to give her the small storeroom as her permanent space, so you'll have to use the back storeroom or the basement from now if you need to put anything aside for a customer to pick up."

"Fine, fine." Natalie took a breath. "It was William who led me to the body."

"Wait a minute. You said he was gone. He's not gone?"

Natalie shook her head, and the beginning of a happy tear formed in her right eye before she blinked it back. "He's barely there, but maybe he just needs time to regain his strength. What he did for me when I was attacked must have taken a lot out of him."

Cassie took her hand. "Nat, I really am happy that he's okay. But, truthfully, I thought, well, maybe it was for the best. I mean, you were trying to build a ward to keep him away like a week ago."

"Yes, but things change. I don't need to explain myself."

Cassie gave her a half-smile. "No, Nat, you don't. But don't gripe to me a month from now when the dead guy is irritating you because he wants to hang out with you all the time." Cassie turned back to the door and exited into the hall, saying, "You might as well tell me the whole story while we work."

Nat started with the call from Denton about Marcus, going on to explain how William had led her to the body and how Denton had found Marcus's sunglasses at the scene. It took a while because she had to talk in between waiting on customers and turning away who'd come for a reading. There were a lot of those. Cinnamon was popular.

"I don't know who the killer is trying to frame," she said at last, "but he's certainly botched it. With Marcus a guest of the Giles PD last night and Denton knowing that the only thing I could do in a serial manner is annoy him, it's taken most of his suspects out of the running. Unless he's holding out on me."

Cassie tried not to smile. "Maybe he doesn't tell the local coven's high priestess all the cop business. That's a possibility."

Natalie snapped her a sharp glance from behind the counter and then looked down at her watch. "Don't you have to run along to your gallery job?"

"When Gillian gets back. I called Dash and told him I was running late and why, so he'll just be glad to get the whole scoop—minus the ghostly part and the framing Marcus part, that is." Cassie bent over and picked up the kitten that had been batting at her shoelaces every time she stopped moving. It purred happily as she ran her hand gently down its back.

"By the way, I don't think I told you this, did I? You know that Lou Frank, the artist?"

"The one Tom doesn't like?"

"Tom has never even really met him. But yeah, he doesn't like him. Anyway, first he seemed nice and then he was terrible to Dash, and then he apologized and fell all over himself to make it up to us. He did this amazing painting of me. And then, when Dash invited him to dinner, he was horrendous again. Poor Dash was devastated."

Natalie harrumphed. "Dash is easily devastated. He'll get over it, dear."

"Yep, he already has," Cassie replied, sounding discouraged. "And I'm not real happy about it. I'm beginning to think Lou Frank is a real psycho. Oh...he said he knew you when he was young. He lived here. I bet you knew all the psychos, right?"

"Lou Frank? Doesn't ring a bell."

"He was at the council meeting. He's the artist who did the bronze of Giles Corey. He sculpted it originally. Dash told me his name was something else when he lived here—Franconi. That's right—Luigi Franconi."

"Was that who that was? Franconi? I'd quite forgotten he did the town's statue." Natalie's mouth worked up a tight grin, then it stopped as she spat out, "Pah! It was a good day when he left town."

"Why?" Cassie asked.

"He was a sponger. Never did an honest day's work in his life. Too busy being an Artist with a capital A. He was always trying to get his hand into William's pocket, and William was so kind that he let him more often than not. But when he tried to worm his way into Lettie's heart with his poetry and paintings while he made fun of her lisp to everyone in town, William's father put a stop to it. She was much older than he was; her father knew what the man was after. I think old Stanford paid him to leave. Lettie was heartbroken, and William disappeared around the same time. Lettie never recovered from the double loss. She was quite a strange old bird by the time she died, living in that house with only her memories to keep her company."

Cassie eyed Natalie with one eyebrow raised. "Strange old bird, huh?"

"Believe me, dear, I'm a sweet, sweater-crocheting grandma compared to Lettie Stanford."

Cassie put Cat down in his basket on the counter, watching as he wrapped his tail around himself before he snuggled his head in just so and promptly fell asleep. As he did, Gillian bustled through the door, and Cassie put her finger to her lips. "Shhh...I've just gotten him down for a nap."

Gillian beamed at the sleeping kitten. "He's such a dear."

Cassie walked into the hall and grabbed her thick blue cardigan off its hook. As she slipped it on, she said, "Nat's been trying to convince me that she isn't considered at all eccentric by Giles standards."

"As much as I hate to admit it, sweetheart, she isn't even close. There are at least two or three residents who are much more eccentric than she is. And if you count the dotty ones, too, well...and, come to think of it, she doesn't make it into the sheer-meanness hall of fame, either."

"That's for sure: I've known Mama Ella Barton since I was a kid... but with recent events, let's just say she doesn't scare me anymore."

"Ella Barton is a pussy cat compared to some of the women I've been introduced to here and in Salem," Gillian replied. "Now, Angelique Franconi, there was one mean old witch! When she died, her own son didn't even come back for the funeral."

"Is her son Lou Frank? Natalie and I were just talking about him," Cassie asked. "I mean, is that Lou's mother?"

Natalie bobbed her head. "Yes, that's her. I still don't understand what he's doing here. He couldn't get out of town fast enough after the Corey statue was installed and people started to notice his work. Like I said, I think William's father paid him to get out of town."

"You'd think he would have mentioned that his mother recently died when I asked him about why he'd come back."

Natalie shrugged. "She didn't. It was years and years ago, twenty at least. But the house has been a rental for that long, handled by what's-her-name—that bleached blonde with the attitude—at Danders Realty over in Salem who handles all the Giles properties. After fifty years, I certainly wouldn't have expected him to return. He wouldn't have a reason to."

Cassie looked at Nat intently as she talked. "Nat," she said slowly, "he lived here during the murders, right? And he's Italian. With what we now know about the evidence from the first cases, do you think there's a chance that he's the killer?" Her eyebrows rose up her forehead abruptly, and she blurted, "Omigoddess...both of you need to be at my house tonight for dinner. I mean it. I just realized something that has never quite seemed right about that man." She looked at the clock above the counter. "But I gotta go. I'm late for the gallery again."

As she grabbed her coat from the hall, Gillian stopped her. "I can't sweetheart. We're having Gerald Akers around for dinner tonight. Not a cancelable event. The poor man is in a state."

Cassie nodded and headed for the door. "Tomorrow then, for sure. And Nat, you're not getting out of it this time. You're coming to the house. No excuses! You're not even on shift tomorrow, so you'll have plenty of time to do anything else you think you need to accomplish well before dinner time."

Then she was out the door, with Gillian calling after her, "Robert and I will be there. And we'll make sure that Natalie shows up, too."

∗∗∗

Robert pushed back the plate which had previously held seared cod along with an interesting fennel and celery salad his girlfriend had prepared . "Gilly, it was delicious. Thank you."

Gerald Akers pushed his own plate away after disposing of the last shred of fish. "Excellent. I have to thank both of you for inviting me. I can't imagine that I'm good company right now."

Gillian patted his hand before she picked up his plate and added it to the pile she'd made with hers and Robert's. "You're always welcome, Gerald. Both of us understand how it feels to lose a spouse. It's hard to believe right now, I know, that life goes on..." she smiled lovingly at Robert, "but it does. Even though the early days are so hard."

Robert mumbled something that Gillian couldn't hear as she left the room with the dishes.

When she returned with three small plates, an artful array of Battenberg cake slices, and a steaming pot of good English tea on a large tray, whatever Robert and Gerald had been talking about trailed off.

"Let me help you with that," Robert said, grabbing the plates and distributing them. He offered Gerald the heaped tray of cake slices before setting them next to his own plate and serving several to himself. Gillian politely hid her smile behind her napkin. Oh well, she had him eating healthy otherwise, and he was still so thin, despite the baked goods. Let him eat cake.

After the men had finished their desserts and were lingering over tea, Gillian asked, "Gerald, have you decided what you're going to do now? Will you be staying in town, or will you go back to Boston?"

"I'm staying here, but it won't—I thought that being someplace as low impact as Giles would be good for Caroline. She was always very highly strung. I thought the easier pace of life would help her relax. But it just made her want to escape, I'm afraid. On the other hand, I was made for it. I could sit on my back porch looking out on the lake for hours."

Robert leaned on his elbows and nodded. The overhead light reflected off the top of his scalp. "That's right, you have lakefront, don't you? One of the lucky ones; we've got to take quite a hike across Giles Woods to get there. It's a beautiful house. There were people in town who worried that a new owner would modernize it so it didn't fit with the surroundings, but you've left it with that natural look."

"The interior has been significantly updated. The kitchen is very high-tech now. You'll have to come for dinner once I've had more time to get to know it, but I'm not the cook that you are," he said, nodding to Gillian. "It's one of those things I always hoped to improve at during my retirement. It could be a while before I'm ready to host a dinner party." He sighed, then perked up a little. "Do you fish?" he asked Robert.

"I do. Not as often as I used to, but I've got a rowboat on the lake. It's always been a good place to clear my head after a long week of business or governing."

"Eccellente! I hope you'll allow me to join you sometime."

Gillian's head, which had begun to dip from the carbs and small talk snapped up again. "I knew the two of you would find common ground! Masters of enterprise, the both of you. You have a lot in common. By the way, Gerald, I noticed your Italian pronunciation is perfect. Do you speak Italian?"

"I'm fluent. I suppose it's an affectation to throw a word in here or there, but I spent a year in Italy after completing college, until father called me home to start me in the business. Since he was a wine importer, it was a useful language to know."

Gillian leaned in. "I imagine it would be. How interesting. And what stories do you have to tell? No one goes to Italy without returning with marvelous stories. I'll show you mine, if you show me yours..."

Gillian listened quietly as Gerald grew more animated, talking about his long-distant youth. A part of her was pleased that the dinner had distracted him from his grief for a while, but another part of her made a mental note to tell Natalie what she had found out about his language skills.

It was just before noon and Natalie was pounding on the front desk at the police station. "Anyone here? There's a restless member of the public who requires your attention."

Denton's voice boomed behind her. "Paula had to go home because one of her boys is sick. Do you think you could wait quietly for something just once in your life?"

She turned and gave him her most patient look, which was less like "I have all the time in the world" than "Do what I want now or I'll turn you into a toad."

"Dear Ms. Taylor, how may I assist you?" he continued as he walked behind the desk, but it sounded more like "I wish you a fiery death, you annoying old bat" than "Gracious lady, I am at your service."

"Have you released the boy yet? If not, I've brought him a hearty lunch and my esteemed company."

"Who says I'm letting in visitors?" the chief growled.

"I say you are unless you want to charge the boy and schedule an arraignment. You need to get him back to school—he's an honors student, did you know that? An honors student who has never learned a word of *Italian*." She held Denton's eyes with her own as she emphasized the word.

"How do you know about that? You didn't dirty my crime scene yesterday, did you?"

"Of course I didn't. But I'd like to make a deal, Denton. Let me see the boy, and I'll give you the gift of knowledge." She continued to hold his eyes. There weren't many who could last long in a staring contest with her. She had to admire that he still hadn't flinched.

"Agreed. But you go first." His gaze remained steady.

She reached into her purse and pulled out the scrap of paper with "impicciona" written on it. "That was in the pocket of the dress I wore the day I was attacked. I didn't realize the connection at first. But one of your people slipped up about that little detail when you were harassing me behind my property this morning, didn't they?"

"I don't recall that they did," he replied.

"I have better hearing than you might expect for a woman of my age. I can still tune in to an overexcited patrolman at his first murder talking just a turn of the knob too loud."

"Fine. Give it to me. I'll enter it in evidence."

"By the way, unless I'm mistaken, the only suspect you have left is Gerald Akers, but I don't like him for this. Do you?" Natalie hadn't actually decided about Akers because he was far too emotional for her to want to make another visit. She hoped Gillian had a better handle on him after their dinner last night. But it couldn't hurt to know what Denton thought.

He turned to dismiss her, "As far as I know, you're not assigned to the case, so who you think is responsible is irrelevant. Let me get one of the officers to escort you to the boy's holding cell. I'll have them move a table and some chairs in so the two of you can eat comfortably."

Natalie was surprised by that and felt suddenly generous. "Thank you," she said. "Let me give you another tip: Lou Frank, the artist, previously known as Luigi Franconi, spoke Italian with his parents as a child. He grew up in Giles and left town right after the murders occurred. He is now back in town, and the murders seem to have started up again. I'd have a look in those old files to see if his name comes up."

She hadn't meant to tip him off that way. She'd meant to look into it herself after she'd talked to Cassie and Gillian. Denton would probably go putting his boot into it now and make a mess of things. What in the world had possessed her? But perhaps he would respond in kind.

"By the way," she said as he led her toward the cells, "What Italian word did you find on Caroline Aker's body?"

"Once again, Ms. Taylor, you're not part of this investigation."

She wasn't feeling quite so generous anymore, but she put her annoyance aside as the officer opened the cell where Marcus was lying on a bunk, staring into space. "Ms. Taylor," he said, sitting up. "You came to visit?"

"And I brought lunch. I have a permanent discount at the Diner of Earthly Delights. I expect it will be worthy eating."

He dug into his food like he'd been starved for days. She knew that wasn't the case; Robert would never let anyone in the town's holding cells go hungry, although she suspected that Marcus had been enjoying a diet of packaged food from the Decent Food Mart, the local mini-grocery. Although its owners spoke English as a second language, she wasn't convinced the store's name was an endearing language mistake. Everyone shopped out of town unless they were looking only for convenience.

She wondered idly what it would cost to feed a teenage eating machine like this one.

***

That night, Natalie barely noticed the rich food laid out on the table as the others dug in, murmuring, "oh yes, pass the..." and "I don't mind if I do..." and "a little won't hurt, I'm sure..." as Tom's menu choices for the night were passed around the table by his appreciative guests.

She picked at her food, distracted. Even the smell of ozone and the faint glimmer as William flashed into existence on the other side of the room only cheered her briefly.

She didn't want to alarm the young people, but she'd had a feeling of unease since the moment she'd entered the house. She wished Cassie had started the evening with her concerns about Franconi, but the girl had insisted, "Fun first! Tom's outdone himself to celebrate that you showed up tonight, Nat. We really thought we were never going to get you here."

She wondered if Cassie had sensed something in the house that didn't belong here. Something that was magic but not Cassie's magic. It was easy to tell the difference; she knew from Cassie's enfolding hug when she'd arrived that all of Cassie's magic burned brightly at her center, wrapping itself around the baby to make a cocoon that nothing bad could penetrate. Natalie was sure she didn't even know she was doing it.

No, this was something lurking, something other. And if Cassie sensed it, she was being very nonchalant about it. Then again, the girl was inexperienced. She hadn't known about her powers for long.

As the meal progressed, Natalie became more and more unsettled and tired of the small talk. Before Tom brought out the dessert, she announced, "I need a tour of the house. Now."

Every conversation at the table stopped, and every head turned to her. "Did you hear me? Your high priestess needs a tour of the house. Immediately. This is not a suggestion."

Tom and Cassie looked at each other, confused, then Tom said, "Sure, Nat. Follow me."

Although she'd been there many times when her mother had been John Stanford's secretary, Natalie didn't know the house well. Back then, she would wait in the big, public parlor to walk home with her mother after work because it was often dark by the time her employer allowed her to go. That was how Natalie had met William. And when he'd offered to drive them home one night, she'd thought he was just being a gentleman. Her mother was frequently tired, particularly after the full moon, but William knew nothing about the secret magic of Giles.

He'd been so innocent when he'd confessed that he had long admired her and would like to know her better. She could just be herself, just Natalie, when she was with him.

She took a deep breath and followed Tom up the stairs with Cassie and the rest of them trailing behind. This was no time to take a walk through ancient memories.

As they climbed, the sense of an intrusion grew stronger. Tom turned to the right at the top of the stairs, but Natalie turned left. "I'd like to see what's over here. Do you mind?"

"Whatever you want, Nat. It's our room, then the room we'll be turning into the nursery, the library, and a smaller room I've already remade into the office. It's the smaller of the two wings, but we like it better—it feels homier to have most of our living space in one place."

"Yes. And less spooky to be in a different wing than William's room, I expect..." She remembered how he'd used to wave goodbye to her from his window, then sneak out later to meet her after she'd delivered her mother home.

She continued down the hall, following the insistent buzz of the magic. She turned into the first doorway on the left, turning quickly back to Cassie. "Your room?"

Cassie nodded.

Natalie put a finger to her lips, cautioning silence. An uneasy silence fell. "Oh, my dear!" Natalie suddenly said, "it's lovely! I see you've kept the period pieces. Such a nice choice." She headed straight for the fireplace. This close to it, it was obvious where the magic she'd sensed was localized.

"This picture? It's heavenly. Beautiful work." She reached out for the frame and grasped the portrait with both hands. As questing magic flowed down her arms and toward the picture, she felt a definite sting. The portrait was protecting itself.

She pulled one hand away and stumbled backward, laying the back of it against her forehead. "I suddenly feel so weak, I..."

Tom rushed forward to catch her as she fell, allowing her legs to fold under her as the hand she still had on the painting grasped it just long enough to lay it face down on the wide mantel. The stinging sensation stopped immediately. There it was. The connection had been broken; whatever the magic was conducting away from the house, it wasn't conducting it anymore.

She sat up, perfectly fine now, and said, "Well, isn't anyone going to help me up?" Making use of one of the hands she was offered, she pulled herself back to her feet.

She brushed off their concern and motioned for them to follow as she led them like a line of ducklings down the stairs and out the front door.

"Everyone in your cars. We'll meet at Robert's house. See you soon." She got into her own car and spun out toward the end of the long driveway, heading down the road toward Robert's.

***

Robert's place was in the newer section of the city, well on the other side of the lake, and Natalie was chilled by the time the others arrived. She'd forgotten her coat at Cassie's in her rush to get the girl and her precious cargo away. She couldn't be sure she'd completely disconnected whatever was flowing into or out of the house, and she hadn't wanted to take any chances. She hugged herself and rubbed at her thin arms for warmth.

"About time!" she said when Robert stepped out of his big SUV and went around to help Gillian down from the passenger side. "I could have frozen to death waiting for you."

Tom and Cassie pulled up in the station wagon behind Robert's car and walked up to join them as Robert said, "We got here as quickly as we could while still obeying the speed limit. It might have helped if you'd let us in on why we suddenly needed to relocate."

"Get me in the house in front of a space heater first. I'm not built for the cold anymore."

Inside, they took their seats in Robert's cozy study. In addition to being the warmest room in the house, it was also the one with the strongest and deepest wards. Natalie needed that more than she needed heat.

She inspected Tom's hands and wrists, which were bare of jewelry—nothing but his wedding ring. Not even a watch. She leaned over to Cassie, "Have you recently gotten any new jewelry, anything you keep on your person all the time?"

Cassie shook her head and furrowed her brow. "No. Just my wedding ring, like Tom."

"That's fine. We know where those came from. Gillian, any new jewelry? Robert, any new furnishings? Any artwork?"

They both shook their heads.

"It looks like we should have no spies then, so let me tell you why I've called you all here, shall I? I believe I've solved the mystery of who committed the Stanford murders, and it wasn't a Stanford at all, just as I have always said."

"You figured it out by taking a tour of the house?" Cassie asked.

"It wasn't only a tour, dear. There was a presence in the house that didn't belong, and no—it wasn't William, although he did stop in momentarily. No, it was something else. I'm not sure quite what. It felt familiar, although I couldn't say why." She leaned in slightly toward Cassie. "I'm hoping you can shed light on it. What was it you wanted to tell us about Lou Frank?"

Tom's head cocked toward Cassie. "Has that guy been bothering you again?"

"No, nothing with me. The last time I saw him, he came into the gallery to bring Dash a bottle of super-expensive champagne to apologize for the second time he'd treated him badly. And he had some big story—Sean had ruined one of his bronzes and put him in a bad mood or something. Like that was a good reason for being so totally out of line when Dash and Jon had him over for dinner."

Natalie drummed her fingers on the table. "You had to have us to dinner for this? There must be more to it."

"There is, Nat. Just give me a minute. The thing is...." Her eyes rolled up and to the left, and her tongue circled inside her cheek. Finally, she said, "The thing that's bothered me is that you both said you didn't tell anyone that I was pregnant. And you guys are the only ones who knew. She looked from Natalie to Gillian. "Are you sure you didn't say anything to anyone, even by accident?"

Gillian's hand went to her heart like a pledge, and her eyes opened wide. "I know I didn't." She moved her hand to lay it on top of Robert's and darted a glance at him before she turned back to meet Cassie's eyes. "Do you know how hard it was keeping it a secret from this one? But I knew you and Tom would want to tell him. So no, I told no one."

Robert nodded his head. "In fact, I didn't know until Tom told me tonight when he handed me a cigar before dinner. I assumed that's what we were celebrating with dinner tonight."

Cassie looked to Natalie, who said, "I told William. But he was hardly going to be flapping his lips to anyone, seeing as how he has no lips to flap."

"Then who told Lou Frank that I was pregnant? He knew about it the day after Tom found out. He brought me flowers to congratulate me."

"Don't look at me," Tom said. "I was too busy loving up my beautiful wife that night to go out and gossip about myself."

Natalie nodded sagely. "Yes, I expected so given the way you carried her out of the shop. Was there talk of the baby that night?"

Cassie rolled her eyes. "Well, duh. Talk of the baby. Kissing of the baby. Rubbing of the baby. Planning for the baby." She squeezed Tom's hand tighter, and they grinned stupidly at each other. "And then more kissing of the baby."

"Did any of this happen in the bedroom?"

Tom gave her the hairy eyeball. "Is there a reason you think you need to get so personal?"

"As a matter of fact, there is. I sensed magic in the house that didn't feel like it belonged there. That's why I had you take me on a tour. That magic was located in your bedroom."

Cassie giggled, still looking at Tom, swinging her feet out from Robert's big leather couch like a child and then swinging them back again. "Well, that *is* where the magic happens."

"Focus, girl! The painting that Franconi gave you. How long have you had it?"

Cassie's brow wrinkled while she calculated. "Yeah, it was, ummm...two days after Caroline Akers came in and returned it. The day after we found her body."

"Has there been anything else that he's seemed to know that he shouldn't?"

"Well...each time he was really mean to Dash and I got upset, he showed up at the gallery with a big apology right afterward. Which is odd because he could have apologized the first time long before that. But he didn't until Dash and I talked about it."

"And, once again, his paintings decorate the walls in the room where you had these conversations?"

Cassie's eyes went wide. "Omigoddess!" she exploded. "That creep has been spying on me."

"Yes. And quite possibly on anyone he's ever sold a painting to."

Cassie huddled in to Tom's shoulder. "Oh ick, ick, ick, and ick some more."

Tom's eyes narrowed and his shoulders tensed. "I'm going to take him apart."

"No, you're not. I'm sure Cassie would prefer you to be at home when the child is born instead of locked up for assault. But you're going to help me catch him at his own game. We need to be sure before we move forward that we have our murderer. I think his motive to kill Caroline is clear—she made him angry when she returned his painting. He could have eavesdropped on everything she said. As to his motivation to kill the handyman. . ."

Cassie gasped, and her hand moved to cover her mouth. When she took it away, her eyes still wide, she said, "Sean broke one of his statues! Caroline insulted his work and Sean ruined his work. I mean, with Lou Frank's ego? Do we know if any of the original victims were connected to his art in any way?"

Robert shook his head. "I'm not aware of a connection, but it was a long time ago, and once they settled on William Stanford as the perpetrator, the investigation stopped."

Natalie nodded. "No, I don't know of one either. But there has to be, don't you think? The spying? The magic pictures? The death of two people who gave him insult or injury? And all of this happening again as soon as he comes back to town? It can't be a coincidence, and it's up to us to prove it. We can't leave it to Denton; magic was involved. My dears, it's time for a huddle."

They all leaned in, ready to follow her into the fray.

18

After a quick breakfast at the house along with a frostily received reminder to Natalie not to reactivate her dormant shoplifting skills on the trip, Gillian buzzed along the pavement at a strip mall in Salem. Natalie stalked ahead at her usual breakneck pace, and the two witches nearly collided when Natalie stopped suddenly to peer through the plate glass window of a medical supplies store.

"Yes, this should be the place," Natalie said. "I don't know why I cleared out so many of the things I'd collected over the years as a nurse. I'm sure I had a cervical collar at one time. But no matter, they're easy enough to replace."

Inside, she quickly identified what she needed while Gillian browsed the assortment of nearby braces. She picked up a particularly sporty knee band and asked, "Do you think this would help Robert's arthritis? Our best healing efforts have only gone so far, and his doctor says that some people find relief through compression, but Robert thinks anything that even comes close to looking like support hose signals the beginning of the end of our sex life."

Natalie replied, not looking back from the counter where she was now carefully counting out change, "Perhaps that would be for the best, dear. Then you would be less likely to discuss your romantic activities in public places with disinterested parties."

As Natalie walked past on her way to the door with the bulky plastic bag, Gillian fell into step beside her. "You certainly would have been interested in Robert's sex life last year before he chose me, so don't act all holier-than-thou when I know better."

Natalie half turned and looked at her through slitted eyes. "Yes. I had some idea that I didn't want to die an old maid. But the fancy has passed. I will be a maid until they plant me in the ground, and that's the end of it. It's not like I could mother anyone at my age anyway, so I might as well remain as I am."

"I understand. Martin and I were lucky enough to have most of the same girls on the softball team he coached through their teens even though we met too late in life to have our own child. Things would have been so different for me, I think, if I hadn't met Cassie that way. I do feel that I somehow made up a little for what her grandmother, Eunice, had become."

Natalie opened the trunk of the car, set her bag inside, and slammed it. "It's a shame that perfectly good children end up with nightmare families. Not that I would know what to do with a child, but surely someone could come up with a better distribution plan."

As both of the women entered the car, Gillian said, "At least Tom and Cassie's little one will be lucky—one real grandfather, one borrowed grandfather, and two grandwitches in the mix. We may not be blood family, but I already love her like my own."

Natalie gunned the engine and started the car across the parking lot toward home. "Who says the child will be a she?"

"I do! Her energy is undeveloped, and with Cassie's magic wrapped around the child, it's hard to tell, but I'm sure it feels more silver than gold. Don't you think so?"

"I have no idea. All I get is the presence of life. Detecting male or female isn't part of it."

Gillian's head cocked to the left as her mouth drew up at the corners. "Do you mean there's something I can do that the great Natalie Taylor can't?"

"There are many things you can do that the great Natalie Taylor can't. For instance, I have never had any talent whatsoever for making an attractive and edible dessert." The car stopped abruptly at a stop light, causing Gillian to throw a hand out to the dashboard to stop her forward motion.

"Of course," Natalie continued, "that doesn't make you the more talented witch, does it?"

Gillian rolled her eyes as Natalie donned her best cat-with-the-cream expression.

"Then again, we might both be poor detectives, no matter how good we are at witching." Natalie hesitated, putting her thoughts in order. "You yourself discovered that Gerald Akers is fluent in Italian. Maybe I shouldn't be so quick to write him off as a suspect. The two victims of this were, after all, his cheating wife and her lover. And his family summered in Giles during the approximate time-frame of the original murders."

Gillian braced herself as the car neared another stop sign. "I can't see it, Nat. The man is a marshmallow, and he's absolutely a mess over his wife. When I stopped by unannounced to invite him to dinner, I found him sitting out on the back deck, still in his pajamas and slippers, without a coat. On a damp and chill day. No, I can't see it."

"I agree. He isn't the type, is he? He's more the sort you'd find cowering in the corner while the other boys make fun of him." Natalie rolled the car to a gentle stop this time, then looked both ways and eased across the intersection. "I simply want to make sure I'm not missing anything. I suppose we'll have an answer soon enough if everything goes to plan with Franconi."

"If Tom doesn't kill him first," Gillian said, her voice trailing off at the end.

Natalie nodded, eyes still on the road. "Yes, that would complicate things." She sighed. "I suppose we can't just let him at it once we've got the evidence?"

＊＊＊

Cassie settled into her husband's strong arms on the couch in the living room at Robert's house where they'd agreed to stay until it was time to put the plan in place. She said, gently, for what seemed like the hundredth time, "Tom, it wouldn't work. Natalie says glamours are extremely taxing and she's not even sure she could glamour herself to look like me, but she's sure it wouldn't work on you. If you had your own magic you might be able to do it yourself, but since Anat bound it all except for your ability to shift from man to cat, there's no point in talking about it."

Tom pulled her slight body firmly against his. *Too firmly*, she thought. It was like he planned to hold her there and keep her from taking part in the plan by force if his words couldn't convince her. "Listen," he said, "I'm not being a Neanderthal if I've got a problem with my pregnant wife using herself as bait for some psycho who's been running around town killing people."

"Tom, I don't know how many ways I can say this—it's not like I'm helpless, right?" She flung out a hand and a heavy leather chair on the other side of the coffee table blew back a couple of feet before she snatched her fingers together, stopping it.

"Yeah?" he said. "How's that going to work with a rope around your neck? Push an attacker who's strangling you with a cord away with that kind of force and it's likely to pop your pretty head right off your shoulders."

Her hand started to rise to tug at her lip, but she realized what she was doing before it got there. Okay, what he'd said made her a little nervous, but there was no point broadcasting it. He'd know he was getting to her if he saw her anxious gesture.

"Look," she said. "It's decided. Nat is our friend, and you know she'd do this for us if the tables were turned."

"I'm not going to argue with that part. I just want to do it differently. Let me go with you, at least."

"You know you can't. He's got to think that I'll be alone and helpless. He doesn't know about my magic. It's not like I talk about it at the gallery or in the bedroom."

"True." He gave her a squeeze, but this time it was gentle, loving. "We always find much better things to do and say in the bedroom."

With his body against her like that, her frustration with his over-protectiveness threatened to turn into a different kind of frustration all together, and that would definitely endanger her resolve.

Her man sure knew how to play her.

She pushed his hands away and sat up. "Oh no, you don't!" She scooted to the other end of the couch. "I know your evil ways, Tom Sanders!"

She paused suddenly, and beamed. There was something else they had never talked about in the bedroom.

"I just realized we don't have to fight any more. We've never talked about Kit and Sheba in our room, have we? And I haven't shifted in the bedroom since the day we found Caroline's body. If you haven't either, he can't know about them. I mean, it's not like anyone would tell him, right? It's an open secret in the choir, but what happens in the choir stays in the choir. Nobody sings outside of the group, right? Even the worst of the gang—the ones who were loyal to Anat—keep that rule with outsiders. They don't want to face the wrath of a coven full of angry witches."

"I haven't shifted in the bedroom, I don't think. So?" he asked.

"Wow, you're slow on the uptake today. I mean, if my faithful cat is right at my heels when I go out tonight, how is a cat a threat?"

His smile lit the room. "Come back over here you smart, sexy minx. I want to show you exactly how I feel about that plan."

19

The school bus dropped Twink off at the end of main street. She was in no hurry to get home. Daria would be sure to hang over her like a big, hungry buzzard until she started on her homework, anyway.

She looked in the window at the little dress boutique, but the stuff in there was for oldsters. It was quality, some nice labels, but not something anyone under thirty would wear. Which made sense—she was one of maybe twenty teenagers in town, judging by the usual crowd on her school bus. Although there might be private school kids or ones who had their own cars; there were lots of fancy houses in Giles, even if they were, like, really old.

The kids she'd met weren't real friendly, either. She'd say "hi" and they'd pretend they didn't see her.

Not that Twink planned on staying. Her mother would come around sooner or later. She had to keep it cool, stay out of trouble, which always seemed easier than it was. Trouble loved her.

The smell of cinnamon and ginger drew her nose to Bountiful

Bakery, making her stomach grumble. She crossed the street and passed by the gallery and a book store, then had to scoot real close to the storefronts to get around some old guy yelling at some other guys working around the bronze statue on the sidewalk. There were ropes attached to a tall metal frame that was set over a pickup truck. A rope and pulley system, right? Who knew what that was all about. It was kind of an ugly statue anyway—some bearded guy in a big hat—so maybe the town just got smart and decided to ditch it.

Unless it was like some bold daytime robbery. That would make Giles a lot more exciting. They'd have to be some really stupid burglars, though. Twink stopped just beyond the truck and turned back to snap a mental picture of the three guys as they lifted the statue into the truck and maneuvered it over the bed. Just in case she had to testify or something.

She wanted to go to the bakery and pick out something good from the trays of fancy decorated cookies and cakes, but she didn't have any money. Just thinking about one of those big chocolate muffins they always had in the window made her stomach start leading a cheer for the home team. She needed to eat now! She darted between two cars that were parked at the curb to cross the street where the mostly healthier contents of Daria's fridge were waiting.

She hadn't looked both ways; when a horn sounded to her left, she realized that had been a mucho stupid thing to do. When the oncoming car didn't slow, her heart raced, and a jolt of adrenaline hit her system. She kicked it into high gear, but lost one of her purple high heels and stumbled. She scrambled up and made it to the sidewalk. She was out of harm's way when she heard the crash.

She looked back into the street, breathless. The driver of the car that had almost hit her had swerved right, slamming the car's back-end sideways into the front fender of the truck, pushing the pickup up against the curb. It still rocked from the force.

The workers were standing out of harm's way. Nobody was

holding the statue steady where it dangled from the crossbar; they watched from a distance as it stood on its own, swaying, while the white-haired man screamed, "Idiots! Get in there and keep it from falling!"

But the workers didn't move. The statue toppled sideways, crashing out the side of the truck and onto the street. When it hit, it cracked all the way down the middle and fell apart in two halves, like a clamshell opening.

And wow. You sure wouldn't see something like that in Boston. Maybe Giles was more exciting than she'd thought. Because she couldn't think of a single statue she'd ever heard of having a skeleton inside it. And definitely not one wearing an ugly old sweater some hipster would go crazy over.

The guy with the white hair screamed at the workers one last time in some foreign language, then ran to a little black sports car and barreled down the street, nearly causing a couple more accidents on his way.

No way was she waiting around for the cops to show up and question her. *Me?* she asked herself. *I didn't see nothin'.* She took off her other shoe and looked both ways before she popped into the street to pick up the lost one, then ran like crazy toward Cat's Magical Shoppe with the cement roughing up her bare feet. She darted through the narrow side yard to get to her and Daria's place, locking the door behind her when she was safely inside the house.

***

The commotion outside drew both Cassie and Gillian out the door of the shop. Gillian shaded her eyes and squinted, then tsked. "Another accident. Parallel parking again, I'd wager."

"Hey Twink," Cassie called as she spotted the teen blasting toward them like she was trying to win the hundred-yard dash. But the girl didn't acknowledge her—she just slipped between the shops and disappeared. Probably still mad at her.

That reminded Cassie that she was going to have to follow up with Daria, and soon. With everything else that was going on, it had been easy to forget that Twink was still running around town with unpredictable magic following behind. She hoped that wasn't what had caused the accident. She followed Gilly back inside.

Ten minutes later, when the sound of too many sirens for a parking accident had gone blaring past, Gillian's phone rang at the same time that Cassie's did.

Their responses were much the same. Gillian's "Oh my" was slightly shorter than Cassie's "Omigoddess," but they looked up at each other with startled expressions and said into their phones at the same time, "A skeleton?"

Their conversations diverged from there with Gillian saying, "Any distinctive features? I mean, the statue has been there since the sixties. Who disappeared back then?"

"Was Twink all right when you talked to her?" Cassie was saying. "She wasn't hurt, was she? She looked okay when she headed for the apartment."

And Gillian was saying, "A sweater? What kind of sweater?"

 Cassie was looking at Gillian. "Look, I don't think they'll even talk to her. No, seriously, there's no reason to. I'll fill you in later. Not tonight, though. I've got stuff to do. And Daria? We have to talk about that other thing, too. Whether or not to tell her..."

She looked over to Gillian who was saying, "Put Denton on alert is all. But don't let him get in our way. You know he won't want to know how we managed to pull Lou Frank out of hiding."

Cassie mouthed, "Robert?" when Gillian noticed her looking, and Gillian mouthed back, "Yes."

Cassie nodded and returned to her call. "Yep, she's got nothing to worry about. The mayor already knows what's going on. The cops won't come around. I promise."

"I love you, too," Gillian said. "Be safe. You never know if he's crazy enough to go after someone else while he's on the run."

They said goodbye to their callers and turned to each other. Gillian's face was drained of color. "She'll kill him, you know, if we don't talk her out of it. Your husband isn't that man's biggest threat anymore. Who else could have been in that statue in an argyle sweater but William Stanford?"

Cassie sat on the edge of her own bed for the first time since she'd discovered that her beautiful painting was enchanted. And the secret in the statue? It made her feel sick. As for the plan—well, too many things could go wrong. Too many people she cared about could get hurt.

She stood up and went to the fireplace, where she set the once-admired and now despised watercolor back up and pretended to lose herself in its beauty.

Tom walked in right on cue. Cassie turned to him. She thought about the big, comfortable bed right behind her. She'd kept the picture at an angle that gave her a clear view of it when she wrapped herself up at night for bedtime reading. If Lou Frank could see them, he'd have had a clear view when she and Tom did something other than read. And she never got much reading done. Or any.

Ugh. Lou Frank could have been peeping at them the whole time. She tried to stay in character, but she couldn't completely suppress her shudder.

When Tom sauntered up to sweep her long hair aside so he could plant a kiss on the back of her neck, the gesture felt wrong, cold. His heart wasn't in it.

"Come to bed," he said.

"In a minute, I...this painting is so amazing. I can never get enough of it."

Tom threw out an arm and knocked a carefully chosen set of objects off onto the ground, where they landed with a series of thuds.

She pulled back from him toward the fireplace. "What's wrong with you? Why are you acting like this?"

"I'm sick of you and your boyfriend Lou. Sick of it! You need to choose. Is it him or is it me?

It sounded so contrived, she thought. Who would fall for it?

But she knew Lou would. He'd fall for it because he thought the world of himself and very little of others.

She continued along in the script the group had put together. "Lou? You think I could ever care about that arrogant old man? You have to be kidding!"

"Every day when you come home from the gallery, it's 'Lou's paintings are so amazing,' and 'Lou and I had a picnic,' and 'Lou got Dash the nicest gift.' Like I wouldn't notice he's all you talk about."

"Don't be stupid. He repulses me! He's so gross. That thing he does with his horrible old-guy hair all the time, always flipping it back like he's some sexy young stud. It's hard not to laugh."

"Then tell me what's been going on between you two!"

"That picture," she said, pointing. "Do you know what that will be worth when he dies? I mean, he's well known now, but when he kicks off—and it can't be long because he's, like, ancient—that will pay for the new nursery. I could care less about Lou 'The Loser' Frank. In fact, if the Giles murderer got him, that would really help us out. But I can probably string him along long enough to get a couple more paintings out of him, don't you think?"

"No! I forbid it!"

Cassie was glad she had her back to the painting because she couldn't manage to completely hide her smirk. Tom couldn't hide his either. As his mouth started to bouy up at the corners, he turned to the table to knock a few more things over. The suggestion that Tom could forbid any of the women in his immediate circle from doing exactly as they pleased would normally have set them both howling.

She took a deep breath and got herself back under control. It wasn't easy.

"You forbid me, do you? You forbid me? Just because Lou isn't my type doesn't mean that someone else isn't. I'm out of here. I'm spending the night at Gillian's."

Tom pulled the keys to the vintage station wagon Cassie had inherited from her grandmother out of his pocket and jingled them as he said, "You think so? You won't get very far without these."

"I've walked there before. I'll walk there now. It'll be beautiful along the lake in the moonlight." She stormed out of the bedroom, grabbing her coat off the chair by the door.

Tom leaned out of the bedroom door and called after her, "Fine. I hope you two have lots of fun."

Then he pulled his head back and went to the bookcase where they had planted a bottle of brandy and tipped it up into the snifter that sat next to it. Cassie spied on him from outside the room, waiting. She'd tiptoed back after she'd stomped as hard as she could down the hall.

Tom lifted the snifter to his mouth and drained it. The brandy bottle yielded a few drops, nothing more. Just like they'd planned. He threw it into the fireplace, shouting, "Blast it! I need a real drink."

He stalked to the door and took his wife's hand as soon as he was out of the picture's visual range. She tiptoed beside him as she matched his footfalls, traveling downstairs and toward the back door.

Before they exited, Tom shed his clothes and hung them up on hooks in the mudroom. Cassie put on a particularly unfashionable and bulky collar beneath her jacket and pulled the jacket's hood up over her head to disguise it.

Tom looked cold, but Cassie knew he wouldn't be covered in gooseflesh once he was dressed in Kit's warm fur coat.

He closed his eyes, calming himself in preparation. His lips moved slightly as he mouthed his shift words to himself and shrunk away before her eyes, folding and warping, winter-pale skin sprouting fur blacker than the moonlit night they would soon be entering. But no matter how well-lit the night was, there were things within it that were steeped in darkness.

21

William slipped through the wall like it was made of mist.

He stood in front of the huge steel door where the words "Unknown—found in statue" had been written on a square of paper and slipped into the nameplate. This is who he was now: Mr. Unknown. He wasn't sure he wanted to see what was behind the door, but if his body was there, maybe it would help him remember what had happened.

He stuck his head through the door. Below him, a skull looked back. His face was level with the corpse's empty eye sockets. Being a ghost had a least one advantage—he didn't have to depend on rods and cones and light for sight. It was pitch black in here, but the head bone on the metal slab was crystal clear to him.

He looked down at what the skeleton was wearing. Tan slacks, a filthy white dress shirt buttoned to the collar, and what would have once been an excellent argyle sweater vest. No mistaking that.

He looked and looked, taking in the empty eye wells that had once loved to look at the world, the bony fingers that had once held the hand of his beloved, but it didn't help him remember anything. It didn't even make him sad. He couldn't feel attachment to the thing. There was nothing for him here; might as well leave.

But something held him back. No. He had to know. He felt sure that the killer stalking Giles in the modern day was the same one who had stalked it fifty years ago. He had to try to open up his own memories so that no one else would be harmed, especially Natalie. William filled his ghostly lungs with a deep, ghostly breath and slipped his ghostly body inside the bones, wrapping himself around them, pretending to be flesh. The only thing he saw from his ghostly eyes was the stainless steel ceiling of the drawer. No memories. He closed them and sighed again. Nothing.

He was ready to give up and go looking for Natalie when his consciousness jolted like an electric shock. His eyes flew open as a bright blue haze lit the chamber. His first instinct was to rip away from the bones, but he was stuck in place, trapped in a mass of emotion that only something living could feel.

Terror. It was terror.

The side of his head felt wet and the pain there engulfed him. He lay face down in the dirt, but he had the sense that he knew this place, knew it well. He turned his head and peered around, his gaze alighting on something white in the gloom that rested on wooden supports. The place smelled of tar and algae.

He was in the shed where his family kept the rowboat during the winter. They'd brought it in from the lake because it had been leaking, and he'd been working on it for several days to make it seaworthy again. Yesterday, he'd added another layer of fresh tar to a couple of areas that needed waterproofing. He didn't want to risk Natalie getting wet when he took her out rowing.

On the water, with no one to tell them no, they could talk about anything. About their plans for a life together. About their dreams.

But today, he'd come to the shed with a canvas bag of supplies he'd picked up at the hardware store and found the door already open. When he set the bag down at his side and pushed the opening wider to let the daylight in, someone turned to him abruptly, a length of rope cut from the loose coil hanging on the wall in his hand, a pen knife in the other.

"What are you doing in here?" William asked. And then he understood. "You? You can't be...you couldn't have..."

The intruder squinted as he moved into the light, and the angry red rash of acne on his cheeks nearly glowed. He slashed out toward William with the knife and William stepped back, stumbling over the bag he'd set down earlier.

That stumble was all the intruder needed; he charged forward and slammed into William's chest with one shoulder. William's head knocked hard against the rough support as he fell. He blinked, his head swimming, his eyes focusing on the blurry shape of the boat at the other side of the shed. Funny, he'd never seen it from this angle before.

Blows rained down as his attacker sobbed.

It was probably the shovel, but it could have been the spade. It really didn't matter—the outcome was the same. The memory, the pain, and the terror faded as William felt himself re-enter the present, feeling the old set of bones sizzle with dancing blue sparks. He looked down at his remarkably opaque body.

It had to be a trick of the light.

He tried to pull himself out of his earthly remains, but he was stuck. And how could he gasp so raggedly without lungs? He panicked. He needed out of that drawer. And as soon as he thought of it, he was outside again. He looked down quickly. Still no light showing through him. And what was that odd sensation? Could it really be the pressure of the floor against the bottom of his feet?

Something unusual had happened to him when he'd wrapped

himself around his bones. He decided to get another look at them, but he bumped his head when he leaned in toward the drawer to go through it.

That couldn't be right. A ghost can't bump his head.

He tried again, and this time, maybe because he knew what to expect, he was able to push through easily, but what he saw inside couldn't be right either.

There were no bones in the drawer anymore.

***

It was silent all around. Dead silent except for the sound of footsteps along the shore. Every so often, Cassie's heel sunk into a muddy patch and made a sucking sound as it released. And then there was her own breathing, coming in loud gasps. She fought it down—she'd need to stay under control if this was going to work. But her skin prickled, and it wasn't from the chilly night air.

She'd been walking for over an hour already, and although that meant she was nearly at the path that led to Robert's place though the woods, everyone had been sure Lou would show up at the lakefront because that's where all of the previous bodies had been.

Although she knew he was there, Kit was silent as a crypt. Tom kept him behind her near the tree line as they walked. Probably so he wouldn't go night blind from her flashlight. She had no doubt that he was vigilant. Although she knew she could take care of herself, she was glad he was with her.

An owl hooted and she tensed. Slowly, she exhaled. She shook her head, smiling at how silly she had been...until a voice sounded in front of her. "I'm so disappointed in you, Cassie."

She nearly jumped out of her skin.

Her hand went to the uncomfortable plastic collar around her neck. Her heart beat more slowly.

The speaker stepped forward, his face hidden in the darkness.

Cassie allowed herself a small smile; the shock of stark white hair curling out beneath the black hoodie was unmistakable. He carried a big leather bag over his shoulder, his hand tight on the strap.

He pushed back his hood, and his pale face shone in the gloom. "I'm sorry. I didn't mean to scare you." His expression changed swiftly, covering the full spectrum from concern to contempt. "Or maybe I did. Maybe you deserve to be scared. You're a stupid, selfish woman to be walking alone at night with a killer on the loose, unless you want to meet the same fate as that middle-aged siren who died out here. I can't believe your husband would risk your safety like this." He stepped toward her.

She stepped back, hearing the unmistakable sound of flesh slapping against the muddy shore as Tom's body flashed through its transformation somewhere behind her. "Oh yeah? Like he would. We know you spy on people through your paintings. Your secret's not a secret anymore. And everybody knows about the body in the statue too!" Her voice rose nearly to a scream. She hoped it alerted the watchers in the boat. She hoped Tom stepped out of the shadows soon.

"Where's your rope, Lou? Is it in the bag? What word have you written down to stick on my corpse?"

He took a step toward her, then stopped abruptly, his face wadded up like a fist. "You think I killed those people? I haven't killed anyone. I just wanted to show you how disappointed I am that the friendship you offered me was false. I believed you were an art lover, a true connoisseur. But now I know you're just like all the rest—you want the money, the fame, and you'll use your pretty face and shapely body to get it. You could have at least slept with me like the others!"

Tom slipped up silently behind Cassie and placed a hand on her back. It gave her strength. She knew he'd be in pain for a while longer—the shift always hurt. But they had time. Lou wasn't threatening her yet.

Lou's eyes shifted from hers to Tom's. "It's cold comfort that your husband wasn't in on the con." And then his expression decayed into confusion. "And why is he naked?"

"None of your business." Cassie's eyes flashed. "This isn't about us. We know you came here to kill me. You were tuning in with that picture of yours, so I gave you something your ego couldn't tolerate, just like Caroline and Sean did. So where's the rope? Is it in the bag?"

"There's no rope in the bag." He looked down at it, his forehead scrunching as he pushed back his cascade of curls. "I'm telling you, I know it looks bad, the body in the statue, but I didn't kill anyone."

"Toss the bag over here," Tom said. "We'll see what's in it and what's not."

Lou took the bag off his shoulder. Cassie could tell he didn't want to let it go. Of course he wouldn't. He was about to be revealed for the killer he was. Except he wasn't acting much like a killer. He tossed the bag toward Tom without an argument; no, he wasn't acting like a killer much at all.

When Tom dumped its contents out on the muddy ground, Lou winced.

When she pointed the flashlight toward the spill, the only items revealed were an expensive-looking wallet and a small watercolor in a mat. It was a chillingly good likeness of Cassie, but her features wore an expression Cassie hoped she could never wear—pure malice. She stretched a rope between her hands, the perspective making the rope appear huge, as if it was coming out of the picture to strangle the viewer.

"Why did you paint this?" Tom asked as he looked up. His expression in the gloom was losing its angry edge. Now, he just looked puzzled.

"Are you completely concrete? Have you no artistic sense at

all?" The artist threw up his hands and released an exaggerated, exasperated rush of air. "It's a metaphor. I planned to confront her and show her what she looked like to me now as she strangles the friendship I offered. It's a rough sketch for a bigger work, but I bet she wouldn't want that one hanging in that ridiculous little man's gallery. Are you telling me you can't understand my horror when your wife said she hoped I'd be murdered?"

Cassie's brow pulled down in the darkness and her hand moved to tug at her lip. This wasn't turning out like she'd expected. The sound of a boat scraping across the shore and footsteps moving quickly toward them signaled the arrival of the rest of their crew. The sound of hushed female voices rapid-fired back and forth as they came closer.

Her friends in their black robes stepped up beside her to join the lynching party, except she was no longer sure that's what it should be. Gillian opened her bag and handed Tom a neatly folded stack of clothes.

"He doesn't have a rope," Cassie said to the assembled witches. "Just a painting of me that's not very flattering. He says he's not the killer, and it sure looks like he wasn't here to hurt me. I don't know what to believe now."

Natalie raised her pointer finger and said, "Don't. Don't let this man talk his way out of what we all know he did just because he decided not to kill you." She turned to Lou Frank, moving toward him with conviction. "You committed those murders so many years ago and framed William Stanford, a man who was your friend and was never anything but kind to you!" Her voice shook with emotion and red sparks danced on her fingertips. "And then you paid him back for his kindness by killing him and sealing his body into a statue to hide the evidence."

"I admit I put him in the statue. My mother helped me by performing a ritual to dissolve his flesh so the statue wouldn't burst apart from the buildup of gasses as it decayed. She would have done anything for me, even kill him if she had to. But William was already dead by then. The killer gave me a lot of money, laughing the whole time about how the town would see how they liked it when they couldn't predict how close the lightning would strike." He suddenly collapsed into the mud, going down to one knee, then both. He pleaded. "Fifty thousand dollars. Do you know how much money that was back then? The boy said he'd stolen it out from under his father's nose because he was the only one who'd seen where his grandmother had hidden it before she died. It no longer mattered that Lettie's father forbade her to see me. Finally, a way to get to New York. I didn't need her. And what would it hurt? My mother and father weren't death witches like yours were. She couldn't raise William."

"What boy?" Natalie demanded.

"The summer boy, the one that the other summer kids humiliated when they stripped him naked and tied him to the water tower in a storm. Gerald Akers. He killed the girl, her boyfriend, and the reporter who put it in the paper, and then he tried to frame William because William was the one who found him. After he killed him, he had to make sure the body wouldn't be found. His frame wouldn't work if it was found." He shook his head. "Like William could have done anything cruel. But I wanted out of this town badly. The money made that possible."

"You knew Gerald Aker was the killer, but you didn't say anything when the murders started again?"

"There was a statue out there with a body in it, and Akers wouldn't hesitate to throw me to the wolves if I said anything. I had easy access to the rope in William's shed, you know. We were friends. We went fishing all the time."

His eyes pleaded, looking for her mercy, but she had none to give. He said, "Look, I tried to warn Sean how dangerous it was to sniff around Gerald's wife, but he didn't listen. I couldn't tell him how I knew without implicating myself."

He sat back in the mud, his long legs splaying out in front. "I'm not a killer, I'm just a voyeur—and even that isn't my fault. Besides, I'd like to see you have me charged with using magic pictures to spy on people. So let me go. I'll take off, I'll go to Paris. I'll never come back."

Natalie's eyes beamed vengeance. "No, I'm not convinced, and even if I was, you're paying for your part in this. I'll let the courts decide if you should hang for the murders, but there's no way I'm letting you walk out of here with your magic intact. You and your mother used your family's magic to abuse William's corpse, even if it does turn out you didn't kill him." Her voice thickened for a moment, then she swallowed and continued normally. "So now your voyeur days are over."

She looked to Robert. "As high priest with a warlock who's abused his magic, you have first right. Do you want to do it or will you pass the right to me?"

Robert's face was impassive. "Nat, this one is all yours."

"Don't touch me, you hag!" the captive shouted. "If you do, you'll be sorry. You don't know what you're messing with."

Natalie raised her hand like she was making a shadow puppet and brought her bunched fingers together with her thumb. The man's mouth snapped shut in response. She'd had enough of his protests. His jaw and head moved frantically, and his eyes went wide as he pried at his jaw.

"Hold him down," she said, looking to the others. They darted toward where Lou sat cross-legged on the ground. Tom seized him by the shoulders and wrestled him into a prone position, knowing what came next. The others grabbed his limbs and held him in place. It didn't take long to pin him; he was in good shape for an old man, but he was an old man just the same. If his crimes had made him feel powerful, he couldn't be feeling powerful now.

Natalie placed her left hand at the base of his spine, probing for the magic that had to be there. His eyes burned with anger, but he'd given up struggling. As she probed, not finding it, she wondered if it was—no, he had to have at least a spark. How else could he have set up his paintings to spy on their owners? Was this something else his mother had done for him?

And then, there it was, but not where she'd expected it. She gripped it psychically, pressing against it. It was far too easy, she thought, but then again, he obviously had very little juice to power his enchantments. No wonder the coven had never known about him.

She relaxed as she worked, squeezing the magic out. She gave him a twisted smile. "You want to know the best part of this, Mr. Famous Artist? When the witches of Giles gossip about your magic—and believe me, I'll make sure there's gossip—the thing they'll giggle about the most is—" and here she held up her right hand, with her thumb and forefinger about an inch apart, "how very tiny it was."

Someone cleared their throat over the sound of the resulting titters. And everyone turned as the newcomer said, "I really don't know why you feel you have to be so bawdy."

Everyone turned. Nat's head snapped from side to side at her friends and then back to where William now stood. How could they know he was there?

She gave a final quick squeeze and the last of the magic Luigi Franconi carried inside him dispersed.

She stood and turned to William, replying, "Yes, well, I'm bawdy, but you're dead. Shall we take a vote on which one is the more annoying characteristic?" she replied.

Cassie's voice, hesitant, squeaked behind her, "Ummm..."

When Natalie looked back over her shoulder, only Tom was still watching over Lou Frank where he lay still in the mud. The others were looking right at William.

". . . should I be able to see him like this?" Cassie finished.

"You can see me?" William asked, his eyes popping wide.

Tom replied for her. "We all can, I think." He looked from Robert to Gillian and they nodded.

William's face lit in a broad grin.

Natalie had no idea what was happening. He hadn't even been able to make her hear him the last time he'd tried to talk to her. What could possibly have empowered him this way? One of her eyebrows lifted in a silent question, and William jumped in to answer.

He shrugged. "I visited my bones and something strange happened. I think I've brought them with me." The statement was flat but weighty. After a pause, he pointed toward their prisoner. "And he didn't kill me. I don't think he killed anyone."

Natalie looked back at Franconi, screwing her eyes up angrily, then turned back to William. "So he says. How do you know this?"

"Because I know who did it. Who framed me with the rope from the boat shed. It was the summer boy with the bad complexion whose family rented the biggest cabin every summer. I can't even remember his name, it was so long ago. The only other time I'd seen him was when I found him after his friends left him tied to the water tower in the woods. I took him home and called the police and his parents, and they came and got him. He was so silent and scared. He seemed so meek."

"Akers," Robert said. "The boy's name was Gerald Akers." His head shook back and forth. He looked angry. "It's just like he told us," he said, nodding at Franconi. "Akers fooled us all."

The group exchanged glances. Gillian's was surprised and sad. Tom looked disappointed.

Behind the group, an ethereal glow burst into life. A low growl split the scene. "You should have paid better attention to whose magic you were removing, you old witch." She pivoted, startled.

William's head turned when hers did, but his eyes scanned beyond the glow instead of focusing there.

Lou Frank's specter stood in front of a waiting portal. "I tried to warn you, but you sealed my mouth and sealed my fate. Don't you remember? My mother brought me to see your mother when I was three. Now who's a murderer?"

He stepped through the portal and it closed after expanding outward in a flash, leaving only the light of the moon.

"No! No!" She turned and rushed to Lou Frank's prone body, shoving the others aside and turning him over as she knelt down beside him. His eyes were closed, his face slack. She dropped her head in her hands. "This shouldn't have happened..."

Gillian understood quickly that things had taken a bad turn and she placed her hands on Lou Frank's chest, ready to help, but Natalie shook her head, letting it drop toward her chest. "No. He's beyond healing. He's already through the portal. He's gone."

"But Nat..."

She sunk to the ground, smearing her immaculate black robe with mud. She was babbling, but she couldn't stop herself. "My own mother, dabbling in raising the dead after what her father had done? How could she? Why would she?" Natalie took a long breath. "But a child...the decision you'd have to make..."

Cassie knelt to her. "Calm down, Nat. Take your time and explain to us what just happened here."

Natalie looked around for something to sit on and settled for a hollow log on the edge of the path. Gillian sat beside her. She tried to rub Nat's back, but Nat brushed her off. The others stood silent, waiting.

William walked a circle back and forth in the general area where the portal had been—at least in the direction she had looked when the portal appeared—talking to himself.

"I feel like I need to call in Denton now," Robert said. "If that's all right, Nat?"

She waved a hand weakly. "Yes, fine. Dr. Don will need to know this is an unnatural death. But I didn't kill him. I won't bear that burden. I believe he's had years of life that never belonged to him. Eavesdropping was just a side effect of what the magic of the paintings did."

Robert walked a little to the side to place his call, but his posture indicated he was trying to listen to two conversations at once.

"What does that mean, Nat? About the pictures?" Cassie asked. "Because I've been near them, like, constantly."

"My mother. I should have recognized her magic, I'd felt it often enough when she punished me with it. The magic inside that man wasn't his, it was my mother's. I didn't know why at the time, I was very young, but Angelique brought her boy to my mother wrapped in a blanket—she was crying and begging, pleading with her. I wondered how he could sleep with all that noise. I suppose it makes sense now.

My mother took him into the shed. Afterward, Luigi and I sat at the kitchen table drawing together while the adults talked in the parlor in whispers."

"Are you saying your mother raised him from the dead?" Cassie asked.

Natalie nodded. "But the essence of life always has to come from somewhere. There's normally a one-to-one sacrifice involved. I think she gave him a jumpstart somehow and then provided him with the means to keep himself going...when he gave me the picture he'd drawn—I remember thinking how much I liked it—my mother took it away, and said, 'You must never again give a drawing to my daughter or I will take back my gift to you.'"

"Oh my," Gillian said.

"Yes," Natalie agreed. "Oh my, indeed."

Gillian stood up and went to Robert, who'd finished his call. He put his arm around her. "Do you think there's any danger to the baby?" she asked quietly.

"I think the paintings drained the people near them at a very low rate to keep him going. He'll have hundreds and hundreds of paintings scattered around the world now, all of them drawing at once. Cassie, you never felt any differently around them—weak or woozy—did you?"

"Not really. I don't think so. In fact, I've been feeling pretty powered up, actually."

"Good. I don't think there will be any long-term consequences. I never knew my mother to be malicious, only sometimes misguided. I suppose that's why he became an artist, to make sure that his drawings and paintings were always hanging somewhere where people congregate."

Tom cleared his throat. "So, to get back to the practical side of things—what's our story on this? Denton will be here any minute."

Robert stepped in. His political side always had a cover story ready. "We were going night fishing. We found him hiding under the boat, and when he tried to escape, he drowned. Tom dove after him to try to save him, but he couldn't find him in time. Doc Don's already prepped."

"What? All of us? In that small boat?" Gillian asked.

"No, only Tom and I. You ladies were up at the house and decided to come down to the shore to have a campfire while you waited for us. That's when you found out about it."

"You'll need gear to pull that one off, won't you?" Natalie said.

Robert nodded. "I'll hustle up to the house."

"No need."

Natalie opened her purse, reached inside, and grasped a rod complete with reel. She kept pulling, passing the end to Tom, who backed away with it, finally ending up with a full-length fishing pole.

Robert took it from him. "This is my favorite rod," he said, looking at her for an explanation.

"I can only shoplift them. I can't create them out of nothing. It's a good thing we're close enough to your property that I can get a hold of them."

Once Tom had his own pole and had taken a dip in the lake, they drenched Lou Frank's body. Natalie handed Gillian one of Robert's better bottles of wine and three paper cups, saying, "It's up to us to go after Akers now. There's no one left except for the ghost of one of his victims to point Denton in the right direction." She cocked her head toward William, who was squatting next to where the portal had been, a puzzled expression on his face. "I doubt the chief would buy it if I suddenly remember who my attacker was."

Robert took a long breath. "Technically, Nat, based on the separation between choir and state we've always maintained, this isn't your business now. It goes to the police. It's up to them to get what they need to arrest Akers. There was no magic involved in these crimes."

"If they had anything, they would have pulled him in already." She turned and called to William. "And you...stop frittering around and make yourself scarce. Denton will be of no use to anyone if he can't continue to pretend that nothing other than normal life and normal crimes ever occur in Giles. We don't need him running around blaming voodoo and ghosties for every strange occurrence."

William moved to her and reached for her fingertips as he said goodbye. She gasped as he held them; his hand was warm and solid. And then he was gone.

***

"I can't say I'm pleased with how it happened, but I'm glad to see the back of him," Natalie said as the ambulance crew wheeled Lou Frank's body away through the woods toward the road. There would be time for her to think about her role in his demise later. She didn't have time to carry that weight along with her just now. "But I don't accept that it's only up to Denton from here. The crime may not have been magical, but it impacted a large number of Giles's magical residents—from Cassie, to me, to our newest budding witch, that Twiniqua or Teeniguo person."

Cassie sounded irritated. "Nat! It's Taniqua, and she goes by Twink, which I'm pretty sure you already know and can pronounce just fine."

"Yes, well, it's a silly name. Whoever she is, she'll need teaching. My point is that anyone who causes harm to the witches of this town must answer to me, and I don't care what our unofficial relationship to the town leadership has always been. It's a foolish rule to keep, given that the mayor is also our high priest. Separation of coven and state? Hmph." She stared Robert down. "What you know obviously impacts how you handle the town."

When Natalie released his eyes, she started walking up the path toward Robert's home, and the others followed her.

Gillian took Robert's hand as she told him, "I'm going to have to agree with Natalie on this one. Since the day Tom first brought me here from England, I've loved this town and its coven. Anyone who tries to harm it will also have to answer to me."

Cassie grinned as she fell in step behind. "Me too. I'm in."

Natalie smiled approvingly, taking her own place in the loose clump of hikers. "We're agreed then. I'll make sure that Denton finds what he needs to take Akers out of circulation. That's our first order of business. However, I doubt he'll believe that I suddenly remember seeing who attacked me. We'll need something far more creative than that. And after that's taken care of, we'll need to figure out what to do with that young man Marcus when he's released. He knows that there's something different about his friend Twink; he's a smart one. And I may also have given him a hint on that score. It's only a matter of time before he accepts what he thinks is happening as the truth. And, of course, when we tell Twink what she is, she'll likely blurt it out to him anyway."

Cassie put a hand on Natalie's shoulder as she walked beside her for a moment. "Daria doesn't know yet if she wants to tell her. I'm still waiting on a decision. Nobody is going to be telling him anything right away."

"It doesn't matter. Either way, we need to keep him close to assure he doesn't do anything unwise with what he knows or what he thinks he knows. That might be more complicated than making sure Denton catches a killer; we don't want to interfere with the boy unduly. I find that I quite like him, which doesn't help Denton any in my eyes. The last time I spoke to Marcus, he was going to be sent back to a group home because his foster mother doesn't want to keep a child who keeps getting pulled in for questioning. From what he told me about that group home, it's not a suitable place for him."

Gillian gave Robert a questioning glance, but he shook his head. Natalie looked at Cassie next, who fiddled with a strand of her long hair, looking at Tom. No one spoke up.

Looks like it's up to me again, thought Natalie. And she'd obviously have to prod them into a plan regarding Akers. Natalie sighed. Then she jumped, almost falling on the uneven ground, when William reappeared unanticipated at her side. Cassie gasped behind her. She could forgive Cassie as the manifestation had been abrupt, but Natalie had never once been so distracted that she didn't notice the whiff of ozone that always signaled a ghostly visitor was on its way—unless there was no whiff of ozone.

No, it's not possible, she assured herself, scrutinizing William as he walked beside her.

Still, most people weren't used to the dead popping in and out as they pleased, she mused, which gave her the most delightful idea.

22

"You'll have to do better than that," Natalie said from her place on the couch, "or you'll give yourself away before you get anywhere near him." She leaned toward William, studying his face. "Your eyes never glowed like that before. You'll simply have to tone it down."

William turned to look in the hall mirror and the blue glow in his eyes lessened. "I'm getting the hang of it. Don't be a worry wart. This will work out fine, you'll see."

"It had better. We have to hand Denton something he can nail Akers with."

"Gosh, Nat, do you really think I'm not every bit as eager to see him caught as you are? I'm the one he murdered, remember?"

She looked away, suddenly intent on arranging the items on the end table. After a moment, she turned, saying softly, "But you weren't the only one he destroyed."

The light in his eyes went out and he started toward her, reaching for her, but she bolted up from the couch and moved away, composing her face as she did. "We'll just have to go earlier than we planned. I would have preferred dusk, but late afternoon will do. Let's say 4 p.m." When she turned back to him, all traces of her earlier softness were gone.

"Keep rehearsing," she said. "I have an errand to run. And don't be late."

✻✻✻

Cassie and Daria exchanged nervous glances where they sat across from each other in the parlor of the shop's apartment. Cassie knew it wasn't going to be easy for Twink, but Daria said she always felt there was something Mama Barton had been hiding behind the threats and bluster. In the end, she'd decided that Twink had the right to know about her family's legacy.

Daria had even asked if maybe she had magic too, and Cassie had probed gently at her friend's spine, looking for the spark, but she didn't find one.

When Twink walked into the parlor, Cassie and Daria both stared at her.

"What?" she half-whined, half-growled at them. "Don't even tell me I'm in trouble again."

Daria shook her head. "No. But we have something to tell you. And you have to promise you won't tell anyone, not even Marcus, at least not for a little while. Because that could end up being trouble. And not just for you, but for a lot of people."

She sat on a chair across the room and set her backpack on her knees, hugging it to her chest. "What people?"

"All of the witches of Giles. We like to keep it on the down low," Cassie replied.

"Why? Are you afraid the witches of Salem will find out your team's strategy and beat you at flag football?" She laughed. "I mean, I'll live behind a magic shop just like I'd live behind a beauty shop, but I'm not buying the whole—"

Cassie raised a hand and a golden glow moved quickly outward from her fingertips toward an unopened bud in a vase on the end table. When the glow enveloped it, the flower unfurled. Within a few seconds, the bud had bloomed into a perfect and fragrant rose.

Daria gasped. Twink took a deep breath too, looking like she wanted to say something, but didn't. She hugged her backpack tighter.

"You want to see a beautician work that kind of magic on anyone? I'm for sure a witch. But so are you."

Twink came back to life then. "Uh, no," she said, her right hand going to her hip and her head rocking forward. "I don't know what you are, but it's got nothing to do with me."

"It has everything to do with you. Teenage witches who aren't being taught, they...leak. I guess that's what you could call it. Their magic makes stuff happen that they don't even know about. It depends on what kind of magic the girl has, but it can be wind, or things getting thrown around and broken, or fires, or flowers growing when you walk past." She leaned forward and rested her elbows on her legs. "But mostly, it's not the good stuff."

Twink cocked her head to one side and her eyes narrowed. "You mean like, a witch could just walk through a room and stuff breaks?"

"Yeah, like that. You know anyone who has that kind of problem?" Cassie gave her a tentative smile.

Twink leaned back in the chair and grabbed her backpack tight again. She shook her head. "No, I don't believe you."

Cassie shrugged. "Then it's just going to keep happening."

Twink bounded up, tossing the backpack on the ground. She pointed a finger at Cassie, angry now. "You, you're crazy!" Then, she pointed at Daria. "And you, why are you going along with this? Did you drink the crazy juice, too?"

Daria started toward her cousin, "Look, Twink, even my mama..."

Twink put her hands to her ears, holding them tightly. "Shut up, shut up, shut up! I didn't do any of those things my mother says I did! I didn't do it!"

The glass in the large, vintage, overhead light fixture shattered with a loud crack directly over Twink's head. She turned her face upward at the sound and froze in place as the shards rained down.

Cassie reacted in a heartbeat. She flung a hand out, and the broken pieces of glass flew backward, embedding themselves like arrows in the wall or falling glinting to the carpet. Cassie rushed forward to pull her close, and Twink didn't fight as she started to cry.

With the girl's face buried in her shoulder and one head stroking her hair, Cassie said, "No. You didn't. You didn't do any of it; your magic did. And you can control your magic with help. I know people. I can make it happen."

***

Natalie had never liked driving in Boston, and she liked it even less today with what she had to worry about. Still, she'd been to Boston City Hall before and found a place to park easily enough, although the walk from the parking garage wasn't as pleasant as the same distance through the woods.

She sat on a bench in the hallway outside the records room and let her mind loose through the stacks, chasing a trail through the bound volumes from the newest birth to the oldest and dabbing out the small changes she needed to make. It was more difficult than she thought it would be, but she quickly got the hang of it. She'd never rearranged ink from a distance before, and had been forced to look it up, but there it was in her grandmother's grimoire, waiting for her. Ink from a pot or ink from a typewriter ribbon, it made no difference. It could be manipulated if you knew how.

She was glad there was so little geographic mobility in the Boston branch of the Taylor family. It made things easier to have the records all in one place.

Only one more alteration, she thought as she opened the books for 1966 one by one in her mind's eye. Ah, there it is.

She enjoyed it, sitting on the bench, smiling at passersby while she created descendants from her unused womb in a straight line to her target.

She stood up and shook off the smell of musty old paper, then headed out to the parking lot. She had to be at Gerald Aker's by four and couldn't afford to get caught in rush hour traffic. William had better have his eye on the clock, too. They'd only have one go at it.

"Ms. Taylor. What a nice surprise," Gerald said, beaming her his company smile. But Gerald wasn't surprised to see her. Busybodies like Natalie Taylor never managed to keep their noses out of other people's business for long. His eyes moved beyond her as he asked, "Did Gillian come with you?"

"No, I'm afraid she had to work today."

"Too bad. By all means, come in. Which do you prefer? Coffee or tea?" He turned his back on her and headed for the kitchen.

"Nothing for me," she told him as she followed him through the big house with its dark wood and natural stone facings. When he motioned for her to sit opposite the sliding glass doors to the deck, she instead placed a hand on the back of the chair. "And, of course, the reason I'm having nothing is because I certainly wouldn't want to give you the opportunity to slip a little something extra into my drink, would I?"

His cheeks reddened at the jab, accentuating the old acne scars, but he played it off, laughing. "I see you're in a playful mood today."

"Hardly playful," she replied. "What's the matter? Don't you have the guts to attack a woman without sneaking up from behind?"

His eyes narrowed, and an angry flush rose higher on the back of his neck.

She beckoned to him with the cupped fingers of one hand, her face impassive. "Come on. I'm sure a big, strong man like you can beat a frail old lady in a fair fight, can't you?"

There could be a wire under her blouse, he realized. Still, all he had to do was keep his calm. But her grin was infuriating. Since when did the Giles police department start sending the town's seniors out to investigate their crimes? They didn't. He laughed. The delusional old hag was here on her own.

She unclasped the mouth of the red purse that hung on her arm and reached inside, retrieving a thick hank of rope. He couldn't understand how it had fit.

"I prepared it for you," she said as she tossed it to him. It dripped in his lap. "There now, isn't that what you need? I've already got your sweet little note and the funny glasses. I suppose those symbolize my detecting efforts? Lacks originality, I think."

He said nothing. She was a fool to come here on her own. He picked up the rope and unwound it slowly, shaking its length loose when he was done. He would have finished her once before if he hadn't been interrupted. If she assumed he wouldn't risk it again, she was even more of a fool than he'd thought.

He pulled the rope out tight in front of him and barreled toward her.

She grasped the center of the rope and used it to push him away. She was stronger than she looked. He let it go and grabbed for her center, pushing her backward.

They fell through the glass together, shards raining down around them. When she hit the ground outside, she rolled over and scrambled to her knees, moaning.

He ran back inside for the rope.

As he stalked toward her, she rolled over stiffly and stood to face him, saying, "You killed all of them, isn't that the truth of it? Your wife, her lover, and even William Stanford and the others, so long ago. You told yourself you were justified because they'd humiliated you, but you really just enjoyed it, didn't you?"

He heard a siren in the distance now, but he had time. It wouldn't take much to dispatch her. He could carry her across one shoulder and take her out to the lake before the police arrived. She was tall for a woman, but she was thin and no more substantial than a bird. He'd tell the police he'd tried to save her after the maniac broke in, but he'd been too late.

"They got what they deserved," he said. He'd enjoy telling her what she wanted to know. She wouldn't have time to harm him with it. "They humiliated me. They stripped me naked in public and tied me up in the rain with the lightning crashing everywhere. Those soshes said I was no different than a dog, that I could never be one of them. I was sure it would only be minutes before the lightning struck the tower and traveled the length of the rope to fry me." He felt the fury rising, overtaking even his instinct for preservation as the sound of the siren drew nearer. "And when I finally return to Giles, a top dog now in my fancy house with my fancy wife, she humiliates me all over again with a man who wasn't good enough to lick her shoes."

Natalie laughed in response, her voice going lower and deeper. Not a feminine voice at all. "Thanks, Gerald, that's all we needed to know."

He could have sworn her brown eyes glowed blue for a moment before he fell on her with the rope, stretching it across and around her neck, choking, squeezing—he let the sensation take him. She fought back, got the rope away, but was no match for him. Even when the siren stopped and footsteps rushed across the wooden deck, he had his hands around her neck. It felt even nicer without the rope. He couldn't let go. He had to make sure she was dead.

He lost his grip when strong but ropey arms wrapped around him as Chief Karl Denton landed in a blast of motion and shoved him off the silent body.

***

The back of Denton's arm slid against the deck painfully as the weight of his body bore the other man away from his victim. Despite his age, Akers came back at him with a fierce strength, shoving Denton's head backward with one palm and fighting to rise with the other.

Denton had no leverage with his head pushed back on its stalk. He released his opponent and moved backward, watching as Gerald rose, raising a foot to shove at him as Denton struggled upward. It slammed into Denton's chest, sending him backward, the wind knocked out of him. He landed heavily on his hands as Akers turned to run.

Denton lunged forward and grabbed an ankle, his hand closing around it like a trap. They were both stuck now. Splinters from the deck stung his arm as Akers dragged him across it. He scrambled to his knees, but was flattened when Akers grabbed the railing and dragged himself forward swiftly, sending Denton sprawling.

But there it was, finally: the sirens of the town's other cruisers growing louder as they speeded closer. Like the persistent bulldog that he was, all Denton had to do was hang on until they got there.

***

Denton scrambled upright and turned back to aid the victim once the patrolmen had Akers firmly in their grip, but there was no one else on the deck now.

Where had she gone? She'd need help after the brutal attack he'd just witnessed. Maybe she crawled away while he was busy. He started toward the steps into the yard. And then he heard her.

"Good day, Chief. Looking for me?" Natalie sauntered toward him from the brush on the left side of the house, her red purse slung over her arm, patting her hair to smooth it. She didn't look even slightly disheveled; something was wrong with this picture.

"Are you hurt?" he asked.

"Just fine, thank you. I'm scrappier than I look. I managed to keep the rope just far enough away from my neck to prevent any damage."

"That's not what I saw," he told her gruffly.

"You must have been mistaken, what with the rush of testosterone and all. I hear the stuff can be muddling." She inclined her head slightly toward him as she mounted the stairs to join him on the deck. "I suppose I should thank you though, so..." She didn't finish. "I assume you have what you need now to take Mr. Akers in for the murders? I don't suppose you heard his confession at the end there? That would be helpful."

"If that was your version of a thank you in there somewhere, you're welcome." He rested his hands on his gun belt. "But as of right now, I can only take him in for attempted murder. With me as a witness, he's not getting out of that one. Unfortunately, I didn't hear anything; if he confessed to you, then you'll be able to testify to what he said. I've also got my men tearing apart the house as we speak. We hope we'll find something to connect him to the other murders. For now, I need you to stay put. If you're not hurt, then someone will get your statement soon. Don't even think about walking away from the scene this time."

"Wouldn't dream of it," Natalie said with a smirk, lowering herself carefully into one of the sturdy canvas deck chairs.

"Chief, you gotta come look at this," someone called from behind. He turned to the officer who was standing in the open sliding door. "The guy had a key to his safe on his keychain. We got right into it. He kept records of everything. We've got a diary. We've got clippings. You just broke open the biggest unsolved cases of two different decades."

Denton grinned, then dropped into neutral again before turning back to Natalie. He raised his finger. "Remember, you stay put."

"Of course."

As he walked toward the house, he was sure he heard a man whisper, "That was fun," followed by a woman's giggle. He turned back to look, but the Taylor woman was digging in her purse for something, still alone.

24

Gillian led the way to Robert's huge library of witchcraft and the paranormal. Natalie and Cassie trailed behind.

"Are you going to tell us what we're looking for, at least?" Gillian asked, as Natalie headed for a wall of bookshelves labeled "Pre-Christian."

"It's ancient stuff. I barely remember where I first encountered the concept. Plato, maybe?" She looked back at Gillian. "Does Robert have any Plato?"

She ran her finger across the titles at the left side of the shelf while Gillian pursed her lips and ran a finger across the titles on the right. She pulled one of them off the shelf and flicked rapidly through the pages.

"There, a daimon, that's what I was looking for," she exclaimed, raising the book in one hand as she beckoned with the other. Her hopeful expression dimmed. "But a daimon is assigned as a guardian at birth. See, right here." She tapped her finger on the page. "It's not quite right. They're still too ethereal. I'm looking for something earthier. Was it Roman rather than Greek? I never thought much of Plato in any case."

Cassie reached for the book, but Natalie slammed it shut and set it down. She turned back to the shelf, frowning.

Cassie put a hand on her shoulder. "You know, if you tell us what you're looking for, we can help. Otherwise, why are we here?"

Natalie's head shook rapidly back and forth but she didn't turn as she shrugged Cassie's hand away. "If I'm right about what happened to William, then even a new ward won't keep him away from me. He's not a ghost any longer. I'm convinced that something transformative happened when he joined himself with his bones. I don't know if it was Angelique's lingering magic or a push from the Goddess to thank him for caring for the dead for all those years I neglected my duties, but he felt nothing when the portal opened for Franconi. It should have pulled at him like it always had before. And have you noticed how his eyes glow blue when he's doing 'ghostly' things like popping in and out or masquerading as someone else? Something happened to him that made him more than what he was. He's infused with magic. Fairly crackles with it. And he's solid now, you know. Completely solid, unless he chooses to fade away."

Cassie put her hand on Nat's shoulder again and pulled her around to face them. "Wait a minute—he's solid? Like firm?"

Gillian added. "Hard."

Cassie giggled.

Natalie didn't bother to glare. Best to just let them have their fun. When the giggling stopped, she said, "I think he's a kind of guardian spirit. I'm just not sure which type. You find different versions of them throughout history, but once you get to Christian times, they all get swept up into the concept of the guardian angel. And William is sweet, but I'm disinclined to call him an angel."

Gillian cupped a hand around her mouth, hiding it from Nat, and stage whispered to Cassie, "Well, now that he's so firm, it would be unfortunate if he did behave like an angel, wouldn't it?"

Cassie giggled again, rushing her hand to stifle the sound. "This is funny to you?" Natalie said. "Do you understand what it means?"

"No, Nat, we don't. That's why I asked for an explanation earlier. Remember?"

Natalie tried to keep herself from looking sad, but she could feel the effort collapsing.

She looked first at Cassie, whose dear, open face was flooded with concern. She looked next to Gillian, whose wisdom and courage she respected nearly as much as she respected her own. Not that she would be caught dead admitting that. If anyone would try to understand why what had happened to William was a tragedy, it would be these two, her friends, the women who completed her through the ritual union of the triple goddess.

"He's alive, that's certain. But he isn't simply human again." She sighed, and all her strength went out of her. She slid down against the shelf until she sat against the books, her legs sprawled in front of her, her black pencil skirt hiked up almost to the tops of her thighs. She didn't care. She honestly did not care.

Cassie squatted down and her blue eyes focused on Natalie's face. "But his being alive, isn't that a good thing?" she asked gently.

"You'd think so, but he waited all those years, and I...I knew he would always be there waiting. I knew I wouldn't be alone when it was my time to go. But if he's no longer an unbound spirit, then when I get to my time, I'll...he won't be able to cross with me."

"Oh," Cassie said, tears gathering in her eyes.

What was she thinking inviting that sort of thing? It was done. There was no rolling it back. She'd adapt. Natalie straightened her skirt, then held a hand out. "Phft! Don't waste your tears! Help me up. It's just now come to me. It's Roman magic we're looking for, I'm sure of it."

Cassie gave her a hand up and turned back to the shelf, quickly finding a book she'd passed over earlier.

"Does William know about this?" Cassie asked.

"I don't think he's taken the time to think about it that deeply. He's having fun playing with his new super powers—he's very strong now, and he can disguise himself as anyone. He's also retained some of the characteristics he had when he was a specter—he can fade to invisibility and think himself from place to place. He keeps trying to test his new sense of touch on me, but of course, I'm having none of it." She sighed deeply. "He's confused because he can no longer see the dead, but I don't think he realizes that means he's alive." She slapped her finger down hard on the page she was skimming. "Here. Genius loci. The light he's bursting with is the magic of protection, and here..."

She held the book out. "See what it says about a boundary around a specific location? Before this, he could only go to places where he'd been in life. So, like most children, he'd been all over Giles Woods, but he had never been able to enter the county hospital because it didn't exist until after he died. Now he can go anywhere in Giles, except he can't put one foot outside the city limits. He's tested it. Not one foot. If he steps out, he pops out of reality and then reappears a few minutes later smack dab where the statue of old Giles Corey used to stand."

The other witches examined the dusty pages, then looked up.

Natalie continued, "See? His abilities and limitations fit exactly with the characteristics of a genius loci. That makes him a type of djinn, one that was created during a magical event. Somehow he's become the town's protector. Our own personal genie." She closed the book and gave a sad smile. "I expect he'll like that, being able to help the living, even if he can no longer help the dead."

Gillian and Cassie each took one of her hands. "Come on then, I'll make us some tea," Gilly said. "And to lift your spirits, we'll discuss the relative merits of your boyfriend being corporeal."

"And firm," Cassie added.

∗∗∗

That afternoon, Cassie finished up Twink's first-day tour of the shop at the rack of clothing items. "And these are the spiderweb shawls," she said, "which, believe it or not, are pretty popular with a particular kind of wannabee witch. I mean, we have to sell this stuff because, like I said, we don't really want anyone to look too close at us. If we play to the tourists, no one takes us seriously enough to think we could be a problem. Still, you never know when people might turn on us. They've done it in the past, and nobody around here needs a witch hunt again."

"Yeah, don't flaunt the magic. Everything that looks like magic is just stage magic for the tourists," Twink replied, reciting from rote. "I got it the first fifty times. Like anyone believes in witches anyway. They'd just think I'm a freak. Because I need people thinking I'm a freak, right?" Twink rolled her eyes for the third time in as many minutes. "Can I tell Marcus about all of this now that I'm starting my training?"

"Just hold on to that for a couple more days, please. It needs to be safer for him to know what's been happening to you, and that change should happen soon. You can tell him then."

Twink eyed her suspiciously. "What kind of change?"

"A good one, I hope. You'll see him more often, at least."

Twink nearly smiled, but her words sounded noncommittal. "That would be okay, I guess."

"Thought you'd like it," Cassie said, then turned toward the front when the shop's bell tinkled. Gillian stepped in with Natalie behind her. Gillian's face lit up when she saw Twink, and she rushed toward her, hands outstretched. Her flight plan was interrupted briefly when Cat went for the hem of her long skirt and nearly tripped her, but she sorted that out quickly by bowing down to scoop him up and hand him off to Nat in one smooth motion. She took both of Twink's immaculately manicured hands in her own hard-worked, chubby ones.

"Twink! I'm so happy you're joining us."

Natalie glared at the kitten, sat it back down, and followed close behind. "Grumbling goose gizzards! Give the girl some space. No need to crowd her all at once. It'll take years to turn her into a respectable witch. Plenty of time to get to know her."

Twink looked over to Cassie with a startled look. "I know, right?" Cassie whispered. "So, Twink," she said out loud, "the friendly one is Gillian Winterforth, and the other one is Natalie Taylor."

Twink's eyes registered recognition at Natalie's name. "You're the one who stood up for Marcus, right?"

"I know when to keep my mouth shut about things that are no one's business, if that's what you mean," Natalie said. She walked around the counter and stowed her red purse beneath it. "Is everyone going to stand around, or are we going to get to work?"

Cassie patted Twink on the shoulder. "You're in good hands. Really. Not only are you getting trained by the best, but you're getting paid, too. Can't beat that."

She picked up her purse from the countertop and flipped the door sign to Open on her way out.

✳✳

Natalie stepped from the car and smiled up at the full moon. The weather was perfect: a warm spring night. She was glad she'd arrived a little early. The sound of the early crickets and gray tree frogs crooning blanketed the woods with peace.

It was the first time in a long while that she felt spring as a rebirth, a never-ending connection to the eternal return. It was the first time in a long time she'd felt the stir of anticipation for new beginnings.

The breeze that moved the leaves brought a chill with it, and she turned back to the open car door and leaned in to retrieve her robe. She pulled it on, but she'd leave the hood down until the others arrived to walk with her solemnly to the ritual grounds. She didn't feel solemn though. She felt buoyed up, happy. She felt like skipping.

She hadn't been unhappy, she knew that. But actively happy? No. It hadn't been her way. She'd been content with keeping busy.

Cars started arriving, and Natalie had greetings for everyone: "Good to see you made it, Lydia. It's a glorious night, isn't it?" and "How's your daughter's pregnancy coming along, Maureen? You must be over the moon with the triplets on the way," and "Darrin, dear Darrin, so good to see you looking so well!"

When she hugged Gillian in greeting, she wondered what insanity had overtaken her, but Gillian just hugged her back and backed away from her with a sly smile.

It wasn't until they were all together that she realized that, with members returning to the coven after the numerous rifts Anat had created, the coven was once again at twelve members. If Twink decided to join them after her year and day of training, it would bring the membership to thirteen. It was a powerful symbolic number, but few thirteen-member covens endured for long without the sheer weight of their member's expectations tearing them apart.

When Tom and Cassie arrived, she moved to them, pulling up her hood, which signaled to the others it was nearly time to get to the business at hand. She followed Tom to the hatch of the old station wagon Cassie had inherited from her grandmother, where he slid out a large leather portfolio case.

The case looked too small for the job she'd asked him to do. "You have all of them?" she asked.

"Man, Nat, keep your hair on. Cassie thought it was a good idea to take them out of the frames to make them easier to carry. Just make sure that Frank's voodoo isn't broadcasting anymore so we can get these back to the gallery. Dash wasn't real happy about loaning them to us. They're apparently a lot more valuable now that Lou Frank is deceased and has been making headlines for his part in the murders. He's not really sure what he's supposed to do with them since no heir has come forward yet to claim them." He held the case out to her.

"They'll be cleared of magic tonight. That's the most important thing. They aren't broadcasting right now, but that doesn't mean someone else can't come along and tie the spell to their own use. You're sure you won't join us, Tom? You'd bring the count to thirteen."

Cassie slipped up beside him and gave him a side hug. "You know he'd rather hunt than be the one without magic in the magic circle."

As Cassie pulled on her robe, Natalie said, "We'll do it someday, Robert and I, figure out how to unbind your power."

Tom shrugged. "I'm fine without it. It never did me much good anyway. I used it for all the wrong things—seduction and my own vanity for the most part. And anyway, as the poet said, 'the woods are lovely, dark and deep,' and with them out there beckoning, I have no interest in any longer being that bad Tom."

With his magic words, bad Tom, spoken, his body transformed. When the juddering ended, a sleek black cat made its way out of the disordered pile of boxers, jeans, and Tom's favorite old dashiki, and brushed against Cassie's legs before springing toward the woods.

Cassie picked up the clothes and tossed them into the front seat of the station wagon. She took Natalie's elbow to walk with her into the woods. The other members of the coven fell in behind, the conversation fading the closer they moved to their ritual grounds.

Marcus had only been at the group home for a week when Mrs. Dean, his social worker, told him that a relative from his father's side of the family had recently contacted the county protective services with an interest in taking guardianship of him. Which was kind of a shock to him, since he'd never met his father.

Mrs. Dean gave him the once-over where they stood on the big front porch of the funky old blue house with its purple and pink trim. "You look really nice. She's an interesting woman, your great grandmother. I'm sure the two of you will do fine together."

Marcus wasn't sure of that, but it had to be better than the group home, and this was the first time anyone had actually asked to have him live with them instead of just taking him because he was placed in their home. It was a real chance. Maybe.

"Ready?" she asked, her hand poised on the bell.

"Sure." He shrugged and pulled his backpack further up on his shoulder. "I got nothin' to lose."

The door opened, and Natalie greeted them with, "Come in then, if you're coming."

"Since the two of you have already met, I'll just run along," said Mrs. Dean. "I have a hundred other appointments today." She put a hand on Marcus's shoulder. "Is that okay with you?"

"Yeah, me and Ms. Taylor, we get along. You said she made it through all the placement checks, right? I'm here to stay?"

"You are," she said, as she pressed his hand. "I'll be by next week to check in."

Natalie led him into the kitchen, where she had a plate of cookies and a cold glass of milk waiting for him. She motioned for him to sit.

"I didn't bake those by the way. If you want fresh baked goods, you'll have to make them yourself. It isn't in my skill set."

He smiled and his head cocked briefly to the side. He reached for a cookie. "These look fine to me."

"And just so there is no confusion—and also to start out together on a basis of honesty, which I will also expect from you, by the way—I'm not your great grandmother."

"Didn't think so," he said between bites. "Even my mother isn't sure who my father is, so..."

"Yes, well...Jeremiah Taylor is what your birth certificate says his name is. Or it does now. He's a distant cousin who would be surprised to discover his paternal grandmother of record has changed. Unfortunately, he died a few years ago, so he won't be protesting the change in ancestors. I have my reasons for the deception, primarily based on the best interests of your friend Twink. But I think we can make it work."

"What's Twink to you?"

"She's my trainee."

"What are you training her for? That mind power thing you can both do?" he asked, setting down an empty glass.

Natalie started to answer, but was interrupted by the doorbell.

"She can tell you that herself." When Marcus didn't move, she had to add, "Well, are you going to let her in?" before he got the hint.

He got up fast and headed for the door.

Twink wrapped herself around him in a hug almost before he had the door open.

"Belligerent brandied beetles! Don't stand in the doorway canoodling. Bring the girl in!"

* * *

At the boundary of Giles, William swung his arms as he walked, thrilling to the feel of the earth beneath his feet and the wind that kicked up as a car whizzed by. Most people wouldn't risk walking along the narrow shoulder, but it wasn't like he had to fear injury or death. All of that had been behind him for a long time.

He pulled out his grandfather's pocket watch, another find from the Stanford mansion. It had fallen behind a chest of drawers, where it was found again when he helped Tom clean out some of the junk in the upstairs rooms. He'd been thrilled when Tom and Cassie had offered it to him, but it had come at a price. He obviously couldn't expect the growing Sanders family to put him up forever, and Tom had taken the opportunity to let William know that he'd have to move on soon. He understood, but he'd never lived on his own. He supposed it would be an adventure.

He could live in an oil lamp if he wanted, like the djinn of old—he'd discovered his magic allowed him to shrink not only himself but a roomful of furniture into a tiny space if he wanted to, but he wasn't quite sure how djinn ended up as slaves to their lamps. An apartment was probably a better bet. If he got stuck there, he could at least have people in.

The old watch had only needed a cleaning to get it ticking again. It told him that it was 3:25 p.m. The prison van carrying Gerald Akers should be coming down the road any minute on its way to the county jail where he'd await trial. Robert had been kind enough to give him the timetable. He hurried to the stop sign. He didn't want to miss his chance.

As the van pulled up, he yelled, "Hey, Gerald!" in his best older-lady voice.

He had no idea what Gerald must have thought when Natalie Taylor smiled at him only to watch her be abruptly replaced by the man whose body he'd paid to have stuffed into a statue.

Gerald blanched dead white as the van pulled away. Maybe William did have an idea what the man thought after all. He turned to follow the van a few more steps, not realizing his mistake until he felt the tug; he stumbled off the side of the pedestal when he reappeared downtown, and didn't manage to catch himself fully before he rolled off the curb. The driver pulling into the parking spot where he landed slammed on the brakes. William's heart raced as he scrambled up, jumping back from the road and signaling to the driver that he was just fine.

He hopped back up on the empty cement pedestal that had once been the base of his tomb and surveyed the main street of the town that had somehow brought him back to life. Then he threw his head back and laughed until tears ran down his cheeks.

Golly, it felt good to be alive.

Afterword

Thank you, dear reader, for making it all the way through to the end! If you enjoyed this book, please consider signing up for my New Release Notification Newsletter at http://www.jillnojack.com/notify/.

At the time of publication of this book (July, 2017), I am hard at work writing The Empty Cradle and The Midsummer Murders, the next books in the Maid, Mother, and Crone Paranormal Cozy Mystery series. You can check out the availability of other books in the series on my website at http://jillnojack.com/books/. If you enjoyed this book and haven't read the Bad Tom series about how Tom and Cassie met, saved the world, and got furry, you can find out more about it there.

As always, you can contact me at jill@jillnojack.com with your comments, questions, praise, or scorn. I would love to hear from you. And, of course, if you decide to leave a review of the book on Amazon, you have my most sincere thanks. Your words can help other readers decide whether or not this book is one they'll enjoy or one they should skip.

www.ingramcontent.com/pod-product-compliance
Lightning Source LLC
Chambersburg PA
CBHW050734180626
46814CB00002B/753